AN UNEXPECTED MURDER

Bill suddenly appeared in at the door of the room.

Janie joshed him. What's the matter, Dad, emergency? Missing some buttons off your shirt?"

He didn't say anything for a moment and Louise knew by the expression on his face that something terrible had happened. She slipped off the bike and came over to him and put a hand on his arm.

"What is it?"

His voice was low. "I heard it on the local news. That professor of yours—Peter Whiting—something's happened to him."

It was as if the bottom were dropping out of the world. "What do you mean? What's happened to him?"

He folded his arms around her. "They've found him murdered, Louise . . ."

Books by Ann Ripley

HARVEST OF MURDER

THE CHRISTMAS GARDEN AFFAIR

Published by Kensington Publishing Corporation

A GARDENING MYSTERY

HARVEST OF MURDER

ANN RIPLEY

KENSINGTON BOOKS
Kensington Publishing Corp.
http://www.kensingtonbooks.com

To Tony

ACKNOWLEDGMENTS

My sincere thanks to those who helped me with the scientific elements of the story, especially Dr. Bill Brown of Colorado State University; Dr. Mancourt Downing of the University of Colorado; and Dr. Matthew Hamilton of Georgetown University. Also lending their expertise were Dr. Harrison Hughes; and Dr. Donald Mykles, both of Colorado State University. I'm also grateful for the help of Keith Brenner; John Pohly; Susan Eubank of Denver Botanic Gardens; Nancy Styler; Karen Gilleland; Sybil Downing; Margaret Coel; my agent, Jane Jordan Browne; and John Scognamiglio, my editor at Kensington.

PROLOGUE

Ramon Jorges glanced lazily around the dingy lobby of the motel. It was on U.S. One, only a few miles south of historic Alexandria, Virginia, and a convenient half-hour trip from Dulles International Airport. Fashionable houses were to its immediate west, and to the south, that distinguished American residence Mount Vernon. He smiled: The motel was a piece of ca-ca set in the midst of Utopia.

It displayed a pink neon sign that had attracted him like a flame to a moth. "Romance Village—Rooms from $30 Up." Ripped pink Naugahyde couches, dirty white walls, and a stupid, pimply desk clerk. Just what he wanted in a motel—at least until he "arrived," under his real name, at the Hilton in Alexandria next week.

"Hi, there," said the clerk, his voice filled with Southern twang. "C'n I gitcha a room?"

"You betcha," said Ramon, not able to withhold a smile from his swarthy face, which appeared to overwhelm the impressionable young clerk.

"You from somewhere abroad?" the youth asked, his pale eyes shining now with interest.

Ramon didn't want a foreign tag, but he saw now he couldn't avoid it, even when he signed in under the phony name of Michael Sanders. Struggling against his Brazilian accent, he said, "Naw—but I've lived a lotta places—especially Mexico." He leaned up closer and smiled whitely. "I'm a little *mestiço, comprende?*"

"Oh, sure," said the clerk, red-faced now, and Ramon was certain the lad's latent homosexual juices were rising. Ramon always seemed to do that for sexually indecisive young men, for his thoroughly worldly history was written in the way he moved his hands and his body, and the way he smiled.

"Lemme sign you up a good room," said the youth.

Ramon leaned on the counter and stared out at the mass of traffic moving in the night on U.S. One. The mystery was almost unbearable: Where were they all going? On one side of the highway, people were heading north to Washington, D.C.—but for what purpose? Wasn't the government closed at night—except for those off on secret assignments? On the other side, they were headed south toward Virginia's more removed, even richer suburbs. It was six o'clock. Many of them must be on their way home after a lousy day at work. Others could be cruising about in their autos only because they were restless Americans. That meant that U.S. Highway Number One was like the traffic-clogged highways spoking out of São Paolo or Rio. In those gleaming cities rimmed with squalid misery, millions of Brazilians clamored for a space to call their own, be it on highways, in expensive suburbs, or in stinking apartments in the barrios. Ceaselessly coming and going, looking for excitement or a place of refuge.

"Your signature, sir." The clerk had filled out the card with Ramon's rental-car license number and the address Ramon had offered. "And your luggage?"

"Right here," said Ramon, and then realized the clerk was paying too much attention again as he gawked at his expensive set of leather bags. Quickly, Ramon added, "Those bags are practically my life's possessions."

"Aw, yeah, I know," said the young man, nodding. Ramon hoped the kid could stretch reality and believe this motel guest was a modest man, with his Gucci bags and rented Lincoln Town Car. As the river of traffic streamed by on the nearby six-lane road, the clerk walked him down the row of rooms. Most of them seemed empty. The clerk stopped at the end room. "This'll give ya a little quiet, Mr. Sanders."

Ramon smiled. A respite from the noise of frantic couplings, most likely.

"And you say you're here a couple of days?"

"Probably three," said Ramon.

"Well, you're in luck as far as food goes. You got a great little place t'eat not more than half mile south of here. Called the Dixie Pig. Y'all try their barbecue—bet y'never got *that* down there in Mexico!"

Ramon gave him a smile and followed him into the faint sour atmosphere of the room. He recoiled for an instant; cheap motels somehow reminded him of death. This room, "best one in the house," according to the clerk, was done in rosy tones, with a deeper rose-colored spread on the queen-sized bed. He pulled out a roll of bills and, remembering how he didn't want to look like a big spender, gave the man three dollars.

Changing into darker sweats after the clerk had left, he shoved his dark ski mask and his weapon temporarily into his waistband and stuck his room key in his pocket. It was time for Ramon to leave the pinkness of his room and go out and do a little surveillance on Peter Whiting, a clever old scientist who used to be his friend. He lived a mile or two west of here, in a showy suburban home.

As far as Ramon was concerned, Peter had crossed that line that friends don't cross.

1

Louise Eldridge hurried up the flagstone walk toward her house in the woods, glad to be home from work. The house sat in a puddle of light created by the converging beams of spotlights set high in the trees that surrounded the place. She walked under the grayed redwood pergola that covered the walk, its twelve-by-two verticals encircled with the untidy but cunning woody vines of climbing hydrangeas. She could almost smell the wonderful fragrance they gave out when covered with white globelike blossoms in summer. But it was November now, and under her feet brown oak leaves, teased by a brisk wind, scuttled across the flagstones like little sea creatures on a beach. Bare branches of an amelanchiar tree clattered ominously against the house, which was low-slung and modern, with floor-to-ceiling windows that made it virtually a glass box. She would have to get out her tree pruners and deal with those branches before they broke a window. But not now, for she had other plans.

She almost ran the rest of the way to the front porch and unlocked the door. Dashing through the living room, dining room, and kitchen, she finally reached the back hall. "Oh, *dar*ling," she crooned to the wriggling white puppy penned there. "We'll go *right* out." With one hand she scooped up the eight pounds of West Highland terrier and walked to the kitchen. With the other hand, she opened the refrigerator freezer section and pulled out a casserole, uncovered it, and placed it in the oven, which she set for 350 degrees.

Then she hurried back to the front hall, and would have been gone before Bill came home if the dog hadn't performed a puppy trick; it entwined the leash between her legs, trapping her like the Lilliputians trapped Gulliver. Just as she succeeded in untangling herself, the door flew open and her ruddy-cheeked husband strode in, accompanied by a gust of raw wind.

"Bill, you're *early*—" She laughed nervously. "Is the State Department cutting its workday?"

Her husband, not noticing her edginess, swept her into a big embrace. He paused only long enough to say, "Isn't it all right to be a little early?" and then gave her a leisurely kiss.

"Mmm," she said, stepping back and smiling at him, and lost some of her resolve to leave. "So nice to have you home again."

"And how was work at the television factory today?"

"Oh, winding things up before we all get ready for a holiday."

He whipped off his overcoat and hat and said, "Wish I could say the same thing, but there's no holiday for State with so damn many crises." He seemed to notice for the first time that she had her coat on, and the dog leashed. "So, I see you're going out again."

"I hate to rush off, but dinner's in the oven, and I have to walk Fella." Though he didn't care for dogs, Bill had agreed that she could take care of Fella for Foreign Service friends called abroad unexpectedly.

He glanced at the scruffy white object fidgeting with anticipation at his feet. Without a word, he put his overcoat and hat away in the front hall closet, then automatically shoved his fingers through his blond hair to neaten it. When he turned back to her, he had an unreadable look on his face. "I know what you're doing—you're meeting that jungle guy again—Whiting."

"I'll probably run into him."

"You've been meeting him every night for more than a month."

"Bill, I want you to meet him. He's great—he's an old professor from Jefferson University, walking his dog."

"Yeah, and you're a good-looking TV garden host walking her dog." Standing in front of her, he put gentle hands on her arms and, with a twinkle in his eye, said, "Admit it, Louise—you've got a thing for him."

"I would think you'd prefer me walking with someone rather than by myself, especially after that incident with the teenager."

"The safety argument—you got me there. Louise, I doubt you would betray me with another man. But there's something about this man and his tales of the Brazilian jungle . . ." He was standing so close now that he had her trapped against the front door. The puppy leaped on Bill's navy wool pants leg, not caring who took him out, as long as someone did. "*This* guy's won your heart—admit it."

She couldn't help giggling. "He's not exactly a Don Juan. He's homely, he coughs a lot, and he's very difficult—I guess you'd call him crabby. But I bet you'll find him just as charming as I do."

"With all that jungle talk, and those wild myths he's laid on you—pink porpoises popping out of the Amazon and impregnating maidens . . . hairy monsters that leap out of the river and steal people's breath . . ." Bill slowly shook his blond head. "I don't think so."

"Well, maybe not." She gave a deep sigh. "But then, you're not me. I need an escape—I *need* jungles right now. And now I've finally found someone who's lived in them, worked in them. Why, he has some kind of a plant laboratory and hinted I might work there—or even go on a field trip next year down to Brazil. . . ."

Bill threw out his hands, a gesture of surrender. "I give up. He sounds like an old-time con artist. I've got to meet this fellow. Well, go and enjoy your walk with Professor What's-His-Name, and don't take any new jobs. Remember, you're a married woman with a loving husband and two devoted daughters, and you've got one job already. Secondly," he said, smiling, "be careful not to let that dog blow away. It's hellishly windy out there."

Louise stepped outside into a wind that was like a living presence. It almost seemed to talk, sending moans and complaints and words of warning humming through the tops of the tall trees. The dog was terrified by the wild night, and she scooped him up in her arms and started down the path through her yard. Soon she was filled with exhilaration, either from the raging elements about her, or else because she was meeting her professor.

Within fifty feet, she'd stepped out of the circle

of light around her house and into the darkness. The only illumination now was from an ungainly three-quarter moon, which soon would become full. But now, as she stared at it, this half-done, emergent moon seemed to look menacingly down upon her.

What *nonsense*, she told herself, to be alarmed by the wind and frightened by the moon. She thought how quickly humans could become spooked by the natural world around them. Then, as if to justify her primitive fears, she saw a sudden, jarring movement in her peripheral vision. It sent her heart racing—but only for a moment. The three figures that dashed toward her were only neighbor boys. They veered away down the path, and she could hear their laughter cast back on the wind. The pup yipped and struggled to get out of her arms and after them. "Shhh," she said.

She trudged onward, walking more carefully now, looking on either side for capricious shadows. But soon, a sense of normalcy returned, and Louise forgot about the shadows.

Fella had now burrowed into her chest as if it were a baby, reawakening old memories of holding an infant against her breast. Her children were now grown; no wonder she clung to this little white dog. And her life was now a complicated balancing of career and home—with her career as hostess of a PBS TV garden show seeming to win out and take too much from her. Perhaps that was why her nightly walks with Dr. Peter Whiting were like precious, irresponsible moments.

The professor never talked about anything ordinary, just the Amazon. Each night they had walked, he had reeled her in further with his delightful tales—of the jungle canopy of lush, flowering trees, underplanted with cactus, palm, bromeliad, and swarming mosses, lianas, and vines, of the noisy cacophony of sounds from exotic birds and animals, of swollen rivers and steep, color-streaked mountains looming up out of thick forests. Of the blue orchid, which he had discovered and given a name. And of the intriguing primitive people living in the midst of it all, with their bare, painted bodies and their mysterious, healing plants.

She saw his tall, bent figure in the distance under the streetlight, looking like a very large bird of prey pacing nervously back and forth. He was thin, even though bundled up in jacket, scarf, and old hat.

Now the man appeared to be dropping to the ground—what was he *doing?* Concerned, she hurried closer, and saw that he was merely crouching down to pet his old dog.

"You're late," the professor barked.

"Sorry, Dr. Whiting. My husband came home as I was leaving. I couldn't—"

"It's all right," he said, cutting her off. Then he raised his thin nose and peered all around them, looking a little like Sherlock Holmes. "Just checking, Louise, to see there are no evildoers around. There doesn't appear to be, so let's be off."

Aided only by moonlight, while the wind continued to swirl around them like a tormented ghost, they made their way into the thickly wooded park. Though the path was narrow, Professor Whiting turned his shoulder slightly to make room for Louise to walk beside him. This meant their heads were close, the better to hear each other.

He shot a beak-nosed look down at her. "And how are you, my friend?"

"Oh, quite well, thanks," she answered, flustered and pleased to be called "friend" by this man. As they proceeded along, his old terrier, Herb, expertly kept up with the professor's starts and jerks, while the tiny puppy Fella went foolishly to and fro, tangling occasionally among their legs.

"You know, Louise Eldridge," he began, and he poked her in the arm with his finger, "you're like a little test for me. We ethnobotanists say that if we can't interest people in rain forests, hallucinogenic plants, and naked people, then we're in the wrong business." He chuckled appreciatively at his own words.

"Then you're in the right business, Dr. Whiting. In five weeks' time, you've certainly hooked me on the Amazon."

"I've entertained you with myths, that's what I've done—and my—no doubt—delightful descriptions of orchids and flora. But we need to talk about the here and now. Things have changed down there, as you well know, just as they were bound to change. The forests were *bound* to be intruded upon, burned, and cleared. Why, the stories I've told you up to now were about the Amazon of fifty years ago. . . ."

"Somewhat like that IMAX *movie* I saw about the Amazon, where not one acre of forest seemed disturbed—"

"Exactly!" he cried. "Back then, Louise, we old-fashioned scientists sweated our way through the forests and gathered samples of rare plants for the sake of pure research. Today, there's an even greater urgency. We must salvage the natives' medical lore before their cultures are completely erased by so-called civilization. It doesn't help that we've been joined by other explorers whose sole purpose is profit."

He snapped the word "profit" like a dog biting a bone. "We call them 'bioprospectors.' They're in the pay of the big drug companies; some are no more than thieves. Why, some even call them bio-pirates."

A weight seemed to have climbed onto Louise's shoulders; she knew that her introductory course in the jungle was over. Tonight the professor was on to much more serious topics.

He suddenly took Louise's arm in an iron grip, pulled her to a full stop, and looked her in the face. The little dog was jerked short at the end of the leash, but old Herb had already halted, anticipating the man's move. "I want you to realize this, Louise. Stealing plants from Brazil and other less developed nations is about the equivalent of someone stealing the United States' secrets from Los Alamos."

"I—I see your point, especially since someone already stole the rubber trade from them. . . ."

He nodded approvingly down at her. "It's why poor Ethiopia so closely guards its coffee germ plasm. Other countries would happily steal it away." Then, he unclasped her arm and set off again at his brisk pace. "Oh, but so much is going on in Brazil alone. A huge country, now sending millions from the squalor in eastern Brazil into those wonderful forests. The irony is the forests have such poor soil that they can never support such a population."

"I've read about the logging and the burning, of course."

"There's more ruin than that," he said crossly, stifling a minor bout of coughing. "The gold mining alone is a scourge on the land. It leaves rivers streaked with pollution, and can ruin drinking water and fishing. Malarial mosquitos multiply by the billions in the backwater pools that are created—beautiful pools of cerulean blue or emerald green that are pure poison. Then there are the herbicides—"

Louise was dismayed. "What are they using herbicides for?"

"To eradicate the coca harvests. They have a powerful new herbicide they want to use that will wash right down from the tropical mountain valleys of Colombia and Peru into the region where I spent so many years—"

His words were interrupted by a crackling sound in the nearby bushes.

"What's *that?*" said Dr. Whiting. He slowed his pace and motioned for silence.

"Maybe it's the three little boys I saw earlier in the woods."

At his insistence, they stood still for more than a minute, while the wind complained above them. Finally, he seemed satisfied that there was no one near. "Ah, let's be on our way again."

When they had gone a few steps, he poked her again on the arm, but this time she wasn't so surprised. The professor was a man who liked to punctuate his speech. "You understand, don't you, Louise, that it's the Indians who knew how to use this paradise? To fish, to farm and raise crops, yet still to conserve the place? Tonight, because I trust you, I want to tell you about a couple of tribes I've been studying. They may have the answer to man's eternal quest for the Fountain of Youth."

She gave a little laugh. "That's always science's favorite topic, isn't it, longevity?"

He stared at her in disapproval. Gruffly, he said, "You sound a little skeptical, as if this were another myth."

"Oh, *no,*" she protested, "I didn't mean to imply that."

"Never mind. Now, you've read about gene therapy—a vast forward step in medicine. But what if I told you of a simple little plant that, all by itself, can create good health and longevity?"

"You've found this plant."

"Yes, and I've watched and seen its almost unbelievable results. It's used by a tribe of Indians called the Makú. They're nomadic people—very timid, very humble. They live around the Rio Tiquié, a tributary of the Vaupés in northwest Brazil. When they decide to move, they just vanish in the forest, so they can be very hard to find." He laughed heartily at the memory of it. "I played hide-and-seek with them for years before they trusted me enough to talk to me. The more settled Indians hold them in low opinion, yet the Makú are masters of the forest. I've stayed with them, studied their language, and grown to know them well."

"And what kind of a magic plant do they have?"

"It's a low-growing, herbaceous species. It's found at the base of the granitic mountains that thrust up through the low hills in the Vaupés region. When taken in a tea, it postpones aging so that ninety-year-old men in the tribe look *fifty*. And what's more, they *act* fifty, if you know what I mean!" This time he poked his elbow painfully into her arm; it was, she realized, a gesture of one old botanist to another.

As far Professor Whiting was concerned, Louise might as well be sexless, able to be let in on everything, male sexual foibles included.

"So they make it into tea—"

"Yes, and drink it twice a day. But notice I said it's only the men who retain this extraordinary youthfulness. That is because it is only the men who drink the *tea.*"

"A male-dominated society, I gather," she said with a philosophical shrug of her shoulders.

He pulled her to a stop again, and she could tell he was coming to a climax in his story. "Most tribes are male-dominated, that's true—women are treated fondly, but not as equals. But I have found another most extraordinary group of Indians with a different pattern." His eyes glittered with excitement. "It's a very small tribe, living in isolation around the headwaters of a tributary of the Vaupés. While in most tribes the men hunt or farm while the women gather food, the women in this tribe hunt alongside their men. They bear some resemblance to the myth about the 'Amazon women'—"

"The ones who were supposed to have seduced and then murdered their male opponents?"

"The very ones," he said with a chuckle. He resumed walking, at a slower pace now. "Herodotus made that myth famous, and a Spanish explorer mistakenly applied it to an Amazon tribe back in the 1500s when he saw the women fighting alongside their menfolk. Actually, these women could be descendants of that tribe he wrote about. For they *hunt* with the men, and probably would fight with them if there was someone to fight these days. The significant thing, Louise, is that these women are privileged to drink the tea with the men. And guess what?"

"They also retain their youth?"

"Ex*actly!*" he said, patting her arm approvingly. "That includes some remarkable results—the continuation of estrus well into their sixties, and its consequences, late childbirth."

"Babies at sixty, ugh!" Louise touched her stomach.

He glanced at her, smiling. "Unlike you North American women, these women welcome babies late in life." He made a sound of disgust. "In fact, if it were not for malaria, and the fact that their Tukanoan neighbors used to sell them as slaves, these little Makú tribes might be much larger."

"These are great *clues.*"

"You understand exactly, Louise. These two small population groups demonstrate the powers of that plant." She could feel the old man's excitement, and saw that he was looking at her again and not the trail. Suddenly he tripped over a tree root and fell flat on his face.

The air was filled with staccato language in another tongue—Portuguese, or perhaps an Indian dialect? Yanking Fella behind her, she ran and bent over his prostrate form. He shoved out a hand and warned her off. "Never *mind,*" he barked. Fumbling around, he located his old hat and jammed it back on his head. "I'm quite all right," he growled, "but get that goddamned *puppy* from under my feet! And fetch Herb—he's blind, you know—blinder than I am."

Taken aback, she pulled her eager dog far to the other side of the path and looked for Herb. He hadn't gone anywhere, just patiently stood and waited for his master to reassemble himself. The companionable atmosphere was gone. It was as if she had committed some terrible breach of etiquette. The professor took over Herb's leash from Louise, and immediately fell back into stride beside her, while she wondered if he would ever speak a word to her again. It took him a few paces, and then he said, "So sorry, Louise, I guess I didn't have to get so cross. My wife tells me I shouldn't lapse into those 'little bursts of anger,' as she calls them. That fall will teach me to watch my step. It's like fieldwork—I guess I'm getting a little old for that, too."

"Oh, surely not . . ." she began.

"I'm not asking you to feel *sorry* for me," he said combatively. "Feeling sorry for me is like feeling sorry for Bill Gates, or, in my generation, Nelson Rockefeller. I've had a good life. And my wife's been in the jungle with me and loved it as much as I have. Traveling peacefully down the jungle's aquatic roads in a boat. Reaching up and plucking an occasional orchid blossom out of the trees that sweep just above our heads. Or helping us bail in rough weather, when our longboat's been tossed by rapids or thrown against huge trees looming out of the water—"

His voice had become so vibrant, and he painted such a loving picture, that Louise could practically see the strong, gray-haired wife: trim, no doubt, and probably in khakis, her pith sun helmet secured by a cord under her chin. . . .

"But back to this wonder plant," he said. "Polly and I are opening a new door to human health by bringing it from the jungle to the United States and propagating it in our laboratory. That's what I was hinting at the other night—that you might want to come and help us."

Since Louise was a bit burned out from nine months of television production, she said carefully, "I'd have to know more about what I would be doing."

"Huh," he grunted, as if she'd insulted him. "And maybe I'd better talk this over with my wife some more. Maybe she won't like me bringing in someone I just met in the woods—she might even think you are an industrial spy."

Louise laughed. "She can check me out; I'm pretty law-abiding."

Getting to the heart of it, Louise realized that Dr. Whiting had set up a for-profit biotechnology firm with super-tight security—and with his profits coming from an endangered plant from Brazil. How was he any different than the bioprospectors whom he'd disparaged?

They went on a few more paces in silence. Louise wished she knew more about Dr. Whiting's personal life, but dared not ask direct questions of this volatile companion. She approached her topic indirectly. "Your wife must be very proud of you."

"And I of her; she is a bright, wonderful woman." They were almost to the end of the trail, and now more light from a distant street lamp illuminated the craggy, hawk-nosed face with its keen, darting eyes. "Once I thought that the person who cared as much as I do about exploring the wonders of the world's richest jungles was my son."

Louise waited for him to go on. After a long pause, he explained. "He left science and became an *actor* instead." The inflection of his voice told what he thought of actors. "Why, my research assistant, Joe, is more of a son to me these days. So that makes two who love the jungle as I do. And my dear, *you* ought to think about going there yourself—it's still a paradise." He lapsed into another coughing spell, and though alarmed, Louise was reluctant to pat him on the back. The truth was that the man both attracted and frightened her.

"Are you all right?" she asked.

As if in sympathy, the old man's dog suddenly began snorting and gasping for breath, at which point Dr. Whiting's spasms subsided. He chuckled, a little hopeless-sounding riff of amusement. "Look at the pair of us—a wheezing old man and a rheumy old dog. How could a wonderful lady like you enjoy our company?"

"I *do* enjoy your company, Dr. Whiting. But I won't see you for a couple of nights, since Bill and I will be out on the town. I'll see you Friday, though, as usual. But I must tell you something quite personal. Jungles are what I dreamed of, all through my childhood. I *love* jungles."

He reached out and put a hand on her arm. "My dear, no wonder we get on so well. So did I, so did I. I'd go to sleep at night in my bed, and invariably **end up in a jungle.**"

2

Dean James Conti was working late, reviewing grant applications that would provide funds for Jefferson University Biology Department's numerous ongoing projects for the coming year.

The door to his office was locked, as was his custom, for he knew full well that security was paramount in the various important jobs he did at this institution. He sat at the desk, shirtsleeves rolled up, considering various requests that would affect the Biology Department's future, occasionally scratching his dark head of hair with a competent square hand. After a while, he leaned his neck back to relieve the tension, and his eyes lit idly upon various pictures mounted on the opposite wall showing himself at home and at play. Then he opened up his right bottom desk drawer and from under a metal strongbox pulled a manila envelope. He withdrew a few well-thumbed snapshots. This was his simple diversion when he deserved a break, and when there wasn't time for a jog around campus or a game of handball.

He flipped rapidly by three pictures of his parents and siblings. The picture at the bottom of the pile was the one he wanted to see. A closeup of a woman with tangled blond hair, her bathing strap falling so that it revealed half of one of her pale breasts. Merely to look at it brought back the old thrill of their lovemaking. Best of all was the expression in her eyes; he had taken that photo at the very beginning of their affair, and she still was so smitten that the love in her eyes was there for him to see forever.

His cell phone began to ring, and he reluctantly left his reverie and answered it. "Conti here."

"James, it's Frank. Bad news. Can you get over here?"

"What's happened? I thought you were getting things under control . . ."

"James, we couldn't know what that viral vector would do. They had an intense immune reaction. It created acute respiratory distress, and multiple organ failure."

"Both of them? You *can't* mean both of them—"

"That's just what I'm saying. They both died, within a few minutes of each other. I'd have called you sooner, but there was some tidying up to do."

James Conti whispered an expletive. "I'll be right there. And it's understood, isn't it, that there's no need to talk about this with anyone?"

"That's why I tidied up. Told the families, of course. No one else."

"I'll be there." The biology dean slammed down the phone and gave himself the luxury of cursing out loud.

He had to calm down; he couldn't afford to go charging out like a madman. Hoping for a moment of peace, he went to the window and stared out onto an almost empty campus, where the tops of tall trees were being tousled as if by a giant invisible hand. He knew the bright lights of Georgetown's M Street glittered two stories below the angle of his view, but there was no light in his life at the moment. In fact, a kaleidoscope of his life's events pushed into his consciousness, irritating him, repeating and reforming into new combinations. It always ended up in a bleak design in dark gray and black. The stubborn, bright little boy, more interested in bugs and small animals than human beings. A budding biologist, adults said admiringly. The invincible, cool young adult, handsome and talented, emerging with top science honors in his class at Harvard University—but achieving no lasting friendships with his peers. The fairy-tale wedding early in his career, to a woman whose face he could now hardly remember, that proved his skills with people were as crude as his skills in science were immense. More scientific honors did nothing to bring him closer to his mother and father and siblings, or any woman he courted—except during that singular, illicit week that he had spent with Polly Whiting. At forty-five, he'd reach a pinnacle of success with no one to share it.

He slammed his hand against the wooden window frame. So much for reaching the pinnacle! Though he was furious, he did not direct this fury at himself. How could he blame himself for the hand that fate had dealt him? It was a fate that stemmed from trying to snatch too much at once—from being enticed to move beyond his own field of biology into the dangerous area of human genetic research. He should have known, after last year's fiascos at other research labs, that Jefferson's genetic research team faced the possibility of trouble. In spite of these premonitions, he'd accepted certain colleagues' reassurances, and willingly put his ass on the line with every human gene experiment in which he participated at this university.

Two patient deaths tonight? His professional reputation, his very future was in jeopardy—his, and the future of the four other doctors who were fellow members of the prestigious "GIT," the Gene Implantation Team at Jefferson University Hospital. They, along with clumps of scientists scattered at universities and private labs throughout the country, were piling over each other to see how fast they could effect cures by injecting helpful genes into sick bodies.

Maybe, he thought darkly, *we tried to proceed too fast.* And now, with two deaths to his partial credit, he could see his meteoric rise in the scientific community sputtering out

Gradually, his wrath began to focus on a man totally unrelated to the murky troubles over at University Hospital a block away.

Peter Whiting became the target of his rage. Here was a man on leave of absence from Conti's teaching staff, but still annoyingly attached, like a barnacle, to his department. What superb irony. The university had sheltered and housed Whiting in roomy labs. Paid him top salary, while suffering his rude diatribes issued from his lofty, tenured position. Helped underwrite his Amazon research for decades. Now, just because James had seen to it that Whiting's funding was cut off, the old man had taken his marbles and gone home. Now Whiting was testing a plant found during those years of subsidized research, and the word was out that it was a gold mine. Buzz in the scientific community was that the plant had huge potential as an herbal medicine, for it was said to prevent senescence. To think that the foul-mouthed bastard would make millions, while he, James Conti, occupier of the prestigious Thaddeus Coleman chair, teetered on the edge of ruin. . . .

He threw on his Italian wool overcoat, and as he hurried through the halls and out the door, he continued to think about the on-leave professor and his wonder plant. This phytoseutical was a sure thing, he'd heard. Why, it would be far bigger than St. John's-Wort and ginkgo biloba—

James deserved part of Whiting's prize, *needed* it, and suddenly thought of a way to get it.

3

"Mindless television, Ma—not good for people doing their exercises." Janie Eldridge sauntered as lissome as a cat across the recreation room, glanced at Louise to see if she objected, then clicked off the set. This left Louise continuing to spin in silence on her stationary bike.

"Thanks for improving my character," said Louise dryly, and ratcheted up her speed to twenty miles per hour.

"I could tell you were bored. Anyone has to be bored when Katie Couric discusses bath aids with a wussy beauty expert." The girl produced a brush and began pulling it through her long blond hair. She wore an oversized sweater and jeans that only seemed to accent her curves. Next, she bent far over, the better to brush her hair down from the crown.

"I'm almost through here, Janie, and since I don't have to go to work today, I'm making a good breakfast for you and Dad."

"Wow, that's outstanding—I thought it was going to be Pop Tarts as usual." Janie smiled faintly at her own joke. Louise's normal morning routine involved a careful selection of clothes, a time-consuming application of makeup, playing Dodge-Em in the kitchen as the entire family ate breakfast on the run, hurried good-byes to the two of them while Bill headed for the State Depart-ment and Janie headed for high school, and then a ten-mile commute to the studios of WTBA-TV, Channel Eight, through suburban Washington's bumper-to-bumper traffic.

But this Friday morning she'd dressed in her gray sweats and old sneakers. For three months she could relax, for her show, *Gardening with Nature*, would require little of her time, and no work on location. Relax, that is, unless she took Professor Whiting up on his offer to work in his plant laboratory.

"Seriously, it'll be a nice change, Ma," said her daughter. "I hardly ever see you anymore."

"What a guilt trip—did you think it might have something to do with those clubs you stay for every night after school?"

"Oh, sure," said the girl flippantly, "that's part of it, I suppose."

"I've been thinking, Janie—I have eight weeks free. We'll have to do something, just the two of us."

Janie ripped the brush through her hair. "I'll believe that when it happens. You'll spend most of the time getting ready for the holidays. First, there'll be Thanksgiving, then it's right into Christmas."

"Not all my time . . ."

"And face it, Ma, you're not too good at that holiday stuff. The guests are no problem, my long-lost sister and that fourteen-year-old you're adopt-ing—though I hope she's not too much of a dweeb. And those guys—they should be fun guests. The main problem is the food. You have to admit you're no Great Granny when it comes to cooking. Even though you've always *wanted* to be known as the Great Cook of the Next Generation."

Louise's little bent-backed grandmother was renowned in the family for her meals. It was true that Louise had begun to fantasize that she was stepping into her Granny's shoes, especially after the old woman had given Louise her favorite linen cooking apron. Now Louise realized what others thought of this outlandish idea.

"As for Christmas," continued Janie, "well, go ahead, but I think you'll need Dad's and my help. And we'll be glad to help you."

"Hmh," said Louise, not knowing until now how it felt to be a charity case. She turned off the bike and pedaled it slowly to a stop. "You don't think I'm good at *much*, do you?"

With a quick movement of her head, Janie swept the entire mass of hair back from her face. "Oh, sure I do—you make a terrific hostess of that little Saturday morning TV show of yours. And you're great at gardening. You, my dear mother, are the master of the nematode, and the mistress of the roly-poly."

"Oh, really," said Louise, chuckling, setting aside the insulting part and actually happy to hear her daughter rattling off the names of garden creatures with such ease, "but I doubt you'd know a nematode if you saw one. . . ."

Bill suddenly appeared at the door of the room. Janie joshed him. "What's the matter, Dad, emergency? Missing some buttons off your shirt?"

He didn't say anything for a moment, and Louise knew by the expression on his face that something terrible had happened. She slipped off the bike and came over to him and put a hand on his arm.

"What is it?"

His voice was low. "I heard it on the local news. That professor of yours—Peter Whiting—something's happened to him."

It was as if the bottom were dropping out of the world. "What do you mean? What's happened to him?"

He folded his arms around her. "They've found him murdered, Louise."

"Don't *tell* me that!" she cried, staring up at him, tears rolling down her cheeks. "Where? When?"

"They found him late last evening, in Ravine Park."

She shuddered against him. "I can't believe it. Who could do that to him?"

"Louise," he said, gently patting her back, "the police haven't caught anyone. But they think it's the same person who tried to attack that teenager."

Janie looked at her father quizzically. "Is this the guy who lived in the jungle?"

Bill nodded.

After a moment, Louise detached herself from her husband and, wiping away her tears on the sleeve of her sweatshirt, walked over to the recreation window. She stared vacantly into the sunny woods. "I would have been with him last night if you and I hadn't gone out, do you realize that, Bill? Maybe that would have saved him—"

"Or maybe you both would have been killed." He followed her to the window. "Louise, I'm so sorry."

"It's strange to get to know someone like that, consider him a friend, and then have this happen. Why, he wanted me to work with him in his lab. He was opening a whole new world for me."

"I know," said Bill. "You'll miss him terribly."

Janie came over and gave her mother a peck on

the cheek. Then she resumed brushing her hair, and looked pointedly at her father. "I don't mean to be alarmist or anything, Dad, but you know none of us can wander out at night anymore in the dark. So—there goes the neighborhood!"

Mike Geraghty was experiencing the usual funk that followed the discovery of a murder in the Fairfax police's Mount Vernon district. A new capital case, unfolding in all its complexity, and with the Criminal Investigation Division at Police Headquarters in the city of Fairfax responsible for solving it. But Geraghty, right here in the neighborhood, would be the one to follow the circus horses and pick up the doo-doo: to filter tips back to the CID, to handle the hysteria of the local residents, to sort out other crimes reported to the substation that might be related to this homicide.

He leaned his large frame back in his chair and laced his fingers together over his ample stomach. The effort created a loud squeak in the chair's ancient spring mechanism. It was times like this when he wished he still smoked. A little nicotine would be welcome to lift him out of this temporary gloom. He extended his huge arms out in a wide stretch, only regretting it when he heard the sound of a little rip in the seam of his worn brown jacket. Prudently, he brought them down again and folded his hands together behind his head. He found this a very comfortable position, and one conducive to thinking things over. However, even in those brief seconds, the number of flashing lights on his phone increased by two, now giving him a total of five to answer—a full house.

He sighed, leaned forward, picked up the receiver, and punched the left button. Time to zero in and get this murder solved. "Detective Geraghty."

"Mike? This is Bill Eldridge."

"Hi, Mr. Eldridge."

"Hey, by this time, you ought to be able to call me Bill."

"Okay, Bill." It was hard to think of this uptight government bureaucrat as anything but a "mister."

"Everything all right with the family, Bill?"

"If you mean Louise, yes. And Janie's fine, too. But I'm concerned as hell since I heard the news. That professor was a friend of Louise's."

"You don't say." He sat back defensively in his squeaky chair, momentarily in shock. But why should he be shocked? He might have known Louise Eldridge, the most viscerally snoopy woman he'd ever met, would have known the old guy. "How did she know Peter Whiting?"

"Actually, it turns out that we attend the same church the Whitings attend, but she never ran into him there. They met on the trail in Ravine Park while they were walking their dogs."

"Oh. Didn't know you had a dog. Always thought you ought to have one."

"It's a borrowed dog," said Bill drily. "A little fellow—named *Fella* actually. Not good for much, but Louise loves him. Yes, she got to know this Whiting just recently, and she liked him a helluva lot. Now that I hear he's dead, there're a couple of things I'm concerned about. The first is the safety issue for Janie and Louise. And the second is that I'm afraid Louise will try to solve the murder herself. The news reports made it sound as if it was a serial killer on the loose."

Geraghty cleared his throat. He had been concerned, ever since the news first got out, that the local neighbors would go into hysterics, and it was already starting—even though he knew folks who could get a lot more worked up than Bill Eldridge.

"The Fairfax CID spokesman didn't say that out-right, Bill, but he did hint at it. Now this is confidential, because we don't want the general public to know the *M.O.* of the murderer. All right?"

"You know me. I'll keep it to myself."

Geraghty was sure that Bill Eldridge would do just that. He knew the man kept plenty of secrets in his mysterious government job. "We gave out that speculation about a random killer because it was such a heinous crime, a slashing crime, very sick. . . . Given the location of the body—in a public park, and given the victim's identity—a prestigious but elderly professor who probably didn't have many enemies, and given that a young woman narrowly escaped being slashed in the same park a couple of weeks before, we think it probably was a deranged person. That's the long and short."

"My God," muttered Bill, "I hope to hell you can find him."

"So do we, Bill. We have plenty of officers checking every lead. I can't think of any reason for Louise to get involved."

"No. She's had enough of that."

"That's for sure. Thanks for calling, and we'll try to keep the community as well informed as we can on our progress. Everybody in the media is calling us wanting more details, but we don't have them yet. In the meantime, and probably until we catch this person, we're assigning a special patrol car to the area near Ravine Park."

Bill sighed. "Well, I'm sure we'll see it, since that's our neighborhood you're talking about."

Geraghty was silent a minute, wondering how Eldridge would take this. "And Bill, now that I know Louise was in the habit of walking with this Peter Whiting, I'm afraid I'll have to drop over and ask her a few questions."

"Mmm. A few questions are okay with me. She'll tell you all they ever talked about was jungles. Make it clear to her that this one's way out of her league."

"I take your meaning. I'll do just that."

He answered his cell phone on the first ring, for this was the appointed time for the call from Carl Rohrig.

"I hear that our principal has met with some very tragic luck," said Carl, the faintest suspicion in his tone. Or was it just cynicism?

"That's right," he replied in a calm voice, "Dr. Whiting apparently was in the wrong place at the wrong time. Second attack in that neighborhood in as many weeks. Washington's suburbs apparently aren't as safe as they used to be."

"What's the net effect of this?" asked Carl. His mergers and acquisitions firm was fronting for Synthez Pharmaceuticals, so he naturally would be stressed out at any possible upset in plans for the takeover.

"It depends."

"It depends?" asked Carl, as if speaking to a servant. "Depends on what?"

He didn't let it bother him, to be treated like a caboclo *by Carl. His own potential gain on this deal was so enormous that he was willing to suffer in silence some stupid remarks from the high-powered asshole on the other end of the line.*

"From your perspective, Carl, it may represent delay...."

"Damn! What kind of a delay are we talking about?"

"Hold on a minute. I told you the setup was fluid: I'd hoped to work with our principal—even though we can all agree he was a difficult old man—but now it's going to be a question of working with Mrs. Whiting. Mrs. Whiting and maybe some others who could be connected to the project."

Carl said, "I wanted to get this on the front burner:

take over that company by next summer. Trials to proceed immediately afterward. FDA approval within three years. Product on the market twelve months later." He rattled the points off in staccato fashion.

"That's a pretty concentrated schedule."

"What the hell, supply is no problem, if Whiting really does have some kind of magic gel that makes these plants grow like schmoos. . . ."

"Schmoos? I'm afraid I'm not familiar with schmoos."

Carl made a noise indicating disgust. *"You mean you've never heard of Lil' Abner? Oh, well, what can I say: Scientists must have one-track minds. It was a little animal out of an early comic strip that grew and propagated so fast that it titillated folks. They were so damned cute that everyone wanted to have one—but they existed, of course, only in the mind of this comic-strip artist."*

"Oh. Well, Whiting's gel does cause things to grow like schmoos. You'll be amazed."

"Good," said Carl, *"and now you've learned a little something to broaden your horizons. Look, you don't know, but I know what's in Synthez's competitors' pipelines—we need this plant of Whiting's—it's gonna make us all richer—and that includes you. Certainly you can move your ass on this a little. Get over there and do what you have to do with Mrs. Whiting. Maybe screw her—or have you already done that?"* A little ribald chuckling. *"Any way you can, get it done. She can't do this alone anyway; she needs somebody like us."*

"Does she? I'm not sure she does."

"Then you better convince her of it, hadn't you?"

4

Louise was surprised when Mrs. Polly Whiting phoned her less than a week after her husband's murder and invited her to tea.

She had sent the widow a simple card with a brief message. It mentioned the five-week friendship fostered by nightly dog walks in the woods, and even mentioned the fact that the Eldridges were members of the neighborhood Presbyterian church that the Whitings also attended. She didn't bother to add that the Eldridges' spotty church attendance in the last year was probably the reason their paths hadn't intersected.

"I was thinking of tea at four." Mrs. Whiting's voice was so low and melodic that it piqued Louise's curiosity. There was that picture in her mind of a well-preserved older woman traveling with her elderly scientist husband down the watery "roads" of the Amazon jungles, plucking blue orchids from the trailing trees.

She pondered that youthful voice: A "longevity" drug was what they had been working on. Suddenly, she wondered if Mrs. Polly Whiting herself was testing the drug. This meeting would be intriguing.

"Yes," said Louise, "I would love to come over."

It took some time to spruce herself up, changing from her old sweats. She pulled a tailored navy pants suit from her closet, certainly the thing to wear for a call on a woman who'd just lost her husband. She added a customary brightness to her lips, and ran a quick brush through her long brown hair. The hair, she noted, would need cutting before she resumed work again in front of the Channel Eight cameras.

As she passed by the back hall, Fella barked at her, and she promptly took him outdoors to relieve himself in back of the bamboo patch. He did this with dispatch, then looked up expectantly, the leash on his dog collar triggering his craving for a walk.

"No, Fella," she said, "Janie will take you on a walk when she gets home from school—I am so sorry but I have to leave now." She didn't feel the least bit silly having a full-blown conversation with the puppy, for the animal had distinctive human qualities. He was a good listener, sometimes even better than her husband, perking his little ears up at everything she said. She'd had to change Fella's routine completely, with all walks taken during the day. The whole family—and the entire neighborhood, for that matter—had battened down safely at night against the mysterious savage criminal. She knew the information on Dr. Whiting's killer had been issued to police throughout the entire state of Virginia, the District of Columbia, and the state of Maryland. But local residents had been the predator's targets—and they were the ones most frightened.

Louise was not frightened, but she was very, very careful.

* * *

She drove out of her Sylvan Valley neighborhood, past the free-form, low-slung modular homes. Even though sunlight slanted through the virtual jungle of tall sweet gums and oaks and glinted on the huge walled windows of the structures, it rarely reached the ground, for the subdivision had been conceived back in the 1950s by creative architects with a liberal bent, and what seemed to some the radical idea of cutting down as little of the woods as possible to provide space for houses.

In a few blocks, she entered the adjacent neighborhood, Northminster Estates, and it was like entering a different, sunny world. Here an architect had decreed uniformity and tidiness and achieved it by building row upon row of orderly, mowed-lawn colonial houses. As always, she wondered about this huge gulf between architectural styles, and knew it didn't play out in other aspects of the homeowners' lives. For instance, her most radically inclined woman friend lived in this colonial neighborhood and fought constantly for the State of Virginia to recognize gay marriages. And the fact was that lots of people didn't even know of Sylvan Valley's reputation as a liberal enclave; Louise had heard the stories straight from the mouths of "pioneer" residents.

The Whiting house was in the first block beyond Sylvan Valley. It couldn't help evoke Mount Vernon, only four miles to the south, since it was buff-colored, with imposing white square columns. Louise had driven by the home many times before, and thought it pretentious. Now that she knew it was the home of a man she had deeply respected, she might have to rethink this view of hers.

At her ring, the door was opened by a fine-featured woman with long blond hair and wearing a rust-colored cotton caftan. Louise was so surprised that she took an awkward step backward on the porch.

"Watch it." The woman laughed in a melodic voice.

She was about forty-five, Louise guessed, and breathtaking in her coloring, which was a burnished brown—or was it jungle tan? Her bright blue eyes seemed to be enhanced with blue lenses, for no one's eyes were naturally *that* blue.

No wonder Mrs. Polly Whiting's voice had been so youthful. *This* was Mrs. Whiting. That image of a gray-haired wife sitting facing her equally elderly husband in a boat faded down the imaginary river.

Polly, who now had a protective arm guiding her guest, said, "You're Louise—I recognize you from your show, and from your mower commercials. I'm Polly. Do come in." Louise entered the foyer and the widow continued. "I've heard a lot about you—all about your wonderful new career."

"And I've heard about you," said Louise. "I'm so terribly sorry to hear about your husband. . . ."

"And to say nothing of those crimes you helped solve. My, you're brave."

Louise was embarrassed by the woman's praise and was temporarily speechless.

"Well," said Polly brightly, "I don't mean to be rude. Come meet Peter's son, and our long-time assistant Joe Bateman."

Two men rose as they entered the traditional living room, one more reluctantly than the other. The slower-moving man was very tall, dark-browed, and dark-eyed, with a hawk nose. She concluded it was Peter Whiting's actor son, since the professor had only spoken of one. He had that lean, graceful aspect that she concluded was a good thing in an actor.

"Matthew Whiting, Peter's son," Polly announced. He nodded and didn't offer his hand.

But the other man, who was a bit older, in his early forties, strode over to Louise and did his own introduction. "And I'm Dr. Joe Bateman, Mrs. Eldridge. I've been Dr. Whiting's postdoctoral research assistant for almost a decade. Now I'm assisting Polly, of course. We're all stricken, as you can see, by the terrible tragedy." In a corner snoozed Peter Whiting's dog, Herb.

The whole tenor of Joe's introduction left no doubt in Louise's mind as to who was in charge. Bateman was a tall, muscular man with light brown hair and penetrating pale eyes. He had a somber look, and Louise sensed immediately that he had been deeply affected by the death of Peter Whiting.

"I was so saddened," said Louise, looking up at Dr. Bateman, "even though I had only known Dr. Whiting a short length of time."

Polly beckoned her to a chair, and began serving tea. Bateman sat beside the widow. Matthew slumped in an overstuffed chair opposite, balancing his teacup precariously on a raised knee, brooding under his thick dark eyebrows. Why did Louise get the feeling the young man had been disenfranchised—or perhaps disinherited?

Suddenly, he blurted out, "It's a hell of an end for a guy like my dad. I'd like to meet the son of a bitch who did it."

Bateman quietly replied, "That might be a better job for the police, Matthew. They think it's a mad killer, and probably none of us are equipped to deal with a person like that."

"Well, I might not be able to retaliate," said Matthew, "but I sure intend to help you, Polly, starting right now." He threw out a hand in an open gesture. "I don't want you to hold against me anything that's happened in the past—I just want to be friends." He leaned forward and gave the widow an intent look with his brown eyes.

As if to give the lie to these words, Herb, Dr. Whiting's elderly terrier, got up from the corner where he had been snoozing and wandered over in front of Matthew's chair. He sat there and growled, in a low pitch.

Dr. Whiting's son put his teacup on the floor at the side of his chair, and tried to reach out to the dog. "Aw, c'mon, Herb, don't be a jerk." The dog quickly moved out of his reach, still growling, and retreated to his sleeping spot.

Matthew shrugged and sat back. "He doesn't really know me very well," he explained. Polly stared at Matthew with an impassive look on her face. Louise was sure now that he had dropped by unexpectedly: the uninvited guest. Then the widow turned her attention from the young man to her visitor. "Louise, I know you must be wondering why I invited you here." Polly sat erectly on the white brocade couch, her caftan skirt sweeping the floor, with just the ends of her handsome sandaled feet protruding. Her hands were folded gracefully in her lap. The large, comforting Joe Bateman sat silently at her side.

"I am pleased to have a chance to meet you," said Louise.

"I have something to ask you," Polly said simply.

Louise watched Polly's stepson, Matthew, re-arrange himself impatiently in the chair. With what was probably a heroic effort, he kept his mouth shut so that his stepmother could get her message out.

"Peter started doing fieldwork in northwest Brazil in 1950," the widow said. "Even then, scientists were sensitive to how the rare plants of the Amazonian jungles could disappear, along with the tribes of Indians who knew how to use them as medicines. Now, a half-century later, these tribes have been ravaged by white men's diseases, or are fast becoming assimilated into modern Brazil. Peter, of course, hated to see what was happening to them—much the same thing that happened to the North American Indians. And the plants—in the past fifty years, the losses of species have been enormous, as you no doubt know. He catalogued thousands of them through the region. . . ."

"It was a huge task," explained Joe. "It took great amounts of time and grant money, and dozens of trips." The big man smiled. "They called Peter and his sort of scientist 'cowboys,' a tribute to the fact that they put up with things that few human beings would put up with."

"Oh, yes," agreed Polly, her blue eyes round and earnest, "snakes, insects, shortages of food and water, death-defying trips through those rapids and cataracts. And disease—why, my husband's life was saved at least twice by the Indians—once when he fell sick with malaria, another time with beri-beri."

Joe reached out and touched her arm. "My dear, you were talking about why you invited Louise over."

She placed a remorseful hand against her tanned cheek. "Sorry, I've wandered. Although samples of these plants were brought home and put in botanical museums around the world, many have never been analyzed, even though they are in danger of extinction; some may hold enormous value as medicines."

Joe propelled the story forward.

"The different Indian tribes have different skills.

Some have highly competent medicine men and women—shamans—and a whole medicine cabinet, so to speak, full of health remedies from plants. Others don't seem as interested in plants for health use. . . ."

Matthew grinned. "Except for getting high—those Indians like to get high. All that coca, all those other hallucinogens . . ."

Polly gave her stepson a level look, the kind that Louise gave her teenager Janie when she made an inappropriate statement. Joe intervened in a matter-of-fact voice. "Not that it bears on this discussion, Matthew, but I have to set you straight for Louise's sake. You make the chewing of coca leaves sound like a yuppie recreational sport, when I know you know better. Coca and hallucinogens are a part of South American Indians' culture and religion. Coca leaves and the cocaine extract are *not* the same, as you know. The leaves, it turns out—in addition to giving them a jolt of energy as we might get from a cup of coffee—have much nutritional value. They are high in calcium and fulfill the Indians' daily requirements in many areas. It's a mild stimulant that's been used without signs of harm for more than two thousand years before Europeans discovered cocaine. Only after that was it viewed as an addictive drug."

Matthew made a dismissive gesture with one of his slim hands. "I know all that, Joe—I learned that stuff at my daddy's knee. I was kidding. Sorry."

"But getting back to my topic," said Polly. "It was during this survey that Peter found two tribes that were especially—fascinating."

"He told me about them," Louise said quietly.

"Tell *me*, then," said Matthew, who looked hardly able to curb his impatience.

She told him about the Makú tribe and their prolonged "youth."

"Do you remember your father speaking of them?" Louise asked.

Matthew shook his head. "Not really, since we practically quit speaking. . . ."

Polly continued. "Certain members of the tribe . . ."

"But not all members of the tribe," interjected Joe, "and that's what's so significant."

"All right," said Matthew impatiently, " 'certain' members of the tribe did what?"

Polly shot him an unreadable glance. "They drank tea made from the leaves of a shrublike species of the *Tabebuia*. One species is absolutely huge. It grows one hundred or more feet high, and brightens the top layer of the jungle with its truly fantastic yellow flowers. This medicinal variety is much smaller.

"And then he began working with another tribe. Indigenous people in the northwest Amazon basin have many idiosyncracies, Matthew, as you may remember from your trips down there, and this tribe is but one example."

Louise knew what was coming next. "Yes, that second tribe—*remarkable* . . ."

Polly gave Louise a look, as if to warn, *Don't give it away now*, then turned to Peter Whiting's son and told him of the tribe where women, because they were hunters, had the tribal status to be tea drinkers.

"*Awesome!*" exclaimed Matthew in a faintly sarcastic voice. "It's like finding the mythical, well-stacked Amazon women—"

Polly Whiting cocked her blond head. "As you know from *being* there yourself, Amazon women are not well-stacked, or blue-eyed, or blond-haired, as in a Hollywood movie. These Indian women are small of stature, dark-haired, dark-skinned, and dark-eyed. Now, back to the plant: Peter realized this *Tabebuia* species, always scarce, was growing scarcer. He had to do something immediately if he were to do it at all." Suddenly a tear spilled from her eye. Joe reached over and patted her shoulder.

Matthew looked on, not knowing what to say, his sharp nose elevated in disdain or possibly embarrassment, and he tapped his foot nervously. The son did not know how to grieve for his father in words, nor did he know how to comfort his stepmother.

She sat a little straighter on the sofa and seemed determined to go on. Louise listened closely, realizing this was the part of the story she hadn't heard.

"To make a long story short," said Polly, "he gained the trust of the tribal leaders, who then were willing to give him samples. Then he worked through all the red tape with the Brazilian government and the USDA for the phytosanitary certificates and import permits needed to bring the plant meristems into the United States. Finally he was able to bring them back to this country. In the past few months we've been tissue-culturing them in our own lab on Route One, only a mile from here. We'll do more meristem culture until we get enough product to do our own field trials."

"To see if it works," Matthew interjected.

"Next we'll put the tea on the market as a food supplement." Polly gave Louise a look that reminded her of how the British queen looked upon her subjects. "You're the kind of person we need to help us—even if it's only on an interim basis."

From the corner of her eye, she saw Matthew lurch forward in his chair. She turned quickly to look at him, and saw the shocked and angry look on his face before he could cover it up in a masterly, thespian style.

"You need this woman to help?" he said, grinning in disbelief. "Why, do you even *know* this woman?"

There was an embarrassed silence that no one seemed to want to fill. Louise decided that if she didn't say something, no one would. "Polly, my family is already about to disown me for neglecting home and family. Though your husband mentioned this, I really am awfully busy. What is it that you wanted me to help you with?" She was painfully aware of Dr. Peter Whiting's emotional son watching all the give-and-take between her and Polly.

Sending a wary look Matthew's way, Polly explained. "With tissue-culturing the plants," she answered. "It's an enormous amount of work. I'm asking you mainly because my husband spoke so well of you; Peter wanted to bring you into the lab. And besides, we've had a couple of resignations."

Louise had thought Peter Whiting's job offer might have died with the scientist. Now, she had to make her own decision as to whether she would step into this brand-new calling: plant research. What on earth would her family say?

Meanwhile, she noticed that Polly Whiting's smile had faltered, and tears weren't far away. "With Peter gone, it becomes all the more enormous a project," said Polly. She glanced gratefully at Joe Bateman sitting beside her. "Joe, as lab manager, has taken over the plant research, of course. . . ."

"Yes, we're studying the genetic structure of the plant," said Joe, "or what we call the plant's genome, and comparing it to similar members of the species which we also brought out of the jungle. That way we can identify the longevity gene and down the road produce it chemically. All this will happen long after we've proven the plant's efficacy, of course. So that's *my* work. And what we need in the lab right now are plant handlers."

Polly sat eagerly forward and explained to Louise, "You'd take care of both plants and, if you were interested, the experimental mice. They're routine jobs, but very important. We can teach you the rudimentary science you'd need, and I think the benefits to you would be enormous—why, you might even want to do a program someday on the subject."

Joe looked at the widow, and with very little body language, just a warning hand out to her, indicated reservations. "But not originating in *our* test tube plant lab, Polly . . ."

"Oh, no," she agreed. "This is the start-up of a very promising company. We maintain a high level of security in the lab. No, we couldn't have anyone looking in our labs just yet." She smiled with some pride. "There's lots of buzz in the scientific community—they already know pretty much what I've just told you, but none of the details, of course."

Joe Bateman explained patiently: " 'Buzz' is what someone else might call the 'hype.' For a new scientific breakthrough, it's almost as important as the breakthrough itself." He smiled wryly. "It's kind of like promoting a movie: Some of them pan out well, some don't. Peter's been highly successful in his work, and everyone knew this was very big. . . ."

"But then along comes a *madman*—" cried Polly, and her grief overcame her again. She bowed her head to hide her tears. Again, Joe put out a hand, and this time he appeared to squeeze her shoulder. "Get a grip now, Polly," said Joe in his monotonous voice. They weren't very tactful words, but then this man was a scientist, whose specialty probably wasn't tactful language to soothe new widows.

The words worked magically. Polly raised her beautiful blond head again and finished her thought. "And then some madman struck him down before he realized the greatest achievement of his life. But I am determined that this project will go ahead and that my darling Peter will get the credit for his marvelous discovery."

It was a perfect widow's speech. Louise, who suffered from occasional bouts of cynicism, wondered if it weren't a little too perfect.

Matthew, who'd been riveted by the conversation, suddenly got up and plopped himself down on the couch on the other side of the widow. "Look, Polly, I'm sorry about my glib remarks. I know this plant project is sound, and that you need people you know and trust. Dad may not have thought I was much"—he self-consciously twisted his body about and threw a hank of longish hair back from his face—"but I'm good in emergencies. Why don't I help in the lab? It'd kinda give me a good feeling to be in his lab. Why, I didn't know it existed before this."

Louise was amazed. It was as if the young man were trying to transform himself before their very eyes from a polliwog into a frog—or in this case from an *artiste* into a scientist. Polly turned on the couch and looked the young man directly in the face. "Matthew, you know how he had trouble accepting your career change."

The young man leaned forward respectfully, as if to present the picture of a dutiful, sorrowing son. "Hey, you know we darn near killed each other over that topic many times, but that's all in the past. And you know I'm no dummy. If you can accept the help of a woman you've just met, why can't you accept my help, too?"

Joe Bateman leaned forward on the couch and stared past Polly over at Matthew. "It'd give you a good feeling to work in your father's lab? Is that all there is to it?"

"Look, Joe," said Matthew, "you could figure I have more than one motive. I admit it—I could use the extra income. It's been a dry season in the Washington theater this fall, and I didn't make the cut when I tried out for an Off-Broadway show in New York. Haven't even clinched any TV commercials lately—they usually tide me over in slow periods."

"You do voice-overs," said Louise.

Matthew looked at her with a new recognition in his eyes. Excited, he pointed a finger straight at her. "Oh, *yeah*, that's it!" he cried. "I knew I recognized you from somewhere—you're on those Atlas Mower commercials."

She returned the smile. "That's me."

"*Funny* commercials, Louise—you have a nice, humorous approach. I should've recognized you right off the bat. None of my jobs have been that big so far, but they sure do help, don't they?"

"I know what you mean," said Louise.

Matthew Whiting's persona was filling out. Not only was he shucking his boorish ways, he'd suddenly become her show-biz buddy.

All this wasn't lost on Polly. She looked from Louise to Matthew, and then at Joe Bateman. As if suddenly bridging a large gap, the widow reached out and grasped one of Matthew's hands. "It's quite a switch—from acting to working in a laboratory. But at least you can come and see the labs. Then you can decide if you want to do such—*mundane* work."

Joe, looking troubled at Polly's offer, murmured something to the widow. "Joe reminds me of something, Matthew." Polly's voice had turned stony. "The labs are secret and confidential. There must be no question but that you keep those secrets, or

I promise you I'll do more than cut you completely out of my life. I'll absolutely—"

"Polly!" said Matthew, grasping her hand tighter. "I promise you I can keep secrets." His voice tore a bit. "You know I wish I hadn't fought with Dad—or if you don't know, I'm telling you now. You might not understand, but I had to fight him—I'm not a bum, I'm an actor—and a damned good one." His voice lifted with new enthusiasm. "But I *know* it won't take long to get back that old scientific knowhow I had in college. Don't forget—*I* went on field trips to Brazil even before you and Dad got married."

The widow looked like someone who had just been checkmated.

Matthew looked expectantly over at Louise as if they were both beginning students in an Advanced Placement science class. In a sense, they were. "When do we start mucking around with these little plants?"

Polly shot another dubious look at her stepson. "Remember, Matthew, security is everything."

"I realize, Polly, I realize."

Next, she turned to Louise.

Louise had been thinking hard as the widow dealt with Matthew. Slowly, she gave the woman an answer. "As it happens, our show's on hiatus for several months. I could lend you a hand for a while—maybe six weeks, though I'm not sure how happy that will make my husband."

"Six weeks would be wonderful. *Do* try to persuade your husband how exciting this will be for you. You and Matthew could start tomorrow. I still need to do some paperwork related to Peter's death, but Joe can train you." She closed her eyes tightly for a moment. "And though I'd like nothing better than to don widow's weeds and go off somewhere and mourn, I just can't do it—can I,

Joe?" She looked up at her dead husband's post-doctoral assistant.

"No, you can't," he answered. "We're onto something very big. The two of you will find that out tomorrow." He gave Louise a careful look, and she wondered how he and Polly could possibly trust either one of them. Louise was almost a stranger, though Polly Whiting had a strong recommendation from her deceased husband about her character, and though Louise also had a reputation as a television garden show host.

Then Joe told them why they could offer the two of them these sensitive jobs. "There is a caveat—we trust you won't mind it. It's standard practice for all of our employees. You're obliged to fill out some long forms giving us a complete history of your past, as well as sign a confidentiality form that makes it a crime for you to divulge what's going on in the company."

"I'm fine with that," said Matthew.

"So am I," said Louise, though it sounded fatiguing.

She could see that, confidentiality agreement or not, it was going to take time for Matthew to earn the trust of Joe and Polly, to say nothing of the professor's old dog, Herb.

Joe Bateman was polite, though he seemed to have reservations about both of the new test tube plant technicians—Matthew more than Louise. He stayed on the other side of the living room while Polly said her good-byes to the two. That way, he didn't have to shake hands with either one of them.

In a pleasant haze, Louise followed Polly to the front hall to get her coat. She hadn't realized until this moment how stressed out her life had become. But now someone had offered her, like a gift on a golden platter, a chance to rejuvenate herself.

She had known as soon as she met him that Dr. Whiting was good for her soul. He had opened a wonderful door for her into the world of ethnobotany, her awakened interest proving his maxim: *If you can't interest people in rain forests, hallucinogenic plants, and naked people, you're in the wrong business.* Her eyes teared up at the memory of that last walk in the woods with the old professor.

And now, by helping his widow, Louise would have the chance to do what she had secretly wanted to do for years, to work in a laboratory with *plants!* It was truly the answer to a prayer.

As Polly brought her coat from the closet, she said, "So, is nine o'clock too early?"

"Oh, no, I'm up much earlier than that," said Louise. As the front door was opened for her departure, she saw that a man stood on the front porch. Polly's face went white underneath her tan.

"Well, can I come in or not?" he asked, already holding the storm door ajar. A tall, dark-haired man with sensuous lips and yellow-green eyes, he wore a superbly cut overcoat with the grace of a fashion model.

"James," said Polly with a little gasp, "it's you—what a surprise . . . but do come in." They exchanged a long look full of personal intimations. The widow reached back with nervous fingers and grabbed Louise's arm for support. Who *was* this man who threw Polly Whiting into such a tizzy?

She turned to Louise and said, "I want you to meet Dr. James Conti. He—he was Peter's boss, shall we say, dean of the Biology Department of Jefferson University. Peter, you know, either taught or was acting dean at Jefferson for fifty years. And this is our neighbor, Louise Eldridge. She is someone special, James, a TV personality in Washington and, I hear, quite a skillful amateur detective."

Looking over her shoulder, Polly saw that Matthew and Joe Bateman were standing near. "You know Joe and Peter's son, Matthew. . . ." The men nodded to each other. Then all three looked curiously at Louise.

"Amateur detective?" said James in a droll voice. "Does that mean she is to solve Peter's murder?"

"Heavens, no," cried Polly, shocked at his words. "Louise has just stopped over to—offer her condolences."

"A pleasure to meet you," said Louise. As he grasped her extended hand, it was if a low-grade electrical shock ran through her; as she stared into his insistent green eyes, she saw that the man indeed was charged—with both sex appeal and power.

Then she gave Polly Whiting a break by slipping out the door, leaving them to work out all the family-employee-friend relationships on their own.

To her surprise, the widow followed her out onto the porch. Louise said, "Thanks so much, Polly."

Quietly, Polly said, "I'll look forward to seeing you early tomorrow." It was quite clear this woman did not want the real reason for Louise's visit known to Dean James Conti.

Louise drove the short distance home on automatic, her head full of thoughts of the challenge she was going to have working with test tube plants. Her real infatuation, which she admitted unashamedly, was outdoor gardens, with their beguiling flowers and graceful bushes and trees. The very *act* of gardening gladdened her heart. In contrast, this lab work would be different. It would call on her intellectual skills more than the simpler tasks of outdoor horticulture. And it would leave her with a greater base of knowledge for all her future gardening pursuits.

It wasn't until she reached her own driveway that the other implications of her visit began to be apparent. Tea at Polly's had not been all it seemed. There was intense feeling among the three people there. Obviously, Matthew had not gotten along with his father, though he seemed friendly enough with his stepmother. But why did he appear to resent Louise? And why would the dog dislike Matthew? Why did Dr. Joe Bateman appear so lukewarm about taking her and Matthew on as plant assistants when they needed unskilled laborers in the lab? Why was Polly so nervous when Dr. Conti arrived? And what kind of a cold-hearted character would make that half-baked joke about Louise solving Peter Whiting's murder?

Suddenly, Louise didn't care. She was so delighted with being offered a part-time job as a plant person that she couldn't be bothered worrying about anything.

All Louise had to do was to take care of baby plants, and stay out of the woods at night.

5

Bill focused in on his chicken à la king, and tried not to look at either his wife or his daughter, who were spiraling down, like two dueling airplanes, into an argument.

"I'm telling you, Bill," said Louise, "it was like a born-again experience. . . ."

"You—born again?" said Janie incredulously. "I doubt it. Let's face it, Ma. God made 'frozen' and 'chosen' Presbyterians, and you're one of the 'frozen' ones."

Louise was silent a moment. Then she said, "You may not believe me, Janie, but I felt something deeply spiritual move inside of me when Polly Whiting offered me that job. And now I realize it's something I've always wanted—to be right there in the greenhouses, working with the propagation of plants."

"Right there with all the minimum-wage Latino workers who can't get any other job?" said their worldly-wise seventeen-year-old.

Louise looked down unhappily at her plate.

"Dear, I'm just trying to tell your father and you how I feel—I didn't want to start a debate."

Janie apparently hadn't noticed that her mother was getting a little annoyed. She shrugged and said, "Oh, sure, I know all about feelings—that's what we teenagers have to deal with on a daily basis for five or six years before we eventually grow up."

Bill gave his daughter a long look. His voice, when he spoke, was very quiet. "A little quick on the draw, aren't you?"

The girl looked wounded, but recovered rapidly. "Hey, I'm glad someone offered her a real down-to-earth job working in dirt. Go on, you two, with your conversation. I'll show you how helpful I can be and go get the dessert." She left the table and went to the kitchen.

He sighed. He knew, too, that Louise had needed a diversion in her life, for her television career was a lot of pressure.

Bill put it as tactfully as he could. "You know, Louise, you could always ditch your job at WTBA. Or—you don't have to be a TV gardening show hostess *and* a shill for that lawn mower company. You could give up one or the other, and then keep on working with the test tube plants."

Louise looked resentfully at him with her large, hazel eyes, and he knew he'd said something wrong. "Shill? I'm spokesman for Atlas Mowers. And I'm sure you haven't forgotten that those commercials are paying Martha's tuition so she leaves Northwestern debt-free."

"Look, I'm proud of you. But your *Gardening with Nature* job is using you up and throwing you away. It used to take you thirty hours a week. Now it must be fifty. That leaves you with only, what? Seventy left to sleep, eat, commute, and"—he grinned—"give your husband a little attention."

"I'll admit it is a bit much. I don't work with the easiest people—there's a reason Marty Corbin's known as the most temperamental producer at WTBA-TV. Though I love him dearly, anyway."

Bill looked at her broodily. "I've never trusted the fellow since I heard he had an affair with Channel Eight's *previous* garden show hostess."

"Oh, but Marty's reformed—and you know it. But then there's John. . . ."

"John Batchelder is such a *cutie*," Janie chimed in, as she served up custard. "What great eyes—he should have been born a girl!"

"My co-host may be cute, but he has his own agenda," said Louise. "He's waiting for me to make a move, such as resigning. He's heard me talk about how we might move to Vienna, and he'd love that. It would leave him to take over the program. . . ." Louise couldn't bear to finish that thought.

"And you would be in a strange country without a career," said Bill.

"Yes."

Bill spooned up some custard onto his spoon and poised it in midair. "Let's not get sidetracked with that Vienna issue. I've no plans at the moment to make any transfer overseas."

Louise sighed. "That's a relief. But really, we've talked enough about me—no wonder Janie's bored with it. Here's the proposition that Polly gave me: to work about thirty hours a week, for about six weeks. I'll be working with test tube plants, and I'll get about fourteen dollars an hour. How does that sound?"

He smiled at his wife. To Bill, Louise still seemed like the leggy coed he'd met twenty-two years ago on the Georgetown campus—even though there were a few lines now in her lovely face. "It won't interfere with you making a wonderful Thanksgiving dinner for all those visitors we're going to have?"

"Oh, no," she said enthusiastically. "This will give me a new lease on life."

"*I* know what you want," said Janie. "Immersion. You want to *immerse* yourself in dirt projects again, like that time you tore up the whole yard for a week and replanted it."

"Janie," said Bill, raising a hand, "enough. But, actually—well put, when I think about it. I agree, Louise, that you'll like immersing yourself in this. And you'll learn a lot about micropropagation, genetic tinkering, etcetera, etcetera. . . ."

He tilted back on the legs of his Hitchcock chair, and it groaned in self-defense. It attracted his wife's attention, which was just what he wanted. "Just one very large caveat."

"What's that?" she said, staring nervously at the chair legs.

He reached a hand out and placed it on her arm, to show her how serious he was. "These people you'll be working with were very close to the professor." He put the chair right again and looked her in the eye.

"Of course. His wife. His postdoctoral assistant. His son."

"Interesting. All the people closest to a man who's been savagely murdered. I don't know if I like that much. Just remember, I don't want *you* involved in the murder investigation."

"Don't worry about that, honey," said Louise. "The police have that under control."

6

Louise drove out onto U.S. Route One, a mile east of her own comfortable home in upper-middle-class Sylvan Valley. Here was a hodgepodge of cheap motels, franchise restaurants, and new condo developments, interspersed with some interesting leftover entrepreneurial efforts such as "The Seeress." The seeress, who told fortunes, occupied a ramshackle house right on a corner of the busy highway near Romance Village, Romance Village being an eye-catching place done in hot pink with deeper pink neon signs. She had heard it was a spot for some fairly fancy Washington people to gain privacy for quick sexual encounters. Louise smiled. They probably were quick sexual encounters among the cockroaches.

Standing neglected in a huge, scraggly field off the highway were two deserted greenhouses, a patch of suburban blight tucked among new condo developments. Louise had driven by the greenhouses innumerable times on her way to the grocery store. Earlier this year she had wondered why someone would erect an expensive twelve-foot stockade fence around this detritus, but once the fence was up, it was out of sight and out of mind.

As she drove through the open stockade gate, she saw folks had been busy behind the fence. Ahead of her was an attractive, low-slung cinder-block building with the two now-modernized green-houses still in the rear. The buildings were set in the middle of a pristine landscape.

Someone anal keeps this place, she thought. The acreage was groomed until it looked almost artificial, the still-green lawn, the well-pruned ever-greens, and the driveways without a trace of debris. The small parking lot was located well away from the building, as if to protect it from the insult of car exhaust. As she walked toward the building, she registered that the structure had glass block front windows, a style in vogue in cities after the urban riots of the sixties. Were these people expecting trouble? On the front door, a small-lettered sign read, WHITING PHYTOSEUTICAL LABORA-TORIES. She entered.

In the small anteroom there was a walnut desk and secretary's chair, but no human being. The only ornaments were two large framed renditions of tropical plants. Louise wandered over and saw they were by Margaret Mee, the famous naturalist painter. *Brazil*, she whispered to herself, and her excitement grew. These were Mee's lush portrayals of the Brazilian rain forest's orchids and bromeli-ads. Most likely, Margaret Mee and Peter Whiting had met somewhere in the Amazon basin, and these were original paintings, gifts from one friend to another.

And to think that now Louise was a little part of an effort to preserve a threatened species.

At the end of this small lobby were glass-windowed

double doors that led into a big, lighted room. Not until she had given one a shove and discovered it was locked did she see the buzzer on the right side of the door. She pressed it, and soon Joe Bateman appeared, wearing a white lab coat. A mask was tied at the neck and ready for use.

He gave her a slow smile, and she realized it was her first sign of acceptance from the man. He had a reassuring presence, she had to admit. "You're on time," he said, "but Matthew was an eager beaver; he's been here a while. First, I tried to explain to him that labs are not casual, laid-back environments such as he's used to, but places where we operate with great care and precision. Right now, he's learning to help prepare media." He showed Louise where to hang her jacket and then gave her a lab coat and mask. "Probably won't need the mask today, but it will give you a sense of the way you should dress because of the multiple tasks you'll be performing. Gloves, of course, too—but you'll find those available in boxes near all the workstations."

He swept his hand around in an arc. "A little tour will help." Fanning out from the central lobby were the workrooms of the lab: first, the media preparation room, where she found Matthew watching a young female lab assistant mix the vital solution that enabled the plants to grow.

"Hey, Louise," he greeted her, "meet Gina." Gina, an attractive woman with long, pale hair caught up in a bun and carefully covered with a net, smiled a greeting, and Matthew fastened his attention again on her as she measured liquid from a bottle into a large beaker. Louise had to admit that he looked considerably more professional in his white jacket than the last time she saw him, and that even his shaggy, dark hair appeared to have undergone a trim. Or was the young actor only *playing* at this lab assistant job? What he wasn't playing at was his infatuation with the pretty Gina.

Joe moved in close to Louise's shoulder, and she noticed he had a pleasant, minty breath. He said, "Gina's in charge of our animals, too, but that will come later in the tour. What you're seeing right here is something new in science. Look at that mixture of agar she's preparing." Louise looked: It was translucent white and mucousy-looking. She placed a hand on her middle, praying it would not fail her now. Such disgusting *goop!*

But Joe didn't think so. He saw only beauty in the murky stuff at the bottom of the beaker.

"It's magical," he said in a reverent voice. "Mura-shige and Skoog, of course, developed the first highly successful media for tissue culturing and growing plants, and they're *giants* in our field. What is not known to scientists yet is that Dr. Whiting has trumped them. He made another breakthrough before he died—and this is it!"

"This—goop?" asked Louise, her stomach nearly turning.

The scientist's pale eyes were alive with excitement. "This media is the stuff of life, Louise. It *accelerates* growth. That's why we have plenty of space on this site—acres of land. One day, we could have a dozen greenhouses here."

"Really."

Joe had lost the attention of Matthew, who was now being drawn in by the mixing process being performed by the lab tech. But Louise had listened carefully, and for the first time began to realize the enormity of this biotech venture. "You mean, a sort of mass production of plants whose leaves can be harvested for the tea?"

"Yes," said Joe, smiling victoriously. "That means we can complete our field trials more quickly and bring the product to market in record time." There was something lamentable in his remarks, but Louise couldn't put her finger on it for a moment.

They left Matthew and Gina behind, and passed through the vestibule to the transfer room. In his near-monotone voice, the lab manager explained, "Like the mouse room, this area has a constant filtered positive air flow. Sterile air builds up in here so that when a door opens, the air moves out, thus not allowing outside air to move in. That makes for the cleanest possible conditions for handling plants and for maintaining lab animals."

Next they moved to the culture-growing room. Louise slowed her pace, captivated by the sight of benches loaded with racks of six-inch-long test tubes in which chubby, green miniature plants were growing. Fluorescent lights hovered above the plants and gave a daylight glow to the windowless room. At one side were a series of big lighted refrigerators with glassed sides to afford a view of more plantlets. She found out they were the lab's "insurance policy," an extra stash in a controlled environment that would survive if some catastrophe hit the lab itself.

Finally they reached two rooms at the end of the building, and Louise could see Joe getting a little excited again—his face flushed, his eyes a little brighter—but not too excited, for that would not behoove a serious scientist. And Joe Bateman was a serious scientist. "Now we approach the very heart of the matter," he told her. The "heart of the matter" turned out to be a drab, windowless space filled with equipment. "This is our research lab— *my* lab," said Joe with quiet pride in his voice. "Gas chromatograph, scales, de-ionizer and distiller, thermocycler, centrifuge, gel electrophoresis system—everything I need for gene research."

A shiver ran through her. "Until a week ago, I bet Dr. Whiting described this room in the same way." She put her hand to her mouth, regretting the words as soon as they were out.

Joe Bateman looked at her in surprise, and then tears filled his eyes. "My God, you are right. This whole big project is rolling on while he is barely cold in the ground." He bowed his head as if in tribute. "Oh, how I know, Louise—he's gone and I'm here, working all alone on this giant project." He pulled out a clean, white, folded handkerchief and wiped his eyes. Louise wasn't sure who he felt the sorrier for, Peter Whiting or himself.

In a minute or so, Joe seemed to have recovered, ready to continue his explanations, and seeming to have read her mind. "A lot of the work is nuts and bolts, constantly monitoring to see if there's any contamination in the plants. Contamination is a big problem in test-tube plants, for we must have clean clones. Polly, who's highly trained as both an administrator and as a lab tech, will step in and help with that as soon as things settle down a bit. Until then, I'm a bit overworked, actually *very* overworked. And then there's the more interesting work on the genetic makeup of the plant itself. . . ."

"You and Dr. Whiting were trying to identify the 'longevity' gene. . . ."

He nodded. "Exactly. I know you must have read about genetic research—it's man's new frontier. It may be that with some genetic manipulation, we can transgenically move the longevity gene into some other plant that produces more plant material. That means we could increase our

yields even further. We might even be able to syn-
thesize that gene chemically at some point down
the line."

Finally, he brought her to the last room, which
was lined with cages, each containing white mice.
Louise immediately approached their cages and
stood there, smiling. "Cute little fellows," she said,
knowing that wasn't a very scientific remark.

Joe beamed at the little animals. "These mice
will soon be the stars of the show."

"How many are there?" inquired Louise, walking slowly in front of the cages.

"One hundred. And we already can see the results of the *Tabebuia* tea on them. Some have a tendency to yaw. We think that's from what might be
considered slight overdoses—while others are
frisky despite the fact they've reached middle age."

" 'Yaw' is what, an imbalance?"

"It's a nautical term," he said, "that means to
move unsteadily and weave about."

"An overdose. Will they die?"

He looked at her, trying to mask his annoyance. "Louise, I know you're not a scientist, but
remember this is a *scientific* laboratory. The mice
may or may not die—we'll have to wait and see."
A dry little chuckle. "You're not an animal ac-
tivist, are you? Those people give trouble to us
scientists all the time. We use animals safely and
humanely—within strict requirements laid down
by the government—to test products that will
benefit people."

She was flustered. "Oh, I do understand. I didn't
mean to come off as some radical. And you say
that some of the mice are acting more youthful?"

Joe smiled, a long smile. "Downright frivolous,
some of them." He led her over to the end row of
cages and stopped at one that housed five so-

called frisky mice. "Here at the front is Perky, as we call him. He's more than a year old, and mice live only two to three years. But just see how he's acting." The creature seemed full of the energy of, perhaps, an adolescent. He jumped up against the cage, as if to personally greet Louise.

"Hi, Perky," she said softly and reached out a finger, wanting to touch him. The little rodent sniffed eagerly at the outstretched finger. "You're part of a noble experiment."

Joe seemed to appreciate her interest. "The mice are given various doses of the tea in their water supply. Some get none. This enables us to test the effectiveness of our magic compound, as well as the optimum time in the mouse's development in which to start dosing them."

"But you have no tea leaves yet, so where . . ."

"Where did we get our *product* for making tea? That's one of the benefits of working with the Makú people. Since Peter was such an old friend to them, we easily got their approval, and later the approval of the Brazilian government to bring in a supply sufficient to begin our animal research. That was more than a year ago—and you can see we're already observing fantastic results. One of Dr. Whiting's dreams was to have the Indians in the tribe raise the plant as a commercial crop. The only trouble is that there are some uncontrollable variables in the jungle, one being the tribe's nomadic nature, another being the weather. One can manage production better in a place like this." He gestured toward the growing room, where hundreds of little plants were busily reaching maturity in the most controlled conditions possible.

"How many plants so far?"

"About eight hundred," said Joe, "and we've just begun. Can you believe—they all started from half a dozen two-inch meristems just a few months ago. As each plant grows, we continue to make cuts and plant them up."

She looked around. "I'm humbled by all this. What can I do, without going back and getting a biology degree first?"

He laughed. "As I told Matthew, our number-one rule is very simple: that you keep your mouth shut and preserve the security of this laboratory. The fewer people who know what goes on here, the better. You can well imagine that we could have trouble down the line from folks—anti-biotechnology radicals have invaded and destroyed laboratories like this. We'll soon have greenhouses filled with mature *Tabebuia* plants that we'll have to protect. Then there are other kooks who object to using animals in experiments." He shook his head.

"I can see you have to be awfully careful."

Joe stared over Louise's shoulder. "Here comes our other new plant handler now. Let me give both of you a short lesson in plant management and then you can get started."

Matthew was walking down the narrow aisle toward them. He stared at Louise for a moment, apparently still not quite approving of her presence. Then he broke into an infectious grin; perhaps the effort of being in a snit was too much effort for him. Or maybe he caught on to the fact that this wasn't *his* lab. Despite this, she could see certain feelings of ownership developing in Peter Whiting's son. "Hey, there, Louise. Waddaya think, is this not cool?"

"It's cool," she said with a laugh.

Joe said, "We'll get started now—let's go back to media prep. We have about sixty test tubes to prepare."

"Hold on," said Matthew, shifting nervously back and forth from one foot to the other. "I need a smoke, Joe, real bad. Where can I go and smoke— where, where?" He started hopping up and down, in a good portrayal of a genuine drug addict, but the grin on his face said he was overacting.

Dr. Bateman looked over at Matthew with faintly disguised disapproval. "The last thing in the world we can afford in this lab is tobacco virus," grumped the lab manager. "That means you'd better be darned careful how you smoke around here." He fished a key out of his jacket pocket and gave it to the young man. "First, hang up your lab jacket. Then go out beyond the front porch area; you'll find a little covered patio. You can use the key to get back through the double doors. When you get back, go wash your hands up to your elbows with soap, and your face, too. Then put a fresh lab coat on. And don't forget to give the key back." He was obviously trying to curb his impatience at the amount of time and trouble the simple smoking of a cigarette was causing. "I hope this isn't one of these things you have to do every five minutes, Matthew."

"Naw," said the young man, starting to pull out his cigarette pack and then thinking the better of it. "I only need one about every couple of hours. I'll be back." And he practically ran down the aisle toward the double doors.

"Take it easy," Joe called after him. "If you slam into those test tube trays, you'll have ruined a lot of the effort that your father worked so hard to achieve." Louise was glad each time she heard mention of the dead scientist. It helped take away the hollow feeling she'd had since she heard that he had been killed.

Joe and Louise were alone again. He arched a friendly eyebrow at her. "Coffee break? We might as well, while Matthew gets his nicotine fix."

She saw the beginning of a kinship with Dr. Joe Bateman, despite his rather stern manner. At least, they shared the same drug of choice—caffeine.

7

By Friday, the new lab techs' second day of training, Louise was in plant heaven.

Matthew's favorite niche was in the media preparation room with Gina, though Louise saw that he pulled his weight wherever he worked. She was impressed both by how fast he picked up lab techniques again after a long hiatus, and how willing he was to do anything, down to the most menial task of cleaning and disinfecting the lab. Cleanliness was a constant effort on everyone's part. As she joked to Joe Bateman, "I can see that in this place, godliness is next to cleanliness, not the other way around."

Louise had gravitated to the transfer room with Joe, where they worked together at a bench with masks covering their faces, latex gloves on their hands, and a net encasing Louise's long, bound-up brown hair. In these most sterile conditions, they divided the plants. As she took up the scalpel preparatory to making her first cutting, she looked over at Joe. Though their mouths were covered, it was clear they were both smiling.

"You like this, don't you?" he said.

"I love it. Maybe it takes a certain personality who likes to do neat, tidy jobs—that's me. I would have gotten into it years ago if I'd only known how much fun it was. I'd like my husband to build me a little lab off the back of our house so I could try some orchids—I hear they're easy to propagate by corm."

"And you don't seem to mind all the detailed procedures—you're quite good at them."

These words helped her lose her self-consciousness as she proceeded to work; she dipped her scalpel in alcohol and then held it in the orange-blue flame of the Bunsen burner until it turned orange in color. Using the sterile forceps, she removed the cultured plantlet from a test tube and placed it on a sterile paper towel, then cut from it the newly developing buds. She put each of these pieces into a fresh test tube, the base of the shoot tip inserted just deep enough in the agar so that it was held upright.

She was working in silence, having forgotten Joe now, and everything else in the world but her little plantlets. Then she heard the buzzer on the double doors. Polly Whiting, who hadn't shown up on Louise's first day, stood outside them, and Joe Bateman got up and hurried to let her into the lab.

Louise was surprised that she didn't have her own key. Dressed in no-nonsense sweater and slacks, Polly had her blond hair pulled back in a bun. When she stopped to talk to Louise for a moment, Louise could smell the flowery perfume that surrounded her. After drawing Joe Bateman aside for a few private words, the distracted-looking widow announced that she had work to do in the office, but had ordered in sandwiches for everyone for lunch.

As Louise and Joe settled back into their work,

Louise's curiosity was aroused, but she didn't feel comfortable asking too many questions. She said, "This place certainly has tight security."

"Oh, you mean Polly—she just forgot her key. But yes, we're a little paranoid." Again, she couldn't see his mouth, but his eyes now looked wary. "Peter was worried about industrial spies after he brought this plant material back from Brazil. Actually, I was surprised when he trusted you after only knowing you a month or so, but it turned out he'd had you thoroughly checked out right off the bat. No, the main object of his distrust was James Conti. You ran into him at Polly's."

"Yes, the dark-haired, green-eyed, certifiably handsome . . ."

Joe gave a little laugh. "Yeah. Dr. Conti is one of Jefferson University's wonder boys in the field of human genetics—though I hear they're having some big trouble with certain of their research subjects. . . ."

Louise could see a smile playing around his eyes. "Trouble—what kind of trouble?"

"When subjects die on you, that's trouble. It must be hard on someone who's risen so high. On the basis of his reputation, three years ago Jefferson gave him the Thaddeus Coleman chair and a salary of two hundred K a year. But he's a vindictive type, to put it bluntly. He probably single-handedly deep-sixed Peter's *Tabebuia* project."

"But the project is well under way."

"Yes, but all this"—and he swept his hand out to indicate the lab and the grounds—"was paid for out of Peter's pockets, because NIH, the NSF, and even Jefferson University refused to fund him."

"I didn't realize one man could have all that power, to cut someone out of funding. Isn't there something called peer review?"

Joe laughed cynically. "Oh, yes. Peer review. Definitely, but if your boss—and you realize, don't you, that Conti was Peter Whiting's boss?—if your boss shoots you down, then who's going to offer you funds for a project like this?"

"What do you mean?'"

"Look, I believe in this project—I burned my bridges and left academia to join Peter Whiting here. But there are still eyebrows raised at the idea of alternative medicines, this despite the fact that NIH has a new National Center for Complementary and Alternative Medicine. It hasn't helped that a certain number of less-than-scrupulous people have entered the field making promises that couldn't be kept, or doing a little biopiracy to obtain their plant product."

"But about James Conti," she reminded him.

Joe was busy securing the glass lid on a test tube.

"He seems to know Polly pretty well," she added.

"He knows Polly very well," Joe agreed neutrally, "but he resented Peter. Peter had succeeded at too much. But worse than that, Peter was too old, too expensive, too uncontrollable because he had both tenure and a bad temper. He also took up too much lab space."

"Goodness, how crass. They're not all kind and gentle people at these universities."

Joe laughed. "That's what happens to elderly science professors who don't go gently into the night. As for Conti, he's the kind of guy who makes me glad I left the university to come work with Whiting. Conti's intensely competitive, and Peter wouldn't have put it past him to do almost anything to find out all about what we are doing here."

Louise said, "He figures Peter owed him something."

"Yes, with Peter being on the Jefferson faculty for decades, and getting some generous funding from the university. Now, Conti will be making an official visit here—Polly just told me she'd had a long phone call from him, asking a lot of questions about the lab. You may think that sounds dangerous, but she can hardly turn him away. At least it will be a controlled visit, and he won't be walking away with samples."

"So Peter Whiting has the exclusive patent on the *Tabebuia?*"

"Yes. But I'm not sure James Conti agrees with that."

"So that's why all the locked doors."

"And the few keys," added Joe.

"I did notice what you said about Dr. Whiting—he was awfully fierce."

He shook his head. "You had to understand Peter. He was a throwback—as I said, a 'cowboy,' who could live off the land, the kind of scientist who slogged through the rain forests and patiently learned the customs and language of the indigenous peoples, and all about the native plants, just for the love of it and the love of science."

"It's as if Peter Whiting was an endangered species himself."

Joe chuckled drily. "That's it. An endangered species himself, poor fellow. His mistake is that he didn't make it clear that he was no longer this unselfish creature, sharing the riches of the Amazon."

"What do you mean by that?"

"Only that, after a lifetime of sharing all his ethnobotanical knowledge, he intended to keep this *Tabebuia* project strictly for himself."

Louise was quietly beginning some work in the vestibule, taking the used test tubes to be washed, triple-rinsed in distilled water, and then put in the autoclave. The staff, Polly, Joe, Gina, Louise, and the increasingly businesslike Matthew, had a quiet lunch together in the small conference room off the lobby. Polly herself was subdued, having spent the morning with lawyers talking about her dead husband's estate, not a fun thing to do, Louise was sure.

As she emptied the contents of contaminated test tubes, she heard the buzzer at the double doors again, and looked up. Joe Bateman, who was in the growing room, strode rapidly forward, and Louise could see the surprise in his face.

He unlocked the doors. Polly stood there with a handsome, olive-skinned man whose white teeth gleamed in a wide smile.

Despite her beauty and dignity, which to Louise had seemed impenetrable, the widow looked as ill at ease as a schoolgirl. "Joe, you remember Ramon Jorges."

The name aroused a dim memory in Louise's mind; somewhere, she had read about this man. She could even remember seeing the name in print. It was spelled "Jorges."

"Sure, I know Ramon," said Joe with his customary brevity, busily transferring a tray of test tubes onto a rack.

"And I want you to meet a new lab assistant, Louise Eldridge. Dr. Ramon Jorges of São Paolo." Since she still was wearing latex gloves, Louise hung back and nodded.

"I'm honored, Louise," Ramon Jorges said, and gave her a little bow.

Polly's blue eyes were a little wider than usual, and Louise had the uncomfortable feeling that she was scared. "Louise, Ramon is a well-known scientist in Brazil, and once did fieldwork with us there. He's associated—"

"*Used* to be associated," amended the wavy-haired Brazilian as he looked fondly down on Polly. "I now have my own consulting firm."

"Both he and Peter used to be associated with the National Institute for Amazonian Research. He's in Washington for the International Science Association meeting and heard of Peter's death."

"I was told the tragic news by James Conti," recounted their visitor, bowing his head.

Joe Bateman came straight to the point. "Polly and I were planning to leave later this afternoon to attend an ISA session. But I suppose you came here because you're interested in a tour of the lab."

Polly looked alarmed, as if her postdoctoral assistant had gone too far in revealing how they felt about Jorges's visit.

"Indeed," Ramon Jorges said, his brown eyes greedily traveling over the room and into the next, "I would be honored to see what you are doing here, Polly—and so would the Instituto Nacional de Pesquisas da Amazoñia. This is the flowering of an idea that your husband and I had years ago, as we journeyed through the jungle together." He laughed, and Louise had to admit it was a gorgeous, sexy laugh.

He shrugged his broad shoulders. "It is a mystery what really happened there, *pois não?*" He left this ambiguous remark floating in air, and Polly looked alarmed.

"Those were the days," he continued, "when I was very young—Peter much older than I. We traveled through the basin together over the savannahs and the forests of the *planada,* the granite mountains, the flooded rivers filled with dangerous chasms. . . . There was nowhere that we wouldn't go to find plants. And among the people, we were never sure what we would find—*cannibals* or merely *campesinos.*" He leaned toward Polly. "Sometimes we had to go to great *lengths* to save one another's lives."

Oh-oh, thought Louise as she heard this talk of the good old days in the jungle. Hanging invisibly in the air of the laboratory, like one of those mythical one-eyed apparitions believed in by Brazilian aborigines, was the insinuation that Ramon Jorges had a stake in this biotech firm.

As Polly and Joe started touring their guest through the place, they passed Louise, and Jorges tossed over a look that alarmed her. For a tiny second, it made her think she had no clothes on. Then she recalled a South American diplomat she had known when she and Bill were stationed abroad with the State Department. Ramon Jorges was running true to a type, the type that unfortunately did not stay home with wife and family.

Two hours later, Louise was through for the day. She slipped out of her lab coat and put it in the laundry basket; she would use a fresh, sterilized one tomorrow. Polly and Joe were getting ready to depart for the science confab in downtown Washington, and she realized that Gina was in charge of closing up the place.

It had been a wonderful two days, and she'd enjoyed working with everyone—even Matthew, whose enthusiasm made up for his occasional tendency to act like a know-it-all. But then along came Dr. Jorges, who had set her teeth on edge—and, unless she was very much mistaken, he'd had the same effect on everyone else at the lab.

As she climbed into her car, she revved the engine harder than usual, partly because the motor of her old Honda station wagon needed encouragement, partly to express her anger through the accelerator pedal.

Whiting Labs, in two days, had become a sanc-

tuary to her, and she didn't like to see people
come in and disturb the tranquil atmosphere.
Whatever the story was on Dr. Jorges, she was sure
Joe would tell her—or maybe she could find it out
for herself. These fretful thoughts, however, only
reminded her of her husband's observation that
she worked with three people who had a motive to
kill Peter Whiting.

What did Bill think the motives were? *Polly Whiting tired of her aging husband, decided to go it alone . . .
Son Matthew elevated ancient father-son strife into a reason to kill . . . Joe Bateman aspired to more—to take
Peter Whiting's place in both the research and in Polly's
bed. . . .*

How ridiculous. She knew the Fairfax police
had the neighborhood bustling with police officers searching out a serial killer who favored
knives as the implement of death. But her
thoughts went back to motive, and she remembered her conversation with Joe about Dr. James
Conti. Did Conti have a motive for murder—or
how about this Ramon Jorges, whose every remark
was laden with a mysterious subtext?

She steered the Honda onto Route One and
headed for the grocery store, disgusted with herself. Talk about avoiding contamination in the laboratory: She was contaminating her *mind* with idle
speculations about who killed the professor. She
loved her job tending baby plants from the Amazon jungle and didn't want to think about murder.

Once she was home, her thoughts strayed back
to the Brazilian scientist. She had time before dinner to do an Internet search, and quickly found
what she wanted. Six months ago, John Noble
Wilford of *The New York Times* had written a long
article about "biopiracy" and "bioprospectors" in

which Dr. Ramon Jorges was mentioned at least a dozen times. Jorges sounded like one of the kind of scientists that Peter Whiting had complained about—a man in the pay of an American pharmaceutical firm who bent the law in his search for desirable plants. Jorges, though a popular speaker about the topic of ethnobotanical plants, had even been brought into Brazilian courts for attempting to secrete plants out of his own country. The case was dismissed for lack of sufficient evidence.

Resting a hand under her chin, Louise stared at the screen, thinking. Finally realizing she was running up her bill, she printed the story, signed off the Web, and went to the kitchen to make dinner. If anyone beyond a madman *were* to be suspected of murdering Dr. Whiting, who would be a better candidate than Jorges?

She set the story aside, and took out her quick-dinner cookbook.

8

Ramon Jorges's taste buds salivated as he saw the small, jolly caricature of a pig high on the building at the corner of U.S. One and Fort Hunt Road. He pulled his rental car into the parking lot of the Dixie Pig Restaurant and ran up the steps to the entrance. He loved their barbecue.

Despite an early dining crowd, his favorite booth in the far corner was still empty. He headed for it, waving to employees as he did—the back-of-the-counter male waiter, and Dorothy, she of the snaggly mop of dark, curly hair, who served the booths and had been so good to him as to serve even more than food. He sat facing the rear of the restaurant.

He could have timed it on his watch. In spite of many others who appeared to need her attention, she was there in three seconds flat. He rewarded her with his most brilliant smile, then decided on a small public display of affection, really only for Dorothy's benefit since visibility into the booth was practically nil. He grasped her hand and held it as only he could hold a hand—sensuously—pressing and rubbing it the way a woman already infatuated with a man wants it pressed. Signaling how he wanted her, until he was sure the woman would be hard put to last through until nine P.M.

"Dorothy," he almost whispered, enunciating each syllable, as if the word had a hard time leaving his tongue.

"Mr. *San*ders," she said, smiling mysteriously, as if they were playing a game, and then keeled back a little, so his hand holding hers was her only means of remaining upright.

"Steady now," he directed, until she'd recovered and he was able to let go of the hand. Then, so that she'd go back to her other customers and not get into trouble, he said, "I'll have the usual."

Sanders. It had been five days since, as Mr. Sanders, he had checked out of Romance Village, traveled the four miles to Alexandria, and checked into the Hilton under his own name. Five days since he'd seen Dorothy, who was easy right from the start about visiting him in his double-pink quarters down the road. Five days since he'd tasted the Dixie Pig's nonpareil pork barbecue sandwich!

While his meal was coming—two pork barbecue sandwiches with big fries and a side of coleslaw—Ramon thought back on his visit to Whiting Labs. Peter Whiting had done a remarkable job of setting up the place so quickly. Ramon had measured it with his mind's eye, estimated they had 4,800 square feet of working space, and plenty of room on that site to expand and ultimately grow plants in the millions. . . .

He picked up his fork and ran it back and forth over the paper napkin beneath it. The new people hired in the lab were a concern. The impertinent son, whom he'd met years before when, as a teenager, the boy had come on a field trip with his father. And Louise Eldridge, leggy and beautiful, who Polly had let slip was some kind of amateur crime solver. Neither lent themselves to Ramon's purposes—very much the reverse.

And then his thoughts converged on Polly Whiting, the woman he'd almost had when she took her first Amazon trip with her older husband. That was fifteen years ago, when Peter had been a bridegroom well into his sixties. Ramon would have thought Peter would be sex-crazy, since his first wife had been sickly for years before she finally died. But he was more infatuated with *looking* at his young new wife than touching her. More taken up with watching her pluck orchids from trees than the earthier activities that Ramon had in mind for her. Ramon, being in his early thirties like Polly, had done his best when they were camped at night to lure the new bride into his tent. And he'd nearly done so, one restless, hot night when she couldn't sleep and wanted nothing better than to have the handsome, sweating Ramon ease her tension with one of his intimate massages. Just as he was laying hands on her, Matthew had arisen and started prowling nearby. The new bride had rushed back to the old scientist's side as if pursued by the legendary pink porpoise that came onto land, assumed the aspect of a man, and inseminated virgins. Polly was like a princess to the stunned natives, and a princess to him as well, a princess whose purity in the end he could not breach.

He hadn't managed it then, and there hadn't been further chances to do so. But he knew the Whitings' love life had been non-existent in recent years, for Peter had sickened with a strange disease he'd not even bothered to have diagnosed. Though they'd taken different paths in recent years, Ramon had kept careful track. And even though no doctor, Ramon had seen it before in the basin. It was tuberculosis, probably contracted from the birds. The net result was a weak husband with scant powers to please a woman in bed. She probably was hungry for sex right now.

Dorothy appeared with his food, and he smiled at the sight of it. "My dear," he said, in lieu of "Thank you."

Once she'd deposited the plate and the salad, and tinkered with his silverware, she said, "Anything else?"

He gave her a hooded look. "Free at nine as usual?"

"En*tirely.*"

"I'll pick you up—I'm no longer staying nearby, but I'll get a room there—maybe the old room." Dorothy, though a simple girl, had a primitive sex drive that made doing it with her a wildly athletic experience. She brought out the roughneck in him, but she was a bit of a roughneck herself. He smiled up at her, remembering it all.

"Maybe. I just *lo-ove* that pink room, too. Or you can come to my place—I'm just down the road apiece, near the Brakes-R-Us Shop."

"Whatever works out for us." And he briefly rested his hand on hers before she went back to serve her other customers.

Janie toyed with the food on her dinner plate as she listened with only half an ear to her mother's animated story of her day. She had to admit her parent told a pretty good story.

The strange tan mixture before her was another

specialty that came from the *Twenty-Minute Dinners* cookbook, but it tasted as if her mother had spent only ten minutes on it. Later, Janie would filch a cheese sandwich out of the kitchen.

Mostly, she was upset about her mother's irresponsible ways, for which this horrible dinner was a perfect metaphor. Janie had her life in order: She was a compulsive neatnik at home and at school, and liked to plan her life right down to the minute. Not only that, she was careful about the life choices she made. Not so her mother, who seemed headed straight for disaster. Janie sighed. She really didn't have the time to keep this woman out of trouble.

There was a pause in her mother's narrative and she leaped in. "It's interesting to hear about how to raise plants in test tubes, Ma, don't think it isn't. But all of a sudden you've started a whole new *second* job, and it's with a lot of people who are under suspicion."

Her mother chuckled and shook her head. "Darling, you have it wrong. *None* of those people at the lab are suspects in Dr. Whiting's death. Actually, they're all pretty nice people, as far as I can tell."

"It just seems creepy, having you work over there with the widow, and the son, and the doctor's assistant. But if you're sure, then I'll stop worrying about it. There's something else that really bugs me. While you're obsessing on this job of yours, did it ever occur to you that Thanksgiving's just around the corner?"

"I know; it's next Thursday. I have it all scheduled, Janie, the shopping, the cooking, the cleaning, the picking people up at the airport. . . ."

"Martha's bringing her beau. Where's he sleeping—in her 'shrine'?" This was Janie's mocking description of her older sister's mauve and white bedroom, kept just the way she left it when she went off to college.

"Of course not," said her mother. "He sleeps in the guest room."

Her dad said, "A beau, a Daley, by God—I'm looking forward to seeing what kind of a guy he is—though any grandson of the famous Chicago mayor has to be an interesting person."

"Oh, retch," murmured Janie, "I'm going to have *two* boyfriends around."

Her father laughed. "Janie, this is not a contest with your sister. You know we think Chris Radebaugh is a fine young man. . . ."

Janie and Chris, now a freshman at Princeton, had been an item for a year now—except her parents didn't realize what a permanent item they were.

"But with that Teddy Horton coming in from Connecticut to see you," continued her father, "you'll have your hands full."

Her mother said, "I don't want to be negative, but there's something—different about Teddy. I hope he gets along all right."

"Oh, don't worry," said Janie, "I can handle him. The one I'm not so sure of is that Melissa McCormick. Ma, I can't understand why you feel an obligation to adopt this kid. . . ."

"Janie, we're not adopting her. Her aunt wanted her to come for the weekend so she could have a break. Why, this poor little girl—"

"You told me she's wily."

"No, I didn't," objected her mother, "I said she was manipulative, like her father. And you might feel sorry for her. Her dad was *murdered* right here in our neighborhood, and he was my old friend."

"Ah, yes," said Janie, "the Mougeys' fish pond

will forever be known for this infamy. But I thought this guy Jay McCormick was your lover." She shot her mother a wise look.

"Not quite." Her parent was not willing to take the bait, and in fact was a lot more unflappable since she'd started her little test tube plant job. "Jay was just a boyfriend."

"If you say so."

Her father said, "We seem to have a lot of neighbors coming, Louise. What's the story there? How come they don't have anywhere else to go?"

Her mother said, "That's just the way with holidays, honey. People are a little troubled, they hint that they have no place to go, and then you have to invite them. Parents are dead, siblings maybe aren't speaking, lots of people are on their own. Chris's parents, Nora and Ron, well, they're not getting along, so they didn't want to go back to their own families. . . ."

"So the Radebaughs are coming *here*," moaned Janie. "Oh, *man* . . . this is *so* embarrassing for Chris, who is *so normal*, to have parents not getting along and the whole neighborhood knowing it. . . ."

"It is a shame," agreed her mother. "We're all hoping Nora and Ron can reconcile."

"By all means," said Janie tartly, "let's let it happen at the Thanksgiving table!"

Her father shot her a dirty look.

"And the Mougeys are coming," said her mother, "because, well, they just don't have a lot of relatives except way out in California. And the Sterns—I'm not sure what their story is. . . ."

"Not yet," said Janie with a toss of her long blond hair, "but you'll pry it out of Sandy Stern. But it'll be all right. We'll all *slide* our way through Thanksgiving, because Richard Mougey will bring lots of fancy wine and make a lot of toasts, and everyone will get a little sozzled. That way, all the misfits and unhappy people and weirdos like Teddy and Melissa will get along just fine."

"Janie," her father warned, "take it easy—you're going too far."

Janie could feel the color rising in her cheeks, and masked her embarrassment by dropping her hair over her face and busying herself with folding her napkin. She said, "It's just that I'm tired of being the only one who thinks about these things— about getting the house organized for Thanksgiving, about planning things so they go smoothly, instead of the usual lurching from crisis to crisis. About such questions as how certain guests will get along with certain other guests. About being sure the turkey is cooked throughout—not like last year, when it was pink and *bloody.*"

Janie now had her parents' full attention; they both were frowning at her. But she still wasn't finished. "Instead of my mom worrying about these things, she's working a second *job,* and of all things, with people who could be murderers! But I'm not going to do it anymore: no more worrying, no more trying to put a semblance of order in our lives. You guys are on your own." She got up from her chair and made a move toward the door. "As for me, I'm going to a rave."

"Oh, *no,* please, Janie!" cried her horrified mother. "I've read about them, and they're— dreadful. Please tell me you're not going to a *rave. . . .*"

Gotcha, thought Janie. "No, Ma, just kidding. I am not going to a rave. Don't you remember—you even said I could drive your car. I'm going to school for a meeting of the English Club."

"Of *course,*" said her mother. "I forgot."

With a parting smile, Janie slipped into the kitchen and grabbed the Honda keys off the hook, even as she heard her parents debating as to whether she should drive her father's Camry instead. She slipped quickly into her bedroom for her things, and then headed for the front door and freedom before they could change their minds.

Once they heard their daughter go out the door, Louise looked at her husband and sighed deeply. " *'Lurching from crisis to crisis'*? I guess I don't inspire confidence in the girl."

Bill sat back in his Hitchcock chair and smiled carefully. "Since you won't worry about what's going to happen on Thanksgiving, *she's* taken over for you."

Louise looked thoughtful. "Maybe we are asking for trouble, trying to crowd five young people into the house. This place is not that big; they're going to be right here in our laps." Her gaze drifted down to the base of his chair. The front legs were tilted off the ground again. "And by the way, we'll need every chair we own, so would you please not treat yours like that?"

He righted the chair and leaned forward and took her hand. "Five kids, plus Chris from across the street—well, we'll just expect them to act as if they're mature adults."

She nodded. "I'm sure they'll get along beautifully."

"Frankly, what bothers me more is why we had to invite all those dysfunctional neighbors of ours—"

"*Bill,* that's *cruel.* These are friends of yours—"

He rolled his eyes. "Sorry—not dysfunctional, then. How about *unique?* All I know is that you'll spend the day giving everyone couch time—hope you have time to fit in cooking the dinner."

"Bill, that is *such* an exaggeration—I hope you aren't going to turn into a worry wart like Janie. As I tried to tell her, everything's all organized. Why, go out and look at them—I have four separate lists in the kitchen right now, spelling out everything we have to do."

Her husband patted her hand and gave her a look which for an instant made her think he was not agreeing with her but just humoring a woman who was already in over her head.

9

Louise came to the lab Monday morning expecting the best of Matthew Whiting. After all, he'd settled down in those first two days of training and become quite friendly, and she foresaw a smooth working relationship with the young man. It took only an instant to have her hopes dashed.

As soon as she entered the lobby, he took her aside, and with eyes lit up like a naughty ten-year-old's, told her of his latest coup. "Look what I've got." He held up a silver object. "A key to the sacred premises."

She gave him a quick glance. His sharp nose almost quivered with the excitement of a trickster; he was delighted to be putting something over on the management. Who? Joe Bateman? Or his stepmother, Polly?

"So, did Polly give this to you?" Louise asked.

"Well, in a sense. It's one of the scarce-as-hen's-teeth master keys that have 'DO NOT COPY' engraved on them. When she and Joe went to that ISA meeting Friday, Polly happened to leave hers on her desk. I looked around in her files and found a folder with authorization papers that you take to a locksmith to get duplicates made, and was able to add my name to it. I got it copied and brought back the original. Joe Bateman would have a stroke if he knew I had one, but Mr. Security needn't know."

Louise just stared at him.

"Oh, never mind," he muttered in a disgusted voice. "I gotta say, I've learned one thing for certain about you, Louise—you're a real product of your little suburban upbringing; you are straight beyond *belief*."

Stung by his words, she trailed him into the vestibule, where, without speaking, they put on fresh lab coats. She began to wonder if she was going to enjoy this job after all. It was hard to work with a capricious character like Matthew. Joe Bateman suddenly loomed large in the vestibule doorway, a suspicious look on his face. "Something the matter with you two?"

"Naw, everything's copacetic," said Matthew jauntily. Joe took them to the growing room and carefully coached them in their latest assignment, which was to inspect every test tube for signs of mold. Mold indicated contamination and meant the plantlet had to be thrown out. As Joe described the work, Matthew interrupted a few times to mock him for his orderly procedures. Finally, the postdoctoral assistant turned to the young man, his face masking what must be considerable annoyance. He said quietly, "It's as if three days in the lab have given you enough expertise to propose lab practices that might suit your personal style, but certainly don't suit mine. Do you want to follow orders, or do you want to get out of here?"

Matthew opened his hands in a sign of submissiveness. "Hey, Joe, don't get hot now." He looked at Louise and shrugged his shoulders, as if saying,

I tried to make this man reasonable. After his initial arguments with Joe, the young man settled down and he and Louise got to work.

"Here's a bad one," said Matthew, holding a test tube up against the light, and then they found more damaged plants. They transferred them out of the rack and into a tub on the rolling cart that accompanied them down the aisle. "It's interesting," he said, "that they're clumped together. I hate to admit I'm wrong, but I'm beginning to see why the boss wants everything done in such an obsessive way. Otherwise we couldn't have picked up a pattern like this. That contamination makes you wonder what the plant technician was doing at the moment he was working with them."

Louise chuckled. "Maybe just breathing too hard did it."

"Maybe it did," said Matthew soberly. "Contamination's one of the reasons I've given up smoking while working here. After all, Louise, even if you and I sometimes disagree, we both love these baby plants. I need to do something in this world to make my mark—I'm sure not being *bequeathed* a fortune or anything. So if I ever decide to return to my first love, science—I mean getting back into it full-time as a teacher, for instance—I know I could make people love plants just like my dad did. Maybe I could find a plant, like he did, that will advance mankind."

She looked at him curiously. It was not the first time she had seen Matthew Whiting change from being an unreasonable boor into a semblance of a fine human being. Either he was practicing his craft and acting, or else he meant it. With a stretch, she could see him becoming a scientist someday, though his use of the diminutive term "baby plants" sounded a little non-scientific.

Maybe he'd pick up more of Joe's professional lingo if he stayed around here long enough.

They had only examined half of the test tube plants in the big growing room when Polly Whiting's first visitor appeared. Dr. Ramon Jorges sailed in, swarthy and self-confident. The only flaws in his perfect physical appearance were ugly diagonal scratch marks on his left cheek.

Joe grinned knowingly and said, "What happened, Ramon, get scratched by a cat?"

Ramon bathed his small audience in a warm smile. "Something rather like that—more like a lioness." But he had scant time for jokes, immediately intruding himself in the lab's daily operations. After a few advisory words to Joe, he focused on the two new employees. He strolled over to the bench where Louise and Matthew were discarding more plants. "Don't you think you should wear masks to work in here?" he said abruptly.

"Not according to Joe," said Louise, "since these test tubes are sealed."

"That may be so," said the Brazilian scientist, "but it's good in these environments to wear them constantly, so that you don't forget them when they're needed most."

She said, "You mean, when working in the transfer room—well, we don't forget."

Ignoring her answer, he drew himself up, reminding Louise of a large bird getting ready to preen. "You must remember where these tiny plants came from—a jungle region of such bigness and such resources that they seem illimitable. But it's proven every day that they are not. These precious little plants . . ."

"Are handled in a thoroughly sanitary way," snapped Joe Bateman, who had come up to see what was going on.

Jorges arched a dark eyebrow and cast his glance down at the discarded test tubes in the tub. "Your losses from contamination seem high."

Joe, normally unflappable, was getting angry. "They're within a reasonable range, Ramon. It might be a good idea if you didn't jump to conclusions."

What was Ramon trying to prove? Louise could not understand why Polly, silent at his side, was acting so intimidated. If Polly and her husband Peter had removed the *Tabebuia* plant material legally from that tiny Indian village in the Amazon, he should have no hold on her. Why, then, did he have such a sense of entitlement?

The South American turned away from Joe, just in time to catch an unguarded expression on Louise's face. He obviously didn't like it; her slightly curved lip, her narrowed eyes. A little tinge of fear ran through her; Ramon Jorges was not the kind of person she wanted for an enemy.

Next, Louise was astounded to see him guide Polly into the research lab, talking and explaining all the way: "This area, state-of-the-art as it is, could have been made larger, for the future of these labs may require a much larger commitment to research. . . ." For all the world, he acted as if *he* were giving a tour of *his* lab. Louise could only guess that under all his show-off talk he was desperate to learn the latest on the research on the *Tabebuia.* Then Ramon and Polly went into the anterooms, and Louise was able to relax and settle down to her work.

Later, Louise had to leave the growing room to use the women's facilities. She emerged just in time to see Ramon and Polly, standing in a corner of the lobby. Not wanting to intrude, she remained in the shadows near the ladies' room.

The Brazilian was like a caricature, swarming

over Polly as if to devour her. "My dear, you are the loveliest thing I have ever seen—a true goddess. . . ."

"Please, Ramon," Polly said, trying to shove him away. It was like shoving an octopus, for as one arm was pushed away, another encircled her.

"Polly, you know how I've always felt. . . ."

"No, I don't know, and I can't do this—"

He withdrew slightly, and decided on another approach. He released his arms, leaned over her, raised a hand, and slowly caressed her cheek. It was a full-scale caress that Louise was shocked to see the widow did not rebuff. Then he placed a lingering kiss on the place he had just caressed, and said, "You need me, my dear, more than you may think."

It was as if Polly was paralyzed, but just for a moment. Then she broke from her seeming trance, and cried, "Oh, *please* . . ." As his arms came out to capture her again, she turned her head and stumbled away from him toward the front door.

"You must go, Ramon," she ordered, pulling her sweater straighter, though it was undisturbed by their little encounter.

While Polly Whiting ushered him out, Louise slipped by and returned to the laboratory. She was disturbed, though she realized she shouldn't be. Widows, she had heard, were prone to being hit on—and this man was a temptation, a walking sex machine. She wondered how long Polly could resist.

When she returned to work, Matthew noticed she was preoccupied. "Wha's happ'nin, Louise? You look a little shell-shocked."

The neat, dark-haired Matthew, with his height and his thin face and nose, reminded her painfully of the murdered scientist. Here he was in his father's lab, helping continue his father's work, and as proprietary about the place now as Joe was. But still Louise didn't completely trust him, and the reason was rather silly: Herb. Dr. Whiting's old dog accompanied Polly each day to Whiting Labs, spending his time snoozing in her office. From the animal's growls, it was clear *he* didn't trust Matthew and wouldn't let him anywhere near him.

"Oh, maybe just not feeling so good," she lied. "How're you doing—find any more contamination?"

Later in the day, Louise's beloved routine was disturbed again when Dr. James Conti showed up for the tour that Joe Bateman told her was in the works. He was even less friendly than the Brazilian, and walked through the place as if he owned it. Another man with a sense of entitlement. But why?

As he passed Louise and Matthew, he paused. He recognized her coworker with a cold "Hello, Matthew." Then he said to Louise, "You're the amateur snoop, aren't you—the one who lives right here in the neighborhood? Well, how's crime in the neighborhood?"

If the remark was supposed to be funny, it fell flat. Polly Whiting, standing in back of the biology dean, looked shocked.

"We're all very concerned about the crimes in our neighborhood, Dr. Conti," said Louise, "but I have nothing to do with them. You have me wrong if you think I run around all the time investigating things. I'm quite busy with a career in television."

He waved a hand dismissively. "Oh, I know about that, too," he said, walking on down the aisle. She looked after him and felt like sticking out her tongue. James Conti was another know-it-all.

Poor Polly. Her audacious old husband had started up a biotech lab that was sure to be hugely profitable. And now, with her husband dead, she was supposed to handle it all, including these scavenger types who seemed to want to take it over from her—or at least to share in the bonanza. One appeared to want to bed her down, the other to twist her arm off.

Fountain-of-youth schemes, she guessed, must always have had their perils, starting with that disappointing venture of Ponce de Leon in Florida. That started her thinking, and she reached up and touched the skin at the side of her mouth, the place where she had perceived a wrinkle the other day.

"It would be interesting to try that tea myself."

Matthew looked over at her. "Doesn't look like you need it yet." She was noticing that Matthew could be rather sweet.

"Thanks, but there are certain wrinkles forming. . . ."

"Hey, Louise, whatever turns you on. Ask Polly. I'm sure she'd make you a part of the trials."

"Polly certainly has a lot of people traveling through this place."

"Yeah," said Matthew. "I feel a little sorry for her—trying to keep the vultures at bay."

"That's what I thought, too."

"You just saw Conti in action. In my book, he's the academic egotist type. I don't think my father ever liked him. But since Polly was a project administrator at Jefferson U when Dad met her, she ought to know how to handle him. Ramon Jorges is another story. I met Ramon once fifteen years ago down in the jungle when we were on a field trip. It was also Dad and Polly's honeymoon, but Jorges didn't care about *that.* I know, because I'd be awake in my tent. The big creep tried to put the make on her, but I managed to stir around enough to scare him off."

He shrugged his thin, sharp shoulders. "She was a lot younger than Dad, so I guess I wasn't too surprised at her for being tempted."

"You mean—" Louise stopped, deciding to leave that topic alone.

"So now I guess Ramon's reputation has gone downhill."

"I know," said Louise. "I looked him up on the Internet and found a *New York Times* article about him."

Matthew grinned at her. "Hey, didja look me up?"

"No, of course not. I just remembered that distinctive name."

He glanced up. "Hey, look—she's dragging another one through . . . except he doesn't look the vulture type. More of a broken-down salesman, I'd say. Maybe he's selling test tubes."

Louise glanced toward the double doors, where Polly was entering again with a big man with a shock of white, curly hair. A man with nice, friendly marblelike blue eyes. He looked at Louise in amazement.

She walked slowly up the aisle to where Polly stood with her visitor.

"Louise, meet Detective, uh . . ." She put a slim, tanned hand on the sleeve of the man's worn jacket. "I'm *so* sorry, I've forgotten your name, Detective . . ."

"Michael Geraghty," said the man.

Polly sounded nervous. "He's just come on a routine visit and wanted to meet the staff and look around the lab."

Louise didn't put out her hand, because she had on latex gloves. She smiled up at the man. "Detective Geraghty and I know one another."

Mike Geraghty took a large sip from his cup, and decided it was about the best coffee he'd ever had. He sat in the overstuffed chair in the Eldridge living room, slanting rays of the afternoon sun coming through the big glass windows and creating a dappled pattern on the thick rug. He was as comfortable as he had ever been in his half-dozen or more visits to this house in the woods, a house that probably had seen more action than any other house in Fairfax County—with the possible exception of a couple of crack houses in some scummy urban parts of the jurisdiction.

As he had told his subordinate, George Morton, "Louise Eldridge attracts crime like a navy blue suit attracts lint."

"This is about the best cuppa coffee I've ever had," he now said.

She smiled. "I'm glad you like it, Detective Geraghty. I favor the kind that stands up by itself—though Bill says it's going to kill me someday."

"Gotta die of something," he said, leaning forward in his chair. "I darned near passed out when I walked into those laboratories and saw you in a white lab coat and hat."

"I bet you did. Bill said you were surprised to learn after Dr. Whiting's murder that I'd known the old man. I told Detective Morton, when he dropped over the day after the murder, that we used to dog-walk together. That led to his widow offering me a job in the lab. And I love it—I'm learning so much." She tucked her feet underneath her on the sofa and rubbed them. "Except my feet hurt from standing up all day."

"I bet they do."

She looked at him uncertainly. "You didn't come here because you think there's something wrong with my working there, do you?"

He set his coffee cup firmly on the table beside his chair, then rested a hand on either knee. "Louise—pardon if I slip and call you Louise, but I feel I know you pretty well—for a change I'm not tryin' to squelch your activities. Just the reverse." His blue eyes stared at her. "Now, I know your husband doesn't want you to get involved—he told me so himself. But since you're already working in that lab, I could use your eyes and ears. I'd like you to do a little checkin' for us."

"You mean—detecting?"

He put up a big hand. "Now, wait. No, no detecting. But you're *in place* over there, with the widow, with that postdoctoral guy, and with the son. We've talked to all three, of course, and the widow twice. I hear folks drop in, people from the university and whatnot. I'd just like you to keep your ears open and report back anything interesting. Nothin' fancy: let's just call it *'research.'* "

"Well, well," she said. Geraghty could see the smile playing around her lips. The woman must be pleased with his offer; now, if only she didn't go overboard.

"So you'll do it?"

"Of course, I'd like to help the police." There was a little irony in this remark, since the woman had solved crimes right under the nose of the Fairfax police force more than once.

"I gotta give you some facts, Louise, so you don't do anything—rash." He nearly said "foolish," which he knew would be a turnoff and might queer the deal. "Quite frankly, the CID in the past eleven days has gotten exactly nowhere on Peter Whiting's murder, despite a three-state alert. No weirdos that we know could have done it. No recently released convicts, or folks like that, who haven't been accounted for. Anyway, we need to do a little deeper investigation of the people nearest the professor."

She shrugged. "I work with them every day."

"We know. We're also interested in a couple of others, a Dr. James Conti—he was Whiting's boss, and no love lost there apparently. Then a man named Jorges, who used to do field research with Whiting and apparently is in the States visiting."

"Ramon."

"Yeah? You already know him?"

"They were both at Whiting Labs today."

"Conti is the one we're most interested in. Dr. Jorges tells us he arrived in the States after the murder, though we have still to check that out."

"I've talked to Conti a little, and it wasn't a very pleasant conversation; he seems to dislike me, though I can't imagine why. And he intimidates the widow, but at least he hasn't told everyone what to do in the lab the way Jorges has."

"Ah," said Geraghty, and he pulled out his notebook and jotted down "Conti intimidating" and "Jorges—bossy in lab."

"Hold on a minute until I get something." She went to her computer and picked up the printout of the story on Ramon Jorges. Returning to the living room, she handed it to the policeman. "There— that will tell you about this man. Even though he's been a popular lecturer on finding new plants for medicines, he's been in trouble lately with Brazilian authorities."

Geraghty perused the article quickly. "Interesting—though not as crucial as something else I have on my mind. Louise, I'd like to get a better feel for the situation at those biology labs at Jefferson University in Georgetown. I don't suppose you'd ever go there—maybe do a TV show at the university?"

Louise put a hand on her chin and thought about it. "Since they have at least a couple of plant laboratories there, I suppose I could get Marty

Corbin to agree to do a program on test tube plants out of Jefferson. I hear someone is raising African trees, for instance."

Geraghty gestured with his big hand. "Perfect. Think Conti'd agree to that?"

"I don't know why not; it's amazing how easy it is to get people to agree to let us do a show about their life's work. It's not Conti's baby African trees, but it's *his* biology lab, and he'd probably love the publicity."

"That way, you could get a read both on Conti and Joe Bateman, too. That takes care of a couple of people. I hear Bateman worked at the university for some years until recently—you could get a little somethin' on him."

"Oh, sure—Joe. He burned all his bridges, as he puts it, to go with Peter Whiting's biotech business, but not too long ago. They should know all about him."

"Great. We're talking about just normal stuff—no surveillances, no sneaky things, nothing even faintly illegal, agreed?"

She smiled broadly. "But I'm going to love this investigating, Mike. I thought my job with test tube plants was good. This one's even better!"

He pursed his lips and frowned, looking carefully out the big living room windows into the woods.

"What's the matter? You don't trust me completely, do you?"

"Naw, but that's okay, Louise. I know your heart is right." He leaned forward again and pointed a warning finger at her. "The reason you can't do anything faintly suspicious is that it could get you *killed.*"

She laughed at him again. "I assumed that to be true, since we're dealing with a killer."

Geraghty heaved a big sigh. "Y'know, Louise, I

don't like to have to tell ya this, but you're being way too lighthearted about your new assignment."

"Tell me what?"

"That Peter Whiting's eyes and tongue were gouged to pieces with a knife."

The words hung in the air between them like a presence. Louise's smile faded and she closed her eyes. "My *God,*" she said finally. "I only hope he was dead when someone did that to him."

"We're not sure, Louise, but at least the knife wounds to the heart area came soon after."

She shook her head and looked forlornly down at her lap. "No wonder you think you have a maniac on your hands."

"I hated to tell you that," said the detective, "but I decided you should know, especially if you're going to go out and ask questions. You can see now what I mean about being real careful."

He sat back in his chair, blew out a breath of air, and tried to relax a little. "If that little pit-bull reporter friend of yours, Charlie Hurd, was covering the story for the *Washington Post,* he probably would have throttled the facts out of the officers who were first on the crime scene. But so far, the information on the disfigurement of the face hasn't trickled out, and that's the way we want it."

"Mike, what about the girl in the woods who was slashed and got away—what exactly happened to her?"

"The assailant grabbed her arm and went for her with the knife, but she's a little, sprightly thing—not a seventy-seven-year-old man in ill health—and she ducked away and outran him. Got a few gashes on her arm is all. So that's two knife attacks—that's why we believe it's a serial killer. It's why we're warning people to refrain from nighttime strolls in the woods around here. On the other hand . . ."

"You could be wrong."

"Yeah, and that's why you are in a perfect situation to rule out these people once and for all."

Louise Eldridge smiled, but her attractive hazel eyes were sad; they'd looked that way ever since he'd told her those details about Peter Whiting's slaying.

It was seven o'clock, exactly one hour beyond the customary time he was used to receiving his call from Carl.

"Sorry I'm late," Carl said. "Terrible day. I hope you have progress to report."

"From everything I have been able to find out, Carl, you'd better chill out. Maybe you had better start altering that schedule of yours."

"What the hell . . . what's happened?"

"Nothing's happened, except the widow's determined to go on with the project, almost as if she never lost her husband and mentor. She has new employees on the scene, and is on the verge of hiring more."

Carl subsided into silence on the other end of the phone. "This is not good. The sooner she sells out, the better a deal it will be for us. God knows how many people will be after that woman."

"There was lots of talk at the ISA meeting. They call it Whiting's 'magic plant.'"

"And we damned well both know that buzz will drive the price through the goddamned roof," snarled Carl.

He didn't like Carl, but he decided that mergers and acquisitions types were all pricks, just like this one. Coolly, he said, "Since it isn't your goddamned money, why are you getting so hot?"

"Because there's heat at that other end," grouched Carl.

"There's nothing much I can do beyond what I'm al-

ready trying to do, in the most tactful way." He hated to
extend this conversation, but he had to. *"One other little
thing—"*

"Not more bad news, for God's sake—"

*"Sort of. One of the new employees is a woman who
lives near Whiting Phytoseutical, and has a reputation,
apparently, for solving crimes."*

Carl's voice was sly. *"Well, we don't know of any
crimes, do we, so she oughtn't be one of our concerns."*

*"She's the kind of person who picks up things fast—
you can tell."*

*"You mean, she could somehow tell you and I were in
league in trying to get the widow to sell the company?
Come on—it's all perfectly legal, even if she got wind of
it."*

*"I guess so. She's just a strange person to be working
in that lab."*

"If you have to, I'm sure you could discourage her,"
said Carl. *"You know, get her to stop being the suspicious
type. Now, about your tactful way of doing things . . ."*
He gave a dirty laugh.

"What about it?"

*"Maybe you should forget tact. It's the widow I'm con-
cerned about, not some dilettante detective. I take it you
haven't bedded down Polly Whiting yet. You must not realize how vulnerable widows are. They long for a man—
it's something visceral in them."*

"Polly is . . . one hell of a woman."

"So I hear," said Carl. *"So get on it. She's awash right
now with emotions—you know, anger, loss, guilt . . ."*

As the industrial bully went on and on, he tuned out.
His sexual fantasy of himself with Polly Whiting was in
place once again, and bigger than life now, a fantasy of
him immersing his longing self in those blue, blue eyes
and that luscious, bronzed body. . . .

When he tuned back in, Carl was saying, *". . . so it's
a good time to put the screws to 'er, if not sexually, at
least psychologically. Make her realize she can't handle*

this, that this is going to be way too huge for her, on that little site on Route One in Fairfax County. It has gotta be moved to our headquarters in Kansas City. It can occupy as many acres and as many buildings as we need."

"Whiting's little magic plant, going big-time . . ."

"Yeah. And your job—and believe me, I couldn't care less how you do it—is to get it for us. I'm not asking any stuffy questions about what you've done so far, and I won't have any questions in the future."

It took a while for Louise to get through to her daughter Martha in Evanston. Roommates in her student apartment reported that she was at the Northwestern University library and would be there until it closed at midnight. This was no surprise, since Martha had always been a bookworm, and had a double major in political science and English. The call came after Louise and Bill had gone to bed. She grabbed a robe to throw on over her silk charmeuse nightie and rushed with the portable phone from the bedroom so she wouldn't disturb her husband.

"Ma, is everybody all right?"

"Oh, yes, I didn't mean to frighten you. *Our* family is all right, I mean. Though something did happen in the neighborhood—to a friend of mine. I thought Janie told you when she phoned the other day."

"Yes, I heard about the professor getting murdered. Have they found the killer?"

"No, but there are lots of police working on it. His name was Dr. Peter Whiting, and it was a horrible crime. . . ."

"I know, right there in Ravine Park. I've been studying, or I would have called and commiserated. I'd heard about your nightly walks with the old professor."

"He was a wonderful man. The reason I called is

that you're the only person I feel comfortable about sharing this with. Guess what? Detective Geraghty wants me to help with the case."

"Oh no," groaned Martha. "Can't you keep out of this sort of thing? It's getting embarrassing for the family."

Louise sighed. It wasn't the response she'd expected from her daughter. "I called you because I felt good about this. I can't tell Janie how I feel about things, because I get the distinct impression she doesn't want to know. There's something going on with Janie. . . ."

"There's always something going on with Janie—don't worry about it. Back to you, Ma. So you're happy about this."

"Yes. Mike Geraghty called it 'doing research.' It gives me a great sense of what you like to call validation"—she chuckled—"or what I like to call self-satisfaction, because I've been good at helping the police in the past, but they've never acknowledged it until now."

"Oh, boy," said Martha. "So, what do you get to do, chase prospective killers?"

"Actually, no. I now work for Mrs. Whiting. . . ."

"The widow?"

"Yes, and that means I can report on the activities of four or five people, all of whom could, I suppose, have some sort of motive to kill this darling old man—even though the police already have a profile of the killer."

"What kind of a profile might that be?"

"A very crazy person." Somehow, Louise didn't want to tell her the details over the phone.

"Swell. The mother I rarely see is now pursuing a serial killer."

"That's not it, Martha—I'm not looking for the person who did it. I'm helping the police eliminate other possibilities: the young widow, the postdoc assistant, the jealous biology dean boss, the pushy Brazilian scientist, the difficult son...."

"That sounds like an easy job," said Martha breezily, *"not.* Ma, you be careful. I'll be home soon; then, if you need help, I'll be there. Why, even Jim will be happy to help you snoop; he's a natural."

"Jim Daley? Your father is looking forward to meeting him, and so am I."

"I know why—you're curious to know what kind of a guy I like."

"That's part of it, I suppose."

"He's down-to-earth, let's put it that way."

"And while you're home, dear, especially since you're staying a few extra days, I hope you and your sister and I can do something nice together."

"Don't strain for it, Ma." Martha's voice couldn't have been more matter-of-fact. "It's hard to turn back the clock to the days when the three of us went out together swimming at the Y, or shopping for clothes. Janie's all caught up with Chris—*big-time.* Why don't you and I just plan to go out for a beer some night?"

Louise suddenly had a foreshadowing of Thanksgiving, and it was not a cozy picture.

10

"Louise," said Marty Corbin, "I don't care zilch about baby African trees."

"But, Marty, millions of plants are raised in test tubes every year, from blueberries to orchids. It's time we did a show on it."

"Then let's feature something the public knows about—*blue*berries, or petunias, or zinnias. A program on raising baby African trees doesn't grab me."

"It would be about how trees mate in jungle areas after a bulldozer has come down and ripped away most of the forest."

"That makes it even less sexy," said her producer sarcastically, "but right in character for an earnest environmentalist like you."

Louise realized she was going to have to tell him the truth. Marty also was on a hiatus from his work at WTBA-TV, so when she phoned him, she knew she probably had fetched him away from his favorite vacation pursuit, watching old movies. That made it tougher to sell him on doing a show at Jefferson University.

"I have a reason, Marty, why we *should* do a show there—or at least check it out."

"Oh, you do? I thought our reasons were usually because it had an appeal to the wide viewing public . . . you know, gardening knowledge to be imparted, even a simple—and I emphasize simple—environmental message to be conveyed to our above-average-in-intelligence viewers—and not some esoteric stuff to which people cannot relate."

"I'm helping the cops with a case."

He started with a chuckle, and ended up laughing uproariously on the other end of the phone. Finally she had to hold the receiver away from her ear. She could just picture Marty, a big man with dark curly hair and liquid brown eyes, slouched in a chair in his family room, with his wife Steffi most likely in the kitchen making one of her tasty lunches for him, tolerating and coddling her temperamental spouse because at least he was faithful again. He would be tapping his fingers on any nearby flat surface, anxious to get off the phone and take the VCR off "pause" so he could get into the movie plot again.

It took a while for him to quit laughing. "You're at it again. What is it this time—oh, yes, let me guess. You knew that professor who was murdered down there in that trendy little neighborhood of yours. So now you're helping the authorities. Good. It's probably the sick son of one of your upscale neighbors, did you know that, Louise? I figured that out the minute I heard it—knew it wasn't some *random* serial killer—let's face it. *Random* serial killers don't hang out in neighborhoods like yours, or mine, for that matter. Our Chevy Chase cops are not that good, but they're better than that. So are the cops out your way. Random killers operate in less *personal,* urban neighborhoods. Tell those Fairfax fuzz that it's some kid sitting in the front window of his house thinking up who he'll carve up next."

"How did you know . . ."

"I read the papers, listen to the news, figure things out." A little chuckle. "Anyway, guys from Philadelphia like me always know the score. Girl is stabbed in woods. Professor is killed in same woods. Police think one person did 'em both. So it's not too hard to figure the professor got it with a knife, too. Tell the cops *I* say it's somebody sitting in a house. Then you won't be expected to go up to Jefferson University and snoop around the biology labs."

"Oh, *Marty*. It isn't that easy. Can't I at least go there with an associate producer—maybe Doug— and scope the place out. Let *him* decide. At least that will get me in."

"That's really all you want, Louise, to get in the door. What the hell are you gonna do once you're there? Pilfer things? Look, you have a certain dignity to maintain, and let's say I don't want you to end up in jail—it would disturb the hell out of our spring shooting schedule."

"I wouldn't do anything like that, Marty."

"Oh, yeah, I know," he said in an unbelieving tone.

"So I talked with Dr. James Conti, the biology dean. Doug and I could drop by on Friday."

"That's the day after Thanksgiving—people don't work that day."

"Some people plan to, like Dr. Conti. He's probably a workaholic."

"But I thought you were havin' lots of company—your long-lost Martha comin' home, and everything. . . ."

"By Friday, Marty, I'll be half-mad and will need to get out of the house. I'll have had six young people hanging around the house."

Her producer chuckled. "All right, let's make it Friday."

"It won't take long. Conti says he doesn't have much time, so he put strict limits on our visit—one hour, nine o'clock until ten o'clock." She remembered the brief, unfriendly conversation with the dean. "He's not a very agreeable person. Actually, he doesn't like me at all. . . ."

"My, my, Louise, quit having to have everyone *like* you. I never worry about that. The only thing you need to worry about is to try not to have people *kill* you."

"Very funny. Well, can we do it? Would Doug go with me Friday?"

"I bet he would, Louise, 'cuz we all love ya, and we'll give in to this little whim of yours. If a program pans out, that's good. If it doesn't, that's not so good. But I figure we owe you a little something."

"Thanks, Marty, and I'm sorry I disturbed your movie."

"That's all right. I've seen it so many times I ain't gonna be shocked to know the man fathered his daughter's child."

"Oh. *Chinatown.* Dark, Marty, very dark."

"Hey, Louise, no darker than some of the stuff you get into. Remember, *I'm* not the one who's helping the cops sniff out a murderous slasher."

11

Melissa McCormick was the first to arrive on Wednesday afternoon, and the sight of her walking up the flagstone path to the house gave Louise a nostalgic flashback. The scrawny thirteen-year-old of last summer was changed. She still had a mass of untamed, curly red long hair and pale skin, but her body had filled out and she had the pelvic tilt of a dancer, which undoubtedly invited the interest of the opposite sex. Louise was reminded powerfully of her daughter Janie at the same age. Fortunately, Janie had moved out of this nymphet stage into being a more mature young woman.

With perfect composure, the girl strode up the walk ahead of a tired but athletic-looking redhead in her forties. Melissa's maiden Aunt Moira, carrying Melissa's bulging suitcase. For Louise this was a bad sign. Yet maybe there was a reason—and still another reason for why the girl had brought enough duds for a permanent stay.

"Auntie *Louise,*" Melissa cried when she saw her, and threw out her arms and ran the rest of the way up the pergola-covered walk to the front door where Louise stood. The girl wrapped her arms around her as if she needed to be rescued from harm.

Louise looked over Melissa's head into the amiable, freckled face of Moira McCormick. They smiled, having known each other briefly years ago, when Louise and Moira's brother Jay were going together while students at Georgetown. When Jay returned to visit Louise last year and ended up murdered, Moira stepped in to take over the care of the virtual orphan Melissa.

It turned out the girl had a strained back. "Nothing serious, Auntie Louise, just too much gymnastics at Arlington High." Ah, thought Louise, gymnastics, not dancing.

Moira smiled. "She fell off the high beam, but she's mending."

"I never would have guessed," said Louise, and began to keep score. One able-bodied teenager helper, sidelined for injuries. Tomorrow's formidable Thanksgiving dinner for fifteen was starting to worry her, and she needed to know whom to count on for support. Melissa did not look like she'd make a good kitchen helper.

"In fact," said Melissa in a voice filled with self-absorption, "I'd love a lie-down. Can I just flop somewhere and take a rest?"

"Go into the blue bedroom, the right-hand bed. That one's yours for the weekend."

When the girl walked down the hall, she now appeared to have a slight limp. Moira exchanged a look with Louise and said, "It's been a hard year for her, with her father killed like that and her mother gone, too. She has problems, but I think she'll make it."

"You go and have a nice change of scenery, Moira. By the way, where are you going?"

"Oh, of course," she said, handing Louise a card. "Here's where I'll be." A dreamy smile lit up the woman's pale blue eyes. "It's a spa in upper Maryland. And I can't thank you enough, Louise."

The woman started down the path, but then turned back. "And don't pay any attention to Melissa's pouts," she called out. "They're like the limp—just attention-grabbers." With that she got into her car and drove off.

A pouty fourteen-year-old? Louise realized she didn't know this girl at all, even though Melissa familiarly called her "Auntie."

She went quietly into the house and sank down into a Hitchcock chair at the antique dining room table. Before her was a lined legal pad with two lists; one, the Thanksgiving dinner menu, the other, "to do" items, such as setting up tables, and rearranging furniture in bedrooms to make room for suitcases.

She put her elbows on the table and her hands under her chin and pored over the lists. It was time for her to get a move on, except the lists looked so long and formidable that they made her want to go take a nap herself. Yet she knew this was not real fatigue, but simply the faint hysteria she suffered at holidays.

What she needed was a good, stand-up cup of coffee. She went to the kitchen, and it took five minutes of machinations. She ground the black, oily beans, positioned the coffee in the filter on the Chemex coffeemaker, waited for the boiling water to descend a few degrees, then poured it over the grounds, and retrieved a deep, brown, gorgeous-smelling liquid. She was sipping a cup of it when Teddy Horton noiselessly slipped in the front door. "Hi, Louise!" he called.

In surprise, she jolted her coffee sideways so that it spilled all over her lists. "Oh, my God,

Teddy, you nearly scared me to death," she said, leaving the mess and going to greet him.

"Sorry to scare you, but here I am." Teddy's toothy smile, his thin, country face with its turned-up nose and pale eyes, and his tan, stand-up hair instantly melted her heart. What a wholesome-looking young man he was.

"The door was ajar, Louise, so I thought you wanted me to just come in. For a minute, I sort of thought of this like the Litchfield Falls Inn." The Eldridges and their neighbors the Radebaughs had spent a memorable weekend at the inn, during which Teddy Horton became attached to Janie. He had invited himself for a reprise at Thanksgiving. The only one who wasn't enthusiastic about this plan was Janie's beau, Chris Radebaugh.

She gave Teddy a hug and said, "I want you to make yourself right at home." He did, rejecting her offer of coffee, and instead went into the kitchen, made a lightning investigation of the cupboards, and got himself a glass of water. Then he wandered around the living room and dining room, while she mopped up the coffee spill on her pad. Finally, he looked at her as if she could tell him where the missing object was. "So, where's Janie?"

She sat back down in her chair. "She's picking up people at the airport—Chris Radebaugh, just in from Princeton, and her older sister, Martha, from Northwestern, and Martha's boyfriend, Jim Daley, who just graduated from law school."

"That's quite a bunch." He looked around, as if measuring the house's dimensions. "Do you have enough room? I can always sleep in my car."

"Oh, no," said Louise. "I have it all planned out. You and this Jim Daley share a bedroom. Melissa McCormick—she's a younger friend of ours who's just arrived—bunks with Janie. And Martha sleeps in her room. *Chris,* of course, stays in his own house across the cul de sac."

She looked at her young guest. "What I'm worried about, Teddy, is dinner." There, she'd thrown him the bait. Looking like a character out of a Norman Rockwell magazine cover, Teddy was deceptive. He was a boy from a poor rural family who had been trained and polished into a maitre d' and general factotum at the posh Litchfield Falls Inn. When she and Bill met him, he was so efficient and debonair that they would never have guessed his humble beginnings. This twenty-one-year-old ran a restaurant kitchen with wizardly ease; surely, Louise's kitchen would be a *cinch.*

He looked at Louise oddly, and she realized how unkempt she was: She hadn't had time to change out of her old gray sweats, and she'd even neglected to brush her hair.

Teddy seemed to recognize a frantic woman when he saw one. Now, hearing the word "dinner," he orbited the table and came around and sat down next to her. "So what's the head count?"

"Fifteen."

He looked at the table for twelve at which they sat, and wrinkled up his nose. "Where—"

"I have another table for four—won't that do? Put it in the living room? Shove it up against this one?"

"We'll do something with it—probably join the two. How about the menu?"

She shoved over the coffee-stained yellow legal pad. "Here it is. To tell you the truth, although my family and friends warned me, I haven't done any cooking yet, though the shopping's complete. I did it after work yesterday—I even laid in a couple of bought pies in case I don't have time to make homemade ones."

Teddy glanced at the stained list. He almost sniffed in disdain. He looked down at his watch, then gave her a snaggle-toothed grin. "We have just twenty-four hours to pull this off, Mrs. Eldridge!"

"Oh, Teddy," she said, sighing, "I'm so glad you came. I—there's something about Thanksgiving that scares me. I think it's my grandmother's reputation. She was a wonderful cook, and ever since I've believed I had to be as good as she was—and I never *am.*"

Teddy looked bored: obviously, he wasn't interested in her deep psychological feelings about the holiday. He got up from his chair. "Just show me what you've got in the fridge and the freezer; that's what counts now. We may have to go shopping for a few items."

"Oh, Teddy," she said, sounding repetitious even to herself. She showed him around the kitchen, and he immediately spied the canned cranberry sauce sitting on the counter.

"Canned?" he asked incredulously.

"That's just in case mine scorches."

He shook his head and grinned. "I can't believe you, Louise." He continued exploring the contents of the stuffed refrigerator; then he moved on to examine the ill-marked packages filling the freezer.

Finally, Teddy stood in the middle of the kitchen with arms crossed. "What you have here are the makings of a really *mundane* meal. And on Thanksgiving? Barbara Seymour would never settle for this." Barbara was the elegant mistress of the Litchfield Falls Inn, where every meal reflected the inn restaurant's four-star rating.

"Let's get outta here, Louise," he said, "and go to a really good market. Do they have any in northern Virginia—or do we have to drive to the District of Columbia?"

"There's one in Alexandria," she said eagerly, and then remembered something. "By the way, the neighbors I've invited have insisted on bringing things. . . ."

"*Oh*-oh," said Teddy, as if someone were trying to intrude on an otherwise perfect scheme. "But we'll manage that, I guess."

"Hold on just for a couple of minutes while I change my clothes, and I'll be ready to go." She hurried to the bedroom, vaguely aware that she was forgetting something. But as she quickly pulled on some slacks and a sweater, she smiled. The arrival of the competent Teddy made her feel like a drowning woman who had just been thrown a rope.

12

It was the arrival of the carload from Reagan Airport that signaled the real beginning of the weekend. In it were also the seeds of the *unraveling* of the weekend, had Louise but known it.

Louise hadn't even come down from the high of shopping with Teddy at Wild Foods in Alexandria. Gourds, bunchy cornstalks, several ears of dried Indian corn—those just for decorations—plus plump organic cranberries, fresh oysters for the stuffing, organic yams, celery root and leeks for soup, and even Jerusalem artichokes.

Most special of all was a jar of white truffles. Surely, truffles were going to make her reputation as a cook!

Then, the four young people poured into the house. Janie, looking flushed and beautiful, introduced the new arrivals as if she were a circus impresario.

"First of all, Ma, here is your long-lost daughter Martha." With long, brown hair and hazel eyes just like hers, Louise almost felt as if she were hugging her twin when she took the tall girl in her arms.

"Welcome home, my darling." But the embrace alarmed Louise; Martha had lost weight.

Janie gently propelled the next guest forward. "And here's Martha's friend, Jim Daley. This is the mother we've been talking about, Jim." Jim was a stocky, assured young man chewing gum. He had bright blue eyes and black hair, and was just a little shorter than both Martha and Louise. He bore a strong resemblance to his famous grandfather, memorialized on TV film as the Chicago mayor who during the 1968 Democratic convention created havoc in the streets by turning club-wielding police out against youthful antiwar protesters.

"Pleased to meetcha, Mrs. Eldridge," he said, in a flat Midwest accent. His gum-chewing went into idle during the introductions.

"And here's our dear Chris," continued Janie, and Chris Radebaugh, tall and blond and more sober-appearing after a quarter of studies as a freshman at Princeton, came over and gave her a big hug. "Hi, Mrs. Eldridge," he said quietly, "you're lookin' good." Even as he embraced her, Louise could see he had an eye out for Teddy Horton, lurking in the background. Teddy met everyone, smiling and deferential, almost as if he were the host.

Soon, Melissa McCormick emerged from Janie's bedroom. Like a proud but shy princess, she approached the group slowly. Dramatically, she said, "I'm Melissa, everybody. So many new people! Oh, I have to meet each one of you."

Over the crowd, Janie exchanged a guarded look with her mother. Louise shrugged her shoulders. Janie patiently introduced first herself, and then the others to the fourteen-year-old. The girl's eyes lit up as she looked from one person to the other, dismissing Teddy instantly, smiling conspiratorially at Martha, her glance sliding appreciatively by Jim Daley, but then lingering and settling on the tall and handsome Chris. Looking as if she'd won a lottery, she sidled over to him and, discovering he was just home from college, began to ask him about how his fall term had been.

A fourteen-year-old going on thirty, decided Louise.

Teddy sidled his way to Janie's side and took her off to the recreation room for a private talk. A minute later Louise spied them ambling outside the house toward where Teddy's car was parked. Surely, thought Louise, they're not going off in the car. . . .

Martha gave her Chicago friend a quick tour of the house. When they had returned to the living room, Jim said, "This house is wonderful." He stared in fascination through the tall glass windows into the woodsy backyard filled with hundred-foot sweet gums. "Nothing like Bridgeport, I'll tell you that."

"I think I've read about Bridgeport," said Louise.

"Yes, ma'am," said Jim. "We've been living there for generations—it's a hotbed of lace-curtain Irish who may have made it, but have never bothered to move out to the suburbs. It's strictly middle-class—more trees than there used to be, that's for sure, but nothing like this."

Louise recalled reading that it was a white neighborhood with an attitude—a place that despised the intrusion of other races. But she would never bring up such a thing, especially since Martha had painted a picture of Jim as a young man who was as staunch a social reformer as she was. Martha was a true believer, even recommending that her parents move from the suburbs and live in downtown Washington so they could learn about how people "really live." Louise wondered where Jim Daley came down on that.

As Louise looked over at Chris talking to Melissa, she could see that he'd had enough. She walked over to the two of them and said to Chris, "Have you been home yet to see your folks?"

He shoved a shock of blond hair out of his eyes and gave her a grateful look. "No, I haven't, and I need to do that, especially since Janie's disappeared with Teddy. Uh—see you later, Melissa." The girl accepted this dismissal and wandered away to talk with someone else.

In a quiet voice, Chris said, "Thanks. That girl Melissa sure likes to talk a lot, but I suppose, considering what happened to her dad *and* her mom, it's not too surprising she's a little, y'know, kooky. And man, the little twerp really comes on to a guy. But Janie will understand."

Louise hoped so—and hoped Chris understood Teddy Horton's need for attention from Janie. And so forth. And then there were Chris's parents, Ron and Nora, mired in marital troubles. And Richard and Mary Mougey, Richard being a bit of an alcoholic who wanted the whole world to join him in it.

Her head faintly ached. It was already getting too much, and the weekend had hardly begun.

Suddenly, Louise realized it was late afternoon, and remembered what she had forgotten in the excitement of the guests' arrival. Since she was taking time off to go to Jefferson University on Friday, she had to get in two hours of work at the lab today. Otherwise she wouldn't fulfill her expected weekly hours.

She looked at the group of young people, who had suddenly been rejoined by Janie and Teddy, and even Chris. He'd been persuaded not to go home after all. The six of them ought to be able to fend for themselves for a couple of hours.

As much as she loved the solitude of the lab, she

hated to go; she had lots of things to do for tomorrow's dinner. But there were plenty of soft drinks and hors d'ocuvres for them, and the dinner lasagna was bubbling away in the oven. Anyway, Bill would be home soon—it would be good for him to get a full dose of the young people without Louise's buffering the process. Meanwhile, in those two hours, she would get done the work that was expected of her.

13

Louise entered the lobby of Whiting Labs, feeling a new sense of ownership, for Polly had given her a door key yesterday for the inner lab rooms so that she could come and go more freely.

The double doors leading to the growing room unlocked so silently that they did not disturb the couple standing inside. They were like a sculpted tableau, thought Louise: *Grieving Woman Supported by Strong Man.* It was Dr. Joe Bateman, in white coat, mask hanging down in front, latex gloves peeled off and held in one hand. And Polly Whiting, also white-coated, leaning, blond and beautiful, against his chest, as if she would fall if not for Joe's support. One of his hands was around her loosely, and her arms clung to his chest, almost like a baby monkey clinging to its mother. It was surprisingly intimate, and Louise wondered if she should back out and come in the door again.

Instead, she hacked loudly. "A-hgh-hgh!" It wasn't hard to do, since she'd just gotten over a little cold.

Joe and Polly broke apart and turned to face

her. Joe looked surprised and guilty. But Polly seemed relieved that it was Louise. She put a tanned hand to her brow and said, "Thank God, Louise, it was you and not somebody who wouldn't understand."

"Hi," Louise said neutrally, and went to work examining plants.

Polly trailed after her, still determined to explain. "I know you've realized how much pressure I'm under, Louise. The only one I have to give me an honest shoulder to cry on is Joe."

"I know that you trust Joe. It's only natural to cry on his shoulder." And in fact, standing this close to her, Louise could see Polly's face was tear-streaked.

"It's just so much more responsibility than I thought, to take over the whole lab by myself," said Peter Whiting's widow. "I don't mind the work, especially since I have such great new employees"— she gave Louise a wide smile—"but it's all these other demands. I'm sick of demands from people."

Louise thought over the roster of Polly's visitors of late. She knew pretty much what Detective Geraghty wanted from this woman—complete honesty about Peter Whiting and his life, and any further details that might help reveal who murdered the man. But she had no exact notion of why either James Conti or Ramon Jorges kept dropping by. She said what she would have liked someone to say to her in similar circumstances: "It's best to stand firm, isn't it, and not make any big decisions until you get over some of the grief."

Polly stared at Louise, who felt almost overcome by the blue of her enhanced blue eyes. Why did this inordinately beautiful woman tinker with perfection? It jarred on Louise's sensibilities and, she had to admit, made her wonder about the widow.

But that was silly; Polly was a very nice, straight-forward woman.

The widow came out of her stare. She said, "That's the best piece of advice I've had. And I'm going to remember it, and be grateful to you." She reached out and pressed Louise's white-coated arm. Then the buzzer sounded.

If Louise thought she was going to find peace at Whiting Labs tonight, she was wrong. The person at the door was the tiresome Ramon Jorges. Even through the glass she could sense his animal charm. Polly approached the door with trepidation.

From the back of the lab, Joe called to her. "Are you sure you want to talk to him tonight?"

"Oh, Joe, I have to, you know I do." She opened the door and the game began anew, according to what Louise could see. As Louise performed her monotonous but rewarding task of examining test tube plants for signs of mold, Polly and Ramon strolled through the growing room, Ramon seemingly without a care in the world. Talking just low enough so that Louise could hear nothing.

She shot a look over at Ramon, and he stared balefully back at her. Louise was no longer on his list of people to flirt with, or even be nice to. She knew herself to be a good person, so this kind of mistrust made her very suspicious. Deliberately, she moved her utility cart closer to the couple and, quiet as a mouse, continued her work. Rewarding snatches of conversation came to her.

". . . Peter's promises . . . insufficient data given the authorities . . . a reopening of the application would be trouble."

There must have been some kind of pheromones in the air, for the Brazilian scientist tried the tricks he used the other day on the widow, and to Louise's surprise the widow didn't seem to object.

This time, he started massaging her back, his hands like serpents. To Louise it was so sensuous that it was embarrassing to watch. But watch she did for a few moments, furtively, in between careful inspections of trays full of plants.

Then she came across a batch of test tube plants with the wilts. She placed them in the discard tub as quietly as possible. It didn't seem to disrupt whatever was going on with Ramon and Polly, and Louise wondered dismally where the two would end—in *bed* somewhere? Just then, Joe burst back into the growing room and broke it up. He called out to Polly, "Are you through?" Then, as if an afterthought, he greeted Dr. Jorges. "Uh, hello, Ramon. Business concluded?"

"Why, yes, Joe, I guess so," said the scientist.

"I'm leaving myself. It's six o'clock. And I'm asking the rest of you to leave as well, so we can lock up tight for the holiday."

Ramon Jorges turned to Polly and said, "Goodbye, my dear. *Do* call me—you know where. . . ." And then he sauntered out the door, with Joe watching to be sure he went all the way to the front exit. Meanwhile, Louise, deciding there was no more work that needed doing, wheeled the cart out of the growing room to the vestibule.

She could just barely see and hear Joe, who was leaning slightly against the double lab doors. He slowly shook his head. Polly approached him, looking slightly embarrassed. "That Don Juan," he said disgustedly, "you know you owe him nothing."

"It's not that easy," she said. "You weren't there for most of those years when he and Peter worked together."

The postdoctoral assistant reached out and grabbed her shoulder. "Polly, for God's sake, toughen up a little. Do you know how many people could come in here and lay faulty claims on you?"

Louise's heart thumped in her breast. She instinctively ducked back into the vestibule just as they probably were glancing in her direction to see if she were eavesdropping. They continued their conversation in lowered voices. She was trapped. Even home was better than this. She finished cleaning out the test tubes that were to go in the autoclave. After a couple of minutes she called out, "Polly, are you there?"

"Yes, Louise," said Polly, strolling into the alcove.

"I heard Joe say he wants to lock up. I'm just finishing—I have about five more minutes cleanup time, and I'll be ready."

"All right," said Polly. "We'll wait."

Polly went back, and Louise could hear Joe complaining in an annoyed voice about something. "People should have normal working hours ... why give *her* a key?" Unlike the key that Matthew had obtained, it provided only access to the inner lab rooms, but would make it easier for her to come and go within normal business hours.

This afternoon, she had come to the lab so she wouldn't fall behind. But she had not been welcome. Unfortunately, she now seemed to be on Joe Bateman's bad side; he didn't like it that she had even limited access to the place. He preferred that the little scenes with Polly and Ramon and Polly and Joe take place in private.

As she drove home, her mind focused in on the central question: What had happened to these people down there in the Amazonian jungle?

Louise doubted she would ever find out.

14

Louise sprang out of bed on Thanksgiving morning at six, hurrying into the fresh slacks and sweater she'd laid out the night before. One needed good traction when cooking a Thanksgiving dinner, so she sat down on her side of the bed and put on her sturdiest running shoes.

Bill stirred. "Are you okay, honey?" he asked. "Want me to get up, too?"

"No, darling, you sleep in," she said, and gave the lump in bed that represented his bottom an affectionate pat.

She walked down the hall past the other silent bedrooms in the house. The young people should be tuckered out; they had gone out the night before to a dance club, one that allowed underaged people like Janie and Melissa to enter. She and Bill had had a pleasant, quiet evening watching a TV movie, during which she had chopped vegetables for turkey stuffing and prepared the celery root and leek soup according to Teddy's recipe.

But now it was D-Day, and she had all the last-minute jobs to do. She was counting on Teddy to make it easier. Entering the kitchen, she felt a sense of hope. This was the year that she might possibly measure up to her grandmother's standards. After all, her ace in the hole was the talented Mr. Teddy Horton.

By nine, Louise had prepared two kinds of potatoes, cranberry sauce, and a huge salad—all the easy stuff. She'd also acquired five gawkers including her husband, all famished, so she put aside her dinner preparations to make the crowd breakfast. The doorbell rang, and it was Chris from across the street, determined not to miss out on anything. This gave her one husband and five strapping young people to feed, right when she should have been mastering the dinner. She still had guacamole, salad dressings, and sauces to make, and worst job of all, peeling those knobby little Jerusalem artichokes; it was worse than peeling grapes.

She was even hoping to whip up a little chili because she knew the ravenous crowd would eventually get bored with leftover turkey. Teddy, of course, would finish the more esoteric dishes, such as truffles with pasta, and pumpkin-flavored crème brûlée.

Glumly, she reflected she should have sent them out for breakfast at Denny's. But she was quite proud when she finally presented an enormous platter filled with scrambled eggs, hash browns, and ready-cooked sausages, surrounded by large, succulent strawberries.

"Cool presentation, Ma," said Janie in a faintly sarcastic voice. Louise took no offense since her younger daughter had produced the huge pile of unburned toast.

"Mother, this is *beautiful,*" said the more gracious Martha. "Thank you."

The others echoed her.

When Louise had a moment to think, she noticed a glaring omission at the table. "Oh, my, where's Teddy?" A chill ran through her. Had he turned around and run back to Connecticut, afraid that she would ask too much of him?

"It's too bad what happened to Teddy," said Chris, fighting a smile. "He had a little too much to drink."

"You don't mean he's *sick?*"

Janie sighed in her most worldly-wise manner. "Yes, Ma, all night. He quit upchucking about five this morning."

The solid, practical Jim Daley stashed his gum in some convenient pocket of his mouth and summed it up for her. "First of all, Mrs. Eldridge, most of us didn't drink much last night—and Janie and Melissa not at all."

"I hardly *ever* drink," crowed Melissa needlessly, stretching her long, thin arms out, as if to bring attention to her red-haired, well-freckled self.

"We certainly hope you don't," said Bill jovially, "for you're way too young."

Jim continued. "But Teddy had quite a few—he's on vacation, you know, and he doesn't apparently get away from that inn very much; they depend on him a lot. As soon as we got home, he became ill. It was a wild night. I finally went and slept in the rec room—hope you don't mind. My guess is that he ate something earlier that didn't agree with him."

Louise experienced a quick moment of panic. *The lasagna.* But then she realized everyone would have become sick if the dish had been contaminated. She was very sensitive about contamination since she'd started working in a test tube laboratory, and newly aware that her home-and-kitchen habits might not pass a health inspection. Cleaning the fridge and removing certain green-with-mold food items had, however, helped a lot.

"Also," added Jim, "I don't think the guy is much of a drinker. He just wasn't used to it."

"Maybe. Also, he *danced* too much," commented Melissa, pulling her mouth into a thoughtful pout. "Ever think *that* had something to do with it?"

"If he danced too much," said Janie with exaggerated patience, "we all danced too much, Melissa. Why didn't we all toss our cookies? Dancing does not make you sick."

Louise interrupted. "So—he's sleeping in for a little while?"

"My guess," said Chris breezily, "from hearing how the night went, is that he'll come to right about the time you're serving dinner. I remember my first hangover at Princeton—and actually my last. I didn't get up until five the next day."

Martha, who hadn't spoken much, now put in her opinion. "Ma, let me tell you how I view Thanksgiving. It is a *spiritual* occasion, so who cares what people eat? Thanksgiving dinner should be simple, but good. I know you thought Teddy would help you. We'll all step in and take his place, but what's really important is to keep it simple." She smiled, her lovely hazel eyes lighting up. "Remember the Pilgrims. They didn't have to serve truffles with that first Thanksgiving dinner."

Leave it to the socially conscious, egalitarian, tofu-eating Martha to shoot down truffles. The mysterious-looking jar stood on top of the fridge at this very moment, waiting for Teddy's magic touch to add to the pasta.

Louise looked out at the sea of friendly faces,

and then at the dirty dishes littering the dining room table. She felt a sense of ruin. Her ace in the hole had fallen out of her sleeve. But quickly she realized there was no time to feel sorry for herself. "Okay, folks," she said, "let's stack these dishes and get them to the kitchen—right now."

15

It might have gone all right, except for the guests who brought food. Had Teddy been around, Louise was sure he would have thrown these contributing cooks out of the kitchen. She, on the other hand, didn't have the guts; after all, they were her friends.

"*Dear* Louise," greeted Mary Mougey in her sweetest tone as she marched into the house. Her neighbor wore a wide-skirted blue designer silk dress and carried a large, flat baking dish. "I need to put this casserole in your oven for half an hour." The small blond woman was a high-powered Washington fund raiser and a surprisingly effective mentor to young people like Janie and Martha, but in some ways rather flighty, in Louise's opinion. Mary discounted cooking, rarely touching a pan in her own state-of-the-art kitchen with its shiny copper hanging pots. Yet today she demanded the use of an apron, as if she were embarking on a culinary adventure worthy of *Gourmet Magazine*.

"Trouble with putting that casserole in the oven, Mary, is that there's no room in the oven," explained Louise. "Wc'll just have to wait until the turkey is out."

"But, dear, surely you wouldn't want me to run back home?" Mary lived directly across the cul de sac, and Louise was tempted.

"Oh, no—let's just see how it shakes out."

Louise lent Mary Granny's worn linen apron, the only one she owned. She was going to wear it herself until she decided it was too frail; instead, she'd tucked a dish towel into the waistband of her slacks. The apron was white, with a couple of holes worn through, and a yellow handstitched band around its edges. "How *unusual!*" cried Mary as Louise tied it over her frock.

Then she lowered her voice and said, "Now, my dear Louise, as we work, we can chat about Polly Whiting. I hear you're working for her. She's one of my very big donors."

Louise was melting a stick of butter, but now turned her attention to Mary. "You mean, she gives you big money?"

"Very, very big," said Mary, widening her eyes and leaning in so others couldn't hear; this was despite the fact that they were the only two in the kitchen at the moment. Louise got a whiff of Mary's expensive perfume, and realized with all these guests, she'd never remember to put some fragrance on herself—which would leave her with that slightly sweaty, gamy smell she had right now.

"She and Peter gave as a couple, of course," continued Mary, "but she handled it. I don't know *what* she'll do now—I assume carry on at the same level if she can afford it. I do know, and I say this reluctantly, that Polly is quite a *scheming* type of giver—she developed a carefully crafted plan that timed their contributions so that they received maximum publicity. They have their own publicity person, no less, handing out the press releases."

"You're kidding," said Louise. "I've never heard of that—unless you're one of the very rich."

Mary shrugged. "You'd be surprised. She's not the only big donor who does that. And there's no telling what you'll do when you might have to raise venture capital—this last publicity coincided with the launch of their new biotech firm."

She laid a cautionary hand on Louise's arm. "But don't get me wrong. I'm sure she's very nice in spite of all this. If I know Polly, that company, even with Peter gone, is headed for big things. So tell me, do you like her?"

Louise turned back to the stove barely in time to save the butter from scorching. "I—like her, what I know of her—and I like my job." She glanced at her bright-eyed friend. "You make a lot of judgments, don't you, on the basis of how people give you money."

"Oh, yes, dear, but I seldom reveal them. Only to you, for you're my *confidential* friend." She patted Louise on the cheek. "You might need that information some day."

"Help!" cried Sandy Stern, arriving with a huge bowl in her arms. A tall woman with strawberry-blond hair, Sandy was staring into the open refrigerator at a solid mass of food. "I need a place, Louise, to put this salad. Also, I have to have a burner to melt brown sugar—then put it on nuts."

Louise was trying to remain calm. She would have thought Sandy, a practical woman with whom she frequently played tennis and occasionally went sailing, might have performed her sugar-melting stratagems at home.

"You'll have to wait a while, Sandy—the pasta will be done soon."

"*Pasta?* Good heavens. I thought we were having turkey. . . ."

"We are," said Louise. "It's a long story." She thought ruefully of how the talented Teddy had led her down a gourmet path, and then had had the misfortune to become hungover.

Sandy sighed, took off her wool suit jacket, and hung it in the back hall, then returned and leaned against the counter, arms folded, and waited for her turn in the sun.

"So," she said, grinning, "tell me all about the pasta, Louise. Does this have to do with your hidden *Italian* side?"

While performing one of her most delicate maneuvers, adding cornstarch to the giblets broth for gravy, Louise told Sandy about the young man's desire to make this a four-star dinner. "Might only be three stars," she muttered.

"*Listen,*" whispered Sandy, grabbing her stirring arm, "do I have something to tell you, or *what*. Can you come outside for a minute?"

"Are you kidding?" said Louise.

"Oh, let me stir," said Mary. "Go on—get yourself a breath of fresh air, Louise."

She and Sandy slipped out the recreation door unnoticed and stood near the bamboo garden, hugging their arms because the temperature was dropping.

"Oh, my God, it's cold," said Sandy. She was a deceptively delicate-looking blonde with an oval face and pale skin, but Louise knew she was a sportswoman who probably could have crossed Antarctica on a dogsled. Nevertheless, both of them were shivering in the biting November wind.

"So, what's the big scoop?"

Sandy looked suspiciously toward the house. "I hope Frank doesn't see me out here; he'll know I'm talking about his patient. Guess what he told me about that Professor Whiting of yours?"

Frank Stern, Sandy's husband, was a urologist, so Louise knew it had to be something below the belt.

"I can't guess," she said, banging her hands on her arms to create a little warmth.

Sandy looked her in the eye. "You must promise you'll never repeat this, for Frank *never* tells me anything like this. The only reason he did was because the man is dead, and Peter himself apparently made no bones about it. He had some serious things wrong with him, the result of a disease he picked up in the Amazon. It's a kind of TB transmitted from tropical birds that he didn't even know he had till Frank did a urinalysis. Anyway, it had made him impotent—and unfortunately, because of the other things wrong with him, Frank couldn't help him."

Louise gave her a knowing glance. "No Viagra, huh?"

"No Viagra, and no surgery, unfortunately. Now I hardly think that this had to do with his murder, but I just had to tell you—"

"Why? Why did you have to tell me?"

"Because I could be wrong about that." She patted Louise's arm. "And knowing you, I bet you're secretly working Peter Whiting's murder, aren't you? You don't have to answer that. But maybe you'll be able to use this information sometime. I tell you this, Louise, with a clear conscience"—and her eyes looked earnestly into Louise's—"because both Frank and I are scared of that crazy killer in the neighborhood. Yet we sit up nights wondering if it really *is* a crazy killer, and not someone else entirely."

They went back into the house. Louise fell behind, lost in thought.

When they returned to the kitchen, Mary had created a virtually lump-free gravy, and received hearty congratulations from Louise and Sandy. Then Nora arrived in the kitchen, looking subdued but beautiful in a fine-cotton beige caftan, her dark hair pulled up on her head with a jeweled comb. She carried a foil-wrapped platter filled with buns. "These, I'm afraid, can't go in the microwave; they have to be coddled in the oven."

With no oven space left, Louise thought she might laugh or cry. As she hugged her friend in greeting, she saw that Nora looked terminally sad around the eyes. When, she wondered, would Nora and Ron get their act together? There would be more than food crises to handle today.

She pulled Nora out into the hall for a moment. "Everything okay?" she asked hesitantly. *Please say yes*, she thought to herself.

"No."

Louise sighed. "So what gives?"

Her neighbor's gray eyes were big and solemn as she told her story. "Ron and I are at a crossroads. I told him I would undergo marriage counseling as long as he went away with me. It's an intensive six-week sex education clinic."

Louise restrained a desire to laugh hysterically. What man wouldn't want to go on a six-week sexual journey with the alluring Nora? Unfortunately, her friend had often been attracted to other men during her marriage. Louise and Bill had seen it happen when they went to Litchfield Falls Inn. Then, recently, Ron had started to roam. Louise was a little embarrassed to receive this intimate news, but Nora was a poet. Maybe that was why, once Louise became her friend, she knew everything about her.

She patted Nora's hand. "It's a win-win situation, believe me." Then she strode back to the kitchen, for party time was almost here. To her intense relief, Martha appeared to give a hand. First she tickled her mother in the ribs and said, "Just pretend I'm Teddy," then with slim, strong arms, helped her maneuver the gigantic turkey from the oven. "C'mon, pretty baby, don't let us down," she encouraged the bird, as if it were a living thing. Its removal broke the traffic jam inside the stove, but not the traffic jam in the kitchen.

Mary Mougey, with her wide skirt, insisted on a permanent station right next to the oven. "I spent too much time cooking this, dears," she said. "It's my *oeuvre*. I have to stay here and hover."

Sandy also crowded in at the stove, where she was caramelizing nuts. "Oh my *God,*" she cried, as her brown sugar threatened to harden, "someone help me!"

"No problem," Martha assured her, and stepped in to expertly toss in the almonds.

Mary, tiring of the crowded environment, slipped off the apron, turned to Martha, and caressed the girl's long, brown hair. "You are such a lovely person, Martha, and it is so good to have you home again. I think I'll get out of here and get your father to make me a good, stiff drink. Can you be sure the casserole doesn't scorch?"

"Of course, Mrs. Mougey," said Martha, putting the apron on herself. She noticed that her mother was approaching the pan of mashed potatoes with the melted butter. "That's a stick of polysaturated *fat!*" she accused. "Are you *kidding*, Ma? Do you want to *kill* people?"

"Oh, no, you don't, Martha," said Louise, dumping the butter in the potatoes. "My grandmother ate butter all her life and she's still alive."

Nora, apparently cheered by Louise's encouraging words, stood at the kitchen door and tried to make Louise laugh with a few droll remarks. "Remember, Louise, Thanksgiving only comes once a year, and if you do it *wrong*, chances are you'll never have to do it again. If you do it right, well, then that's your own hard luck."

Janie was sent into the bedroom to get the truffles recipe from the prostrate Teddy. Reporting back, she said, "It's like he's on his deathbed in there, Ma. His last words to me were, 'For my sake, don't blow it.' "

Louise could detect a slight smile around her younger daughter's mouth. "He did not—did he?" Finally, it was time for Louise to drain the pasta and add the truffles mixture—which was to be done, according to Teddy, with "panache."

"Here goes nothing," Louise said, and mixed the dish with a flourish, then set it absentmindedly on the back burner of the stove.

Finally, they were at the table—actually, two tables placed together under one huge tablecloth—with eight adults and six young people, including the quiet twelve-year-old son of the Sterns. They held hands while Bill led them in a simple grace.

"And bless my dad and mom, too," Melissa piped up, after the common grace was said. Louise looked at the frail girl and had a rush of memories about her parents and their unfortunate demise. No wonder Melissa was an attention-seeker, as her Aunt Moira put it.

Louise picked up her fork and ate. It was disappointing, except for the gravy. "Great *gravy*," she kept hearing from around the table. Perhaps the biggest letdown was the truffles dish, which had

sat on the warm burner and now resembled shriv-
eled innards.

"So *these* are truffles," said Janie, taking a sip
from her water goblet as if to remove a bad taste.
"So *pigs* snuffed them out of the ground. No wonder they are so hard and earthy . . ."

". . . but an *int*eresting flavor," said Mary Mougey.

Suddenly Teddy Horton appeared at the dining
room doorway. His face was the color of parch-
ment. They cried out welcomes to him, followed
by little clucks of sympathy and condolence. "Poor
thing, in bed all day." "Missing out on all the fun."

"I've come to try to eat dinner," he proclaimed.

That was enough reason for Richard Mougey to
gather himself together for his role as toastmaster.
With his long, oval, Modigliani face and wearing a
rich-looking cashmere turtleneck sweater under
his light tweed jacket, he looked quite the picture
of the European man, Louise thought, and he
would have appreciated someone telling him that.
Although sweet, Richard was a bit of an unconscious snob, probably resulting from a lifetime of
European country-hopping for the State Department. Thus, Richard and her husband were colleagues, though Bill's State job was simply cover
for his actual employment as a CIA operative.

Just as she knew he would, he'd brought both
wine and his own high-end French brandy with
him, and this was just one of many toasts he would
make during the meal, no matter how lackluster it
was. He had always liked booze better than food.

"Let's welcome our absent young friend,
Teddy," said Richard, reaching an arm out wide toward the young man, whom he and the other
neighbors had never met before. "Now, we are all
together, and it's time for a toast—to the Eldridges
. . . and to Mrs. Eldridge's most—*exceptional* dinner!" Everyone raised their glasses.

She acknowledged the toast, took one sip, and put her glass down. She had to work tomorrow and didn't intend to drink. Anyway, she doubted that this dinner was worth toasting. What was more worthwhile was the information about Peter and Polly Whiting that she'd heard from her friends. It had told her two disturbing things: that Polly was perhaps not the guileless widow that she appeared to be, but much more conniving. And that the marriage of the Whitings—in which normal sex was missing—could have been an unsatisfactory union, especially for Polly, who had been young enough to be Peter's daughter.

Teddy clinked on his water goblet for attention, then got shakily to his feet and raised the glass to make his own little toast. He probably had heard some good ones in Litchfield, thought Louise. "Our warmest thanks to Louise and Bill Eldridge for graciously inviting us all here to their house. It's wonderful to spend Thanksgiving with such a nice family. We have enjoyed Louise's, um, great cooking, the, uh, turkey, the—ah, truffles dish, the *fantastic* gravy and soup, those interesting Jerusalem artichokes, and the dynamite mashed potatoes. . . ." The young man was beginning to look faint, probably from the stress of exaggerating.

"Thank you, Teddy," said Bill, rescuing him. "That's the best toast we've ever had at the Eldridge house. Now you need to eat and regain your strength." He raised his own glass. "Bless you, and everyone here for making this a very special Thanksgiving. We're bound to remember it for a long time."

Louise caught her husband's eye and they smiled at one another.

16

"Louise," said Bill, "are we sure that Janie and Melissa aren't in there drinking wine?"

Her husband had taken a peek into the recreation room, and then come into the kitchen, where she was putting away the last couple of serving dishes. Her back ached, and she longed to go to her bedroom, get undressed for the night, and think more about what she'd learned today about the Whitings.

"Bill, I honestly don't know. If they're sneaking a glass of wine out of those opened bottles, it's going to be hard to know, since I doubt any of them would want to squeal."

He leaned over her, bent down, and kissed her forehead. "All right. I won't worry about it. And no matter what that Teddy Horton thinks, *I* think you're a great cook, and a charming hostess. I know you had to bear most of the burden of the conversation at the table today, people being obsessed as they are about Whiting's murder."

She said, "I'm awfully glad the newspapers haven't picked up on the fact that I know the family—and in a way, that's strange. . . ."

"Yes," said Bill. "It means Charlie Hurd must be out of town. Otherwise, he certainly would have called you up, since the two of you have been such great pals over the past year."

Louise gave him a wry glance. The intrepid Charlie, now a suburban reporter for the *Washington Post*, was not a close friend, though he had done her important favors in the past. Sometimes she despised the man, but couldn't help admiring his gutsy determination to get a story. He must have left Washington, or who knows, maybe he'd been run out. Otherwise, he would have perched on her doorstep the minute he heard of a murder in Sylvan Valley.

Wine had flowed heavily during the Thanksgiving feast, in Louise's opinion, but then she was practically a teetotaler. It had seemed to help some in the crowd, for by the time Nora left with Ron, her face was flushed and so was his, and she was leaning into him in a promising sort of way. Louise guessed that one of their whispered conversations might have involved his agreement to go to the sex clinic. As the other neighbors drifted away, Richard Mougey insisted that the Eldridges keep the left-over wine, including, of course, the opened bottles.

She strolled to the door of the recreation room, and it seemed as if the delicate fabric that held together this disparate group of young people was beginning to wear thin. *Just like Granny's apron,* she reflected. Martha and Jim looked politely bored. The two left the rec room, walked past her, and joined Bill in the living room.

Her husband could have guessed right, about Melissa anyway; she seemed scrappy and ready to pick a fight with Janie. Louise sailed into their midst. "How would you like to play a game of Scrabble?" she proposed, and got mixed reactions. Teddy, still the worse for the wear, seemed indifferent. Chris was agreeable as usual, his real feelings hidden behind a bland expression. Janie, usually an enthusiastic Scrabble player, was silent with downcast eyes.

Melissa said, in a high voice, "I bet we could find something lots more exciting to do than *that.*"

Louise looked at Janie and quietly said, "What's wrong, dear?"

Janie stood up, made her way over to her mother, and draped a slim arm around her neck. "Nothing, Ma," she said in a normal voice, then whispered in her ear, "This is going to be a long weekend. But don't let it get you—and don't you dare steal away on us again to go work in that lab. I don't think it's particularly safe."

Louise gave the girl a hug; who would think this lovely young daughter would become the official family Cassandra? Just then, Bill called Louise to the living room, and she decided to let the four kids settle their problems themselves. She sat down with Martha, Jim, and Bill, and joined their discussion of Chicago politics.

"Jim intends to run for Chicago alderman next year," said Bill.

Louise must have looked surprised. Martha had told her that Jim Daley was twenty-four years old, which seemed young to enter politics in a big city.

The young man read her look. "What's the matter, do you think I'm too young?"

She smiled, trying to soften what might come across as criticism of Jim. "No, not too young—I guess Chicago has no age limit for people to enter city politics."

"Absolutely none, Mrs. Eldridge." He shrugged his shoulders. "Look, I probably won't make it the first time, maybe not even the second—but you gotta get started. You have to get your name out there, you have to have the guts to take a loss. And you have to know how to develop loyal supporters." Louise noticed he refrained from chewing gum while discussing his career.

Why wasn't Louise surprised to hear this about Jim? Why, every inch of him proclaimed "politician"—the familiar Daley Irish face, the winning smile, the forthright delivery, and the political know-how. He could be a perfect match for their reformist daughter.

"How wonderful, Jim," said Bill. "And how about you, Martha, are you going to be part of this campaign?"

"I sure am," she said, looking very comfortable sitting next to her stocky beau. "I'm going to try to get credit for it, too, at Northwestern, as an independent study."

Bill looked at her with admiration. "My, that's having your cake and eating it, too."

Martha gave him a beautiful smile. "More like multi-tasking; we hardworking students have to do that every chance we get."

Louise heard, but didn't really notice, the opening and closing of doors around the house, until it was too late. Suddenly, she realized all four were gone: Chris, Janie, Teddy, and Melissa. Remembering the state of alert following the professor's murder, she got up and said, "I hope they realize they can't wander around out there in the neighborhood and be safe."

"When Martha told me about what's been going on," said the young man from the heart of Chicago, "I could hardly believe it. It sure seems like a safe kind of place."

"Not right now," Louise said grimly, and got up and went out the front door. She promptly tripped over a couple of gourds, as the wind whipped the storm door from her hand and slammed it shut. "What a mess," she grumbled, seeing the disarray in her Thanksgiving decorations; she crouched down and set things back in place. Then she hurried down the walk to see if she could find the missing four.

Two of them were visible in the glow of lights from the front of the Radebaughs' house. It was quite a sight: Chris Radebaugh, with Melissa first clinging to his arm, then breaking away to dance wildly around in circles like a wood sprite. The teenager definitely had gotten into the wine. Her tinkling laughter floated on the wind, and Louise could hear Chris's tense voice trying to quiet the girl down.

Around the corner of the Eldridge house appeared Teddy and Janie, the young man with his arm loosely around her daughter's shoulders. Janie looked furious. She came up to her mother and said, "Have you seen Chris and that Melissa?"

Louise nodded her head. The couple was approaching from across the cul de sac. Chris hurried up to Janie and said, "So *there* you are!"

Janie stood with arms akimbo, and said, "And there *you* are." In the generous light under the front door, everyone could see the smeared lipstick on Chris's mouth and cheek. "And just look at you!"

"Hey, Janie, you ran off first, with Teddy," said Chris accusingly.

Teddy stood there with an innocent expression on his face. "Janie and I just decided to step out on the patio for a minute so I could get some air."

"But you weren't there. . . ."

Melissa stepped up to provide her part of the story. "Chris took me for a visit to *his* house, and we had fun, just stumbling around in the woods." She tried to attach her hand to Chris's again, but he pulled his away.

Louise, dead tired now, felt like giving them all a good paddling. Instead, she said, "All right, folks, I declare a unilateral disarmament, as of right now." She put her arms out and encircled Janie with one, Melissa with the other, and said, "I hope you all had a good breath of fresh air—and now you must be freezing. Why don't you come in and I'll make you some hot cocoa."

Melissa, who was coming down from her alcoholic high, said, *"Now* maybe we could play Scrabble—actually, I *love* Scrabble." As they reached the front porch, the girl added, "I was fooling around here, too—oh, I see you already got those little dinghooeys back where they belong. Sorry, Aunt Louise—like my Aunt Moira says, tomorrow I'd better try growing *up!"*

Hot cocoa and cookies restored peace to the young people, and they became absorbed in the game. Louise heard the dog whimpering in the back hall, and so had a perfect excuse to escape for a while.

She put on her jacket, scarf, and gloves, knowing the temperature had dropped into the high twenties, with the windchill factor bringing it down even further. Fella eagerly piled after her as she strode out the door. She was confident he now knew enough to follow her when he was off the leash.

With the dog at her side, she tramped across the woods to the other side of the bog garden. This was the prescribed area for Fella to be trained. It was just beyond the pool of light provided by the overhead lights mounted in the trees, but safe enough since the moon was full. The little Westie, however, had heard something, and took off toward the huge stand of bamboos in the neighbors' yard that bordered the Eldridge property.

Dismayed that her dog training was so faulty, she called, "Come on, Fella, get *back* here." The diminutive white pup had darted into the bamboos. She ran through the rustling leaves after him, pushing her way through the thicket. The tough, thick stalks grabbed at her clothes almost as if trying to impede her from an approaching danger.

Then she felt a hand on her shoulder, whipping her around. She saw a dark figure with a face mask—and was that a glint of metal in his hand?

She was horrified to hear the person speak her name: "Lou*ise*"—or was it just the wind, complaining again in its high, sinister voice?

Then she heard Fella's raucous growl and saw the white bit of fluff that was her dog leap at the figure. Without thinking, she twirled around and shoved through the junglelike growth. "Oh, *God!*" she cried. Behind her, she could hear Fella's frantic barks and a few male grunts. The puppy had attacked the assailant—it surely would be caught and throttled to death!

"Fella!" she cried. "Come!" And fled. She knew she could be killed if she didn't keep going, and that was no way to save the dog. Making herself take deep, even breaths, she wrenched her body through the thicket of canes, and finally broke through the last of them. Her pursuer, she could hear, was right behind her—but where was the dog? Then she heard the welcome sound of his yipping.

Ahead lay her chance—the bog garden. It had stood her in good stead once before when a rash young man had tried to pursue her. Yet would it work? Its masterful plants, the skunk cabbage, the *Iris pseudacorus,* and the *Sagittaria,* were diminished, shrunken with the fall frosts. At least its surface was covered with fallen leaves and browned duckweed. So it sat there, a chimera, ten feet in diameter, filled with three feet of water. In the middle of this pondlike garden Louise knew there was a flat, slightly submerged rock, a support to the bog plants, and soon to be hers. She ran to the garden's edge and leaped to the rock, frantically fighting for balance so she didn't fall in the turbid water. Once she steadied herself, she leaped to the far edge and safety.

The dark figure behind her followed the same path, and not recognizing it was water, landed in the muck with a splash. She could see the person flounder and grab the sides. The thing that terrified her most was that the person made no further sound. She could make Fella out in the darkness. He stood by the edge of the bog garden and barked, as if determined to harass this stranger until he was caught. She darted around and grabbed him in her arms. She ran to the house, went in, and slammed the front door. "Bill!" she screamed, bringing her husband at a run to the front hall.

"Louise, what . . ." He came up and gripped her arms.

Gasping for breath, she explained, "A man chased me in the backyard."

He pulled open the front door. "Somebody's climbing out of the bog garden. . . ."

He started to open the storm door, but she shoved herself in front of him. "Don't go out there. He has a knife! I could see it in his hand."

"Hell, I have a gun!" said her husband, and he ran to the bedroom to retrieve his Beretta from its lockbox. In the few seconds he was gone, the young people gathered around the front door, demanding details from Louise. Jim Daley stood in the middle of them, talking to the police on his cell phone. When Bill returned from the bedroom, Jim looked at him and said, "Mr. Eldridge, the police said to wait—"

"Later!" Bill said, and ran by him without stopping. As an afterthought, he called back, "You people stay here," and then pulled the front door open and lunged into the yard. Louise shoved out the door behind him. "Go back!" he yelled when he saw her, but she didn't. With her heart beating like a small drum, she stumbled after him as he searched the edges of the property. "Dammit, then keep close if you have to come."

They ended up in the front yard just as the police arrived with flashing lights. He turned to her and said, "Let's leave it to them now. He isn't here anymore."

As they came in the front door, Jim said, "Nothing?"

"Nothing," said Bill.

Louise leaned against her husband, shuddering uncontrollably.

He gathered her tightly in his arms. "Honey, are you all right?" he said, kissing her temple.

"I'm all right as long as you stay here with me."

"I'll stay."

In a few minutes, she had calmed down, with only an occasional tremble rocking her composure. Martha brought her a cup of herb tea, and Janie sat beside her for a while, consoling her. As they waited for the police to arrive, Bill reached down and scratched Fella's head as he lay at

Louise's feet. He'd heard of the Westie's heroic exploits out in the woods. In moments, she knew, police would fill the house. She turned to her husband and gave him a tired little smile. "Just like you said, Bill, it's a Thanksgiving we're bound to remember for a long time."

Louise couldn't help smiling a little. The brusque Detective Morton, never known for his people skills, had his hands full at the moment. Six young people were milling around him in the living room and peppering him with questions. "Naw, naw," he said, putting out a defensive hand as if he were a running back, "I can't tell ya any particulars right now. Sure, they're combin' the yard for clues—maybe the perp dropped something. . . ."

He looked over at Bill and Louise on the couch and gave them an exasperated look, then turned back to the six. "So none of you know anything about the incident?"

"That's right, officer," said Martha.

Trying his best to be tactful, Morton gave their older daughter a placating smile. "Then, may I please ask you and all these other young folks to move into whatever that room's called back there." He pointed to the rec room. "That way, I'll have a little privacy in which to question your parents. And I assure you that you'll all hear the details later."

While Martha guided the rest of them into the recreation room, their younger daughter didn't move. With a toss of her blond hair, Janie positioned herself in front of the detective and crossed her arms over her chest. "I want to be here when my mother is questioned—I like to keep track of her. After all, she might need my help."

A message was coming through on the two-way radio hooked to Morton's belt. "Hold *on* a minute," he said into the mike. He turned to Janie. "Young lady," he said crossly, "you look *here* now—" Louise could see his composure shaken by still another human—and another Eldridge woman at that—who refused to do exactly what Morton expected.

Louise got up from the couch and came over and said, "I'll take care of it." As the detective went to the front hall to talk more privately on the radio, she put an arm around her daughter and escorted her slowly out of the room.

"It is nice of you to be concerned, Janie," she said softly, "but believe it or not, I can take care of myself. I'll tell you all about it later, so you really won't miss out on a thing."

"All right, Ma," said Janie, "but don't forget— *everything.*"

In a minute, Morton had returned to the living room, an excited expression on his usually expressionless face. Louise wondered what he'd heard on that radioed message.

"Let's get some details from *you* now," said Morton, sitting down in the only straight chair in the living room, her grandmother's walnut chair with wicker seat.

Bill continued to hold Louise's hand as she described the events in the yard. As she talked, her gaze was attracted by the flashing lights in the woods. She and Bill exchanged a glance, remembering another unhappy time when the police had had to search this yard for clues to a macabre crime.

Knowing Louise well, George Morton felt comfortable reverting to his scolding ways: "Why did you go *out* in the woods when you knew that there was someone wanderin' around out there killin' and threatening people?"

"Because I had to get my dog—he'd run off into the bamboo. I was only sixty feet from my own front door, so I thought I was safe. *My* mistake, Detective Morton."

"Yes, it *was,*" said Morton quickly. By the time Mike Geraghty came in, she had finished her story and she and Morton were trying not to glare at each other. Hearing his partner's voice, the detective hurried to the front hall to confer. Then the two swept back into the living room, a distinct swagger in Morton's step, and a pleased look suffusing the face of the blue-eyed Irishman.

"Hello, Louise—hello, Bill," Geraghty greeted them. "A tough night, huh, Louise?" Then without waiting for a reply, he went to the rec room doorway and took in the six young people lounging about on chairs and couches. With a friendly grin, he said: "So this is the Thanksgiving crowd Mrs. Eldridge talked about—"

As he palavered with them for a moment, Louise realized she hadn't told Morton, or even her husband, about how the attacker might have called out her name. What had stopped her was that she didn't know whether she was hearing things or not.

Perhaps she'd simply been anthropomorphizing the November wind again.

Geraghty came and joined them, making himself at home in an overstuffed chair opposite the couch. "George here tells me he's gotten most of your story, Louise. Pretty darn scary for you."

"Yes, it was."

Geraghty cleared his throat. "Well, let me share some news with you that I just told George here. It might help explain things. Right after you folks called, there was another incident involving a couple of kids. They're being questioned right now. They were walking on Rebecca Road about fifteen minutes ago when they noticed someone following them wearing a ski mask."

"My attacker was wearing a mask," said Louise.

"Yes, ma'am," said Morton. "I told Detective Geraghty that."

Mike Geraghty continued. "The person got close enough so they thought they could see a knife in his hand. They began to run, and this guy gave chase. But these were young folks who know every hill and dale in Sylvan Valley. They just sprinted off the road and cut through a half-dozen yards until they came to a house where they knew the people."

"My God," she said, "then it *is* some random killer. . . ."

But then why would the person know my name? she thought.

"Is that supposed to be comforting?" said Bill in a discouraged voice. "A crazy person who operates right here in our own *backyard?*"

Geraghty was sitting forward in the big chair, looking uncomfortable now. "It's just that it narrows down our possibilities. Now we know we're gonna have to zero in on every resident, every visitor that's been stayin' around here—"

"Because it looks local, huh?" said Bill.

Geraghty nodded. "It looks local."

It all made sense. The assailant, who knew this neighborhood so well, had now killed one person, wounded another, and scared the living daylights out of Louise and two more residents. Since the person was local, there was no reason not to know Louise's name, as well as the names of scores of neighbors—all potential victims to be threatened or killed. She was just one of many. She needn't mention it, for it would upset Bill and create the false impression that she was a special target.

17

James Conti sat at his desk, placing his important and confidential papers into one neat stack. It was hardly worthwhile to start going through the stack, though, for Louise Eldridge would be here soon with her Channel Eight associate producer. As his thoughts turned to the nosy Eldridge woman, he slapped the paper pile straight with the palms of his hands.

The woman was up to something and had to be stopped. Doing a TV show about Jefferson's biology labs was a thin ruse. She was coming to snoop, but she would learn nothing from him.

When his cell phone rang, he gave a start, for he wasn't expecting a call. Slowly, a dark web of fear dropped over him. He didn't need more trouble today. If it had been the ringing of his desk phone, it would have been in the realm of things he could have handled—administrative details, the Eldridge woman delayed perhaps, or a grad student with a baffling research problem.

But a call on the cell phone, reserved as it was

for the business of the Gene Implantation Team at Jefferson University Hospital, heralded disaster.

"James, it's Frank."

"Christ, please don't tell me. . . ."

"I'm telling you—it happened again. And we all have to face this, James. All four of us are in this equally, and must take equal credit—or blame, in this case. We shouldn't have used that medium. . . ."

"It was perfectly justified," growled James. "Why didn't you try the new protocols on this one?"

"I tried, but the patient didn't respond to them. There was another intense immune reaction. And then all the organs failed."

James Conti slumped back in his leather desk chair. "I'll come over to the hospital."

"You'd better." Frank sounded as if hysteria was not far away. He'd been right there when those people had died in agony, with every aperture spewing fluids. Conti couldn't blame him.

"Don't think you aren't part of this," said his colleague. "The family, in fact, is right here now. Take your turn, James—*I've* taken mine, and so have the others. Tell these people their son's gene therapy didn't work, and that he's dead."

James turned the phone off, folded it, and put it in his pocket, then stared down at his desk and the pristine pile of papers centered on it. A feeling of rage overcame him, and he gave the pile a vicious swipe with his square hand, sending papers flying all over the otherwise meticulously neat office.

The violent action seemed to reinvigorate him. He got up from the desk and spun out of the office, determined now to change his life. James Conti had to be defined in some way beyond being a member of the "GIT" team at Jefferson Hospital. Why, an intern at the hospital had even made a black joke that it stood for "Gross Internal Trauma"— an acronym for death!

* * *

Louise could see that her associate producer Doug did not mind being called out to work on a holiday weekend.

"Darned good cup of coffee, Sarah," he said, aiming a discreet glance up at the beautiful woman pouring him a refill.

Sarah Shane was Public Relations Department assistant at Jefferson University. Under her bob of light brown hair was a finely boned face dramatized by big, soulful gray eyes. The whole effect was of subtle radiance, and this was with no makeup. Makeup, Louise reflected whimsically, would have turned Sarah into a raging beauty who, with the flick of a finger, might have lured her homey, middle-aged associate producer away from wife and family.

As it was, the three were having a cozy time of it, sitting and talking in the university's deserted and plain-as-dirt public relations office. Louise had made sure they arrived early, just so there would be time to cultivate the P.R. assistant. Louise needed Sarah Shane, and she'd already established a delicate link with her. At an evening adult education class, Sarah had chanced to meet Rachel, one of the writers for Louise's *Gardening with Nature* show. Louise intended to milk this tenuous relationship as far as she could.

Now, the young woman stood uncertainly before them, holding the half-full pot. "I can pour you a fourth cup or, if we're ready now, I can show you the way to the dean's office."

"I'm ready," said Louise, "and I can't thank you enough for your hospitality on a chilly morning like this. Would it be possible for me to get in touch with you later for some background information? You know, on the university, and maybe

on notable biologists who've come from here?"
She hoped that didn't sound too pushy.

What Louise actually wanted was something
quite different: some personal scuttlebutt on both
James Conti, and on Joe Bateman, who had worked
there for almost ten years. It wouldn't be easy, but
the first step was making friends.

Sarah responded to Louise's request with a
charming smile. "Look, that's what I'm here for—
to help you. Now let's go to Dr. Conti's office."

As they walked up the long flight of stairs to the
second floor, Louise suddenly felt breathless, and
realized how traumatic the events of last night had
been. By the time police had left, it had been two
in the morning. But there was no time for fatigue
this morning.

Trying valiantly to keep up with the spry Sarah,
she grasped for a conversational gambit. "Schools
have distinctive smells, don't they?"

"The smell we're comin' to makes my nostrils
curl," Doug joked, stroking on his salt-and-pepper
beard.

"Oh, please," said Sarah, laughing, "say it's not
that bad in here. Of course I'm used to it. I always
attribute the odor to hydrochloric acid, though
I'm not sure what it is."

"Maybe we don't want to know everything that
we're smelling," said Doug.

The second floor, Sarah told them, was where
generations of Jefferson biology students had
cooked up experiments, and where James Conti's
office and the plant laboratories were located.

They approached an office with the dean's name
stenciled on the door. The young woman shoved
her straight hair back from her face. "I'll intro-
duce you, and then I'm going to leave you with Dr.
Conti. He said he'd take you on the tour of the

plant labs—and that's quite an honor. He's definitely the best one to do it."

"Thanks a lot, Sarah," said Louise.

She knocked on the dean's partially open office door. "Dean Conti?" she called.

A distracted-looking grad student scurried by. "Looking for the dean? He ran out of here a minute ago on an emergency at the hospital."

"Oh, darn," said Sarah, looking at her watch. "This is so awkward—I have someone coming in downstairs to see me. . . ."

Louise smelled opportunity. "Would it be appropriate for Doug and me to wander through the plant labs by ourselves? They're not secret, are they? And I gathered that some of Dr. Conti's students will be in there working. They can probably help us a lot."

"Well, that was one of them who just went by toward the labs," said Sarah. She looked at Louise and Doug. Louise had worn a royal blue corduroy dress with princess collar that made her look as innocent as a child. Doug, with his friendly beard, rosy cheeks, and pleasant manner, was almost irresistible. How could two public television employees cause any trouble for Jefferson University or the prestigious Dean James Conti?

"Of *course,*" said Sarah, "that's a splendid idea. Shall I go with you to the labs?"

"Just point us in the right direction," said Louise, "and then you go before you're late."

Sarah gave them directions, then trotted off, her high heels clicking on the asphalt tile of the hallway. Doug looked at Louise inquiringly. Marty Corbin had briefed him on why they were here. "Well, I hear you're the police's little helper," he said, "and I can see that your detective antennae are quivering. So what do you want *me* to do, Holmes?"

She put her hand on his arm. "Doug, dear, go scope out the labs—I'll be there in a jiffy."

He took one look at the partially opened office door and gave her a serious expression, eyebrows raised. "Louise, this isn't funny. Did you ever consider you could end up in jail?"

"But no one will catch me," she assured him. "I am very fast." With that, she darted into James Conti's office, closed the door, and turned around and gasped. Papers were strewn on the desk and the floor, and for an instant she wondered if a thief had entered. But it was a rather artistic display of papers, undisturbed since they'd fallen— or perhaps been thrown. She crouched down to read some of them. Quite a number appeared to be applications for research grants—big research grants. A cluster of others interested her because they were letters from pharmaceutical companies, including the giant, Synthez. Though she was too nervous to take the time to read them all, she scanned a few. They sounded like proposals for Dr. Conti to collaborate on drug research projects. Though interesting, this wasn't what she was here for.

Carefully stepping around the papers, Louise went straight to the desk. Tentatively, she sat down in the expensive, high-backed leather desk chair, and felt the thrill that thieves or criminals must feel. Dr. Conti, called out just moments ago to a hospital emergency—surely she had at least five minutes to paw through his desk.

Giving a last quick look at the door, she turned her attention to the desk and began to make a quick survey of the drawers. They proved uninteresting, full of university files and papers. Then she sat back and forced herself to relax. She needed something to supplement the meager personal information she had pried out of Sarah Shane—

James Conti was divorced, no kids, and very much a big shot on campus. The public relations assistant had gushed about Conti's work in genetic research, and she'd frowned when Louise said she'd heard there was trouble with patients undergoing gene therapy. Sarah claimed to know nothing of it, but Louise bet she did, and was just trying to protect the university.

It wasn't until she stared into space that she discovered signs of a personal James Conti. Three pictures hanging on the opposite wall told the story.

She went over and examined the framed photos. First, there was the dean, standing, tall and suntanned, on the stern of his sailboat. He was holding a big fish and wearing nothing but a brief bathing suit and a victorious smile. In the foreground of the picture were tools for cleaning the big catch. Next was a photo of James Conti in polo garb, astride his horse, leaning far over to try to hit the ball. A third picture showed Conti in expensive jacket and leisure pants, emerging from a huge red brick colonial house with a six-window span across the front.

It was a wonder he hadn't hung up a photo of himself standing near whatever kind of expensive car he owned, thought Louise sourly. Knowing Conti just a little bit, she guessed it would be a Beemer. The most interesting thing about the photos was that no other human being was in them besides the proud dean.

So the man lived in an expensive house, played polo, and owned a huge sailboat. She was not surprised. Her eyes darted around the office to see what else could reveal a little of the real man. She wandered back to the desk, again stepping around the strewn papers, and decided on a new search strategy. Where does one put one's secrets, if one has secrets?

She pulled out the right bottom drawer all the way. To the very back of the drawer was a locked metal box. That didn't interest Louise, but the worn manila envelope under the box did. She carefully pulled it out and dumped the contents on the dean's desk.

Four small snapshots lay in front of her, obviously pictures that James Conti treasured. A shot of an older woman and an older man, probably his mother and father; two shots of a group of three young people, two men and one woman. Siblings, perhaps?

"Well, well," she said as she came to the fourth picture. Finding it, she hoped, would justify her illegal and impolite entry into Conti's office. It was a snapshot of Polly Whiting in a bathing suit. The picture was taken with the sun streaming down upon her. Her wet hair was flowing down in a most becoming manner, her bathing suit in dishabille, with one strap far down and thereby mostly exposing a breast. Peter Whiting's wife looked into the camera with longing; the woman obviously was infatuated with the person who took the picture. Louise turned the photo over and saw the date. Eighteen months ago, Polly Whiting, married to Professor Peter Whiting, had had an affair with Whiting's boss, Dean James Conti.

Almost too excited to think, Louise reassembled the photos and stuck them back into the envelope, thrust it back under the metal box, and closed the drawer. Then she quickly rose from the chair and navigated her way through the papers. Time to get out of here.

She was tiptoeing over the last paper when the door slammed back on its hinges and James Conti came in. His eyes were like an animal's, yellow-green, with dilated pupils. As frightened as if she were facing a wild animal, she backed up, her feet sliding from underneath her on the papers. She feared she would land ignominiously on the floor, until her rear end came to rest against the dean's big desk.

"I *knew* it!" he cried. "You're a *spy!* And I'm going to have you up on charges." He stood right in front of her, his eyes staring into hers.

"I just came in a minute ago," she lied. "I meant no harm. . . ."

He looked around to see if anything else was disturbed, beyond the mess of papers. Then he laughed bitterly. "Do you think I believe you, Mrs. Eldridge? You are so transparent. Has this something to do with Peter Whiting? Well, you're *ridiculous!*"

He practically spat the words into her face. She leaned back on the desk, trying to stay out of his space and wondering what he would do next. To her relief she heard Doug's voice at the door. The associate producer looked and sounded so normal that just maybe he could pull her out of this mess.

"Hi, there," he said. "Dean Conti? So you're here after all." He stuck out a hand and forced the dean to reciprocate.

Then he turned to Louise. "Since I made my reconnaissance of the labs, I thought I'd come and get you—but I see you *have* found the dean in his office."

"Thanks, Doug," she said in a businesslike voice. "I told Dean Conti that I'd just come in for a minute, to be sure he wasn't working in some little alcove there—" She waved her hand toward the back of the office, as if it might contain a warren of hidden rooms.

"Yep, just left her for a minute. Now I've come to fetch her." Doug was convincing, Louise thought.

Dean Conti stared at the two of them, less sure now. He told them, "I don't want people nosing around here while I'm not on the premises. My office is *very* private, for good reason. It's full of grant applications and important things you people would have no *idea* of. You have no right to be here."

"I'm *sure* that's true, Dean Conti," said her associate producer.

He looked coldly at Doug. "I've had some unexpected things turn up this morning, so I couldn't have given you the tour anyway." He turned to Louise. "I want you out of here, Mrs. Eldridge."

She released an anxious breath. There was no need to say anything, for the dean's face was closed with anger. Still, she reflected, people who expressed remorse always got away with more than those who didn't. She murmured, "I'm so sorry. I didn't mean to offend." The aggrieved dean stood by the door until they filed out, then firmly shut himself in his office.

As they hurried down the hall, Doug murmured, "I thought you said you worked fast."

"I *do*, but I ran into something really interesting."

"I sure hope it's worth it to you, since that man could be calling the cops on us right now. If you get frisked, they won't find anything, will they?" His friendly face looked at her dubiously.

"No, Doug. I don't do burglary—only illegal entry."

18

"I realized I'd gone a little too far when the campus police stopped and asked me if I would consent to a voluntary search," said Louise. "They didn't find anything, of course, because I didn't take anything."

Louise found this an embarrassing confession. She had come directly from Georgetown to see Mike Geraghty at the Mount Vernon District Station. She needed to tell him about her problems with the dean before he got word of it from someone else. She hoped to soften Geraghty's heart so he wouldn't fire her, but she knew it was hopeless to try to win the sympathy of his colleague, Detective George Morton, who shot her suspicious looks from across the dingy office.

"So, what I'm saying is that they let me go. And what was so strange, Mike, is that they seemed to *want* to believe I was innocent of whatever Conti accused me of."

"Conti wouldn't have much of a case of illegal entry anyway," said the detective. "That is, if the

door to his office was open, the way you claim it
was."

"It was open—that's why it was such a terrific
temptation."

"You should have resisted it, Louise." Spoken
like a Catholic, she was sure; maybe in another life,
Geraghty would have been a priest. He sat back in
his squeaky chair, and Louise could see her detective friend had gained weight again; sometimes
she worried that he would have a heart attack.
"When I asked you to help the police, I didn't
mean things like this." He opened his big hands in
a helpless gesture.

"Keep up stuff like this and you could end up
being an embarrassment to us, Mrs. Eldridge,"
added Detective Morton needlessly. Morton was
an impassive-faced man with good features, and he
sat tall in his chair. But Louise knew when he got
up, he'd be no taller than she was, for he was long
of trunk and short of leg. She found it hard to like
the man because of his brusqueness; he always
seemed to have it in for her.

"Detective Morton," she said with exaggerated
politeness, "not in a million years would I deliberately embarrass you and Detective Geraghty."

Morton seemed to accept her remarks at face
value, and even looked a little more amiably on
her, loathsome miscreant that she was.

Geraghty leaned forward in the chair, creating a
tremendous squawking sound. His face broke into
a big smile that lit up his bright blue eyes and
made his white hair look whiter. "So, didya find
anything we can use?"

She scooted her chair closer to his desk. "I sure
did."

Morton got up to his full height and said, "I sure
would like to stay and hear this, but I gotta go out
on a call, Mike." He cocked his head toward

Louise, and added, "Maybe you'd better warn her, y'know—"

"Why don't *you*, before you go?" suggested Geraghty.

The somber Morton turned to her. "If you found something good in that office, then maybe you think that makes it worthwhile. But it's risky business what you did there, all the same."

"I see what you mean, Detective Morton. Thanks. In retrospect, I might not have done what I did."

When he left, she turned to Geraghty, putting her elbows on his worn wooden desk and clasping her hands together. "Now, let me tell you about it. . . ." She described in detail the disheveled interior of the office, and its most personal item, the revealing snapshot of the beautiful Polly Whiting.

"But how do you know that James Conti took that picture?"

She sat back, a little deflated. "Because no husband would give out copies of that picture to other men. It bordered on pornographic—it was very sensuous. And anyway, the man had it hidden in the most obscure spot in the bottom of his desk. He didn't want anyone to know he had it."

"So what's your take on it?"

"The two of them had an affair, period. That would be a year or so after Conti came to Jefferson. Who knows, maybe Polly got tired of her old husband. I heard just yesterday that Dr. Whiting had become impotent because of a disease he suffered. He picked it up in the Amazon—a kind of TB contracted from birds."

"Speakin' of pickin' up, who'd ya pick that up from, a urologist?"

She grinned. "How did you guess?"

"Impotent, huh?" But then Geraghty slowly shook his head; he wasn't buying her theory. "It's interesting, but you might be misinterpreting a little snapshot. Folks take snapshots at beaches all the time where someone's falling out of their bathing suit. Maybe he does have the hots for her, but that picture, minus other corroborating information, isn't going to prove anything."

"Of course, we're trying to prove a negative, aren't we?" said Louise. "Prove that no one around Jefferson University had anything to do with Dr. Whiting's death. Well, this didn't help take Dr. Conti off the hook—just the reverse. One thing I can prove for sure about him. . . ."

"Yes, what?"

"He's a conspicuous consumer." She described the three photos showing Conti's opulent lifestyle. "Nothing but top-of-the-line goods for him."

"Hmm," said the detective. "Now the question is whether that included Whiting's wife."

"Let me see what else I can come up with. After all, there's also Joe Bateman to inquire about."

Geraghty shook his head. "No, no, Louise, no more overtures at Jefferson University. I think you've blown it there. In fact . . ."

"Oh, please don't fire me. I promise I'll be discreet. I can't get in much trouble—after all, this is only research. If you don't want me to return to Jefferson, the only other place I was going to go was to my own church. Is that all right?"

"That's Whiting's church, too, right? Doubt there's much to find. What I do want you to do is to steer clear of the dean. He strikes me as dangerous."

"Funny you should say that," said Louise. "The main reason the campus police let us off the hook so fast was that they thought Conti was overreacting. One of them suggested that he was paranoid. Apparently, he's having big troubles over there at the University Hospital, and lots of people on campus know about it. Someone at Whiting Labs told me Conti's gene replacement therapy subjects are dying. . . ."

"Whaddaya mean by that?"

Louise lifted an eyebrow and smiled. "Just that, dying. How much worse can you get? And then there are the letters—you should know about the letters. . . ."

"What letters?"

Louise shrugged her shoulders. "Maybe it's nothing, but in the mess of papers on his office floor were probably half a dozen from pharmaceutical firms—including Synthez, the biggest one of all. One has to ask whether they have something to do with Dr. Whiting and his new laboratory."

Geraghty made a few notes. "We'll look into those angles. Now let me say this again, Louise: you be careful. And I think you've done enough research for us. . . ."

"Oh, no, you *are* firing me!" She gave him an indignant stare, and felt tears of anger springing to her eyes. She wiped them away with a quick movement of her hand.

The detective stared silently at the blotter on his desk, as if it might have a magic message there among the blots. Finally he said, "Darn it, Louise, it's hard to deal with you. I'll give you one more chance, though this *should* be a 'one strike and you're out' situation, you know that, don't you? But I'm gonna be nice." He managed a smile. "Now don't muff it at church next week."

19

It was late Saturday night, but the only ones who were really tired were Louise and Bill. They passed in the hall, one coming and one going to the bathroom, and stole a kiss. They had had only a few moments alone in four days, and she could see signs of strain in her husband's face. A good part of it was his concern over the safety of his family with a killer on the loose.

And it didn't help that the house was full of company.

"I know," she said, "you want to be alone in your own house."

"Or maybe just with our own kids . . ."

"This is the last night. The visitors leave tomorrow, and Martha gets to stay on with us until the middle of next week. But think of it this way, Bill. If we'd had six kids of our own, it would be like this all of the time."

"Oh, yeah? Impossible."

"Melissa, fourteen. Janie, seventeen. Chris, eighteen. Martha, nineteen. Jim Daley, twenty. Teddy

Horton, twenty-two. We could have produced them all."

"Thank heavens we didn't. When are they going to bed?"

"Soon, when the game ends." When they returned to the living room, they found that Martha and Jim Daley had broken away from the Scrabble game for some advanced nightlife elsewhere. Bill accompanied the two to their car, for safety's sake, then retired to their bedroom.

Their departure left the four other more "problematic" people, as Louise thought of them. Except that Melissa McCormick had changed for the better in the past two days, and Louise realized that Janie was responsible.

Her seventeen-year-old daughter gave a cautious report on the young houseguest after the group took a sightseeing trip downtown. "Melissa's not *that* bad. She started out being a real jerk, showing off and being terribly loud. At first I thought I would die of embarrassment, so I took her to one side. Actually, we stood on the mezzanine of the East Gallery, and she might have thought I was going to throw her off—and I told her we'd drive her back home again if she didn't straighten out."

Louise smiled at Janie's methods. "Then what did she do?"

"Oh, we went to the ladies' room, and that gave her a chance to cry a little. She talked a little bit about how hard it was to live with a maiden aunt, and how much she missed her father—and mother."

"What did you do when she cried?"

"It was more than just crying. She threw herself into my arms like a movie star and sobbed her heart out. So I *patted* her—it worked really well.

Now, of course we're buddies for life. Not that she's that easy to like, but I do feel sorry for her now, where I didn't Thanksgiving night when she was trying to take Chris away from me."

"Has she quit doing that?"

"Of course not," said Janie, airily gesturing with a hand. "I don't mind her flirting, as long as she doesn't act stupid about it. She's just practicing. I told her lots of fourteen-year-olds are messed up, and that the teen years get better, so that by the time she's *my* age, she'll be just fine."

Janie flipped her long blond hair back and gave her mother a smile of total confidence. "I helped her rearrange that red mop of hers, too." Now Louise realized why Melissa looked so much better. Her wild hair now had side-twists of some kind that reduced its volume and added maturity.

Louise put her arm around her daughter's shoulders and squeezed. "Wait until her Aunt Moira sees her."

"I'm not saying any of this is going to last," said Janie.

By the time Saturday night's activities were coming to a close, Melissa had regressed. She had dropped out of the Scrabble game, and sat stiffly nearby with thin arms extended on either side of the chair to balance herself. From this vantage point, she directed resentful looks at the other three. They barely noticed, and just continued their lively scrapping over words.

Louise came up to her. "Why did you quit playing, Melissa?"

The girl gave her a glance, then put her hand in front of her mouth so the others couldn't tell what she was saying. "Too many already *in* this game." Louise hung around for a while and watched. Chris, a quiet but systematic player, was ahead. He would lay down his tiles for big scores, then shove his blond hair out of his eyes and grin happily.

Teddy, his country-boy face relaxed and happy, was close behind. Louise thought he seemed to have an extraordinary vocabulary for a young man with no college training. "A*ha!*" he cried. "*Hegemony.*" And arranged his seven tiles around a free-standing "m" on the game board.

"What's *that?*" said Chris, frowning.

"Oh, it's something about the authority of nations," said Janie.

Teddy glanced smugly at Chris. "She's right. It means the predominant influence of one country over others—like the U.S., for instance." And he happily retrieved seven more tiles from the bag in which they were kept.

"Good job, Teddy," said Janie. It was as if she were the referee, and both young men were struggling for victory just to win her attention.

After a few moments, Louise leaned down and cupped her hand so the others couldn't see, and said to Melissa, "I see what you're talking about." She cocked her head. "Why don't you come with me?"

At that, the girl leapt up out of her seat and followed Louise to the kitchen. "Can I help you clean up these stray snack dishes?" the fourteen-year-old asked.

"How nice. I'd love to have you help."

Soon after they'd finished, Melissa wandered off to her room, and Chris showed up in the kitchen. He had a hangdog expression on his face as he announced that he was going home.

"Where's Janie? Where's Teddy?" Louise asked.

Chris shrugged his wide shoulders. "I don't know, Mrs. Eldridge."

It was as if a cold wind had blown over her. "You

don't *know?*" she cried. "They're not out in the yard, I hope." She set down the sponge with which she was wiping the counter and hurried to the front door.

"They're probably all right," Chris assured her as he trailed her down the hall. "He does this, you know. Gets Janie to step out for a breath of fresh air—and then, man, they're out of sight." He smiled, bravely trying to make the whole thing into a joke. "You know, the old sleight-of-hand trick: First you see her, then you don't."

"We've got to find out."

Chris said, "For all I know, they went off together in his car. He's pulled this, oh, I don't know how many times—and it doesn't really matter, because he'll be outta here pretty soon."

"Come on," she said. They walked together down the flagstone path to the street.

"Yep," said Chris, "car's gone. He's persuaded her to take another joyride."

Louise sighed. "At least they'll be safe in a car. But I'm so sorry they left you behind, Chris. They're just rude."

"Well, that's life, Mrs. Eldridge," said the tall young man. "I'll walk you back to the house and then I'm outta here." He leaned down and gave her a little hug. "Good night and thanks for dinner again."

When Janie and Teddy didn't return by the time everyone else was ready for bed, Louise was considering calling the police for the second time this weekend.

Just as she was thinking of punching the fast-dial police button—it had been marked "Fuzz" by her younger daughter—she heard that very daughter and Teddy enter the house through the front door. She stood at her bedroom door and listened. Teddy was making some solicitous little argument in his good-night speech. Janie grumpily replied, "Go to *bed*," and they went to their respective rooms.

Maybe Janie had an excuse for this behavior, but Louise doubted it. The young man from Connecticut seemed bent on making trouble, or maybe his judgment was clouded with young love.

When she stumbled back into bed, Bill turned over sleepily and asked, "They back?"

"Yes, they're back."

"Good girl."

"For what?"

"For not running out there in your nightie and beating them to a pulp."

"Mmm, I restrained myself."

"Now what do you say we never admit company to the house again?"

20

The Northminster Women's Association met in the social hall of Northminster Presbyterian Church on the fourth Tuesday of each month, in an atmosphere of muted chintz and faux French Provincial. Members were surprised to see Louise, who'd attended only a few times before in the three years she and Bill had belonged to the church. She sat on the end of one of the rows of chairs, a place where the sunlight through the stained-windows splashed orange, red, purple, and gold down on her head. She felt as if God had painted her with color.

Next to her sat Marge Allgren, a woman in her late fifties with a gray pageboy—ordinary-looking in every way except for her large, blue, oracular eyes. Marge was said to know everything about everyone in the congregation.

Truly, thought Louise, a conversation with Marge was like surfing Yahoo. But Marge got away with it because everything she offered was objective and able to be proved in court. With her, gossip was almost a talent. She poured out the truth about people the way Chopin poured out preludes.

Though Marge turned off certain people—that small, ever-shrinking clique of paragons who never gossiped at all—there was much to be said about people like her, in Louise's opinion. Some of Louise's best tips on crimes and criminals had come from gossip—or what she preferred to call "hearsay." She smiled, remembering the warm ambience of her Thanksgiving kitchen. Filled with people of goodwill, armed and ready with useful, chatty rumors, hearsay, and idle talk about the Whitings. Seeming to know that Louise *needed* that information.

In the few times Louise had met Marge at coffee after church, she had never invited Marge's confidences—or used her services, so to speak. But she intended to do exactly that today.

Therefore, she'd found it fortuitous that this seat near Marge was empty—a seat that provided the wonderful spill of color upon her head, the embodiment of autumn.

The business meeting took precisely forty minutes, with Louise resisting the temptation to raise her hand and volunteer for any number of jobs that would have looked good on her spiritual resume. She already *had* two jobs—one of which, her lab job, she'd ditched to attend this meeting. Plus, she needed to get on with her research for the police. Certainly, she had no time to volunteer for the special church committees on social service, retirement home service, liturgy, vestments, or missions.

The two women got up and looked at each other with the joyous relief people feel at surviving another meeting. Louise stuck out a hand. *"Marge—* Louise Eldridge. Good to see you again."

"Oh, yes, Louise. A break in your TV schedule? I watch you every Saturday."

Louise guessed this woman knew all about the Eldridge family, even down to the adventures they'd had this August in Colorado. She rather doubted Marge knew Bill was undercover CIA, but she just might—for his cover wasn't nearly as deep as it used to be years ago. "Yes, a three-month break. But I'm working during the break, isn't that silly?"

She felt she had to apologize for being a workaholic in the face of these stalwart women. They declined paying jobs to do everything else well— cooking, cleaning, volunteering, serving God. . . . Louise could actually remember when she didn't have a paying job, and found staying home was a very lonely business, even when she interspersed it with volunteer work. She decided she was made to hold a paying job, preferably until the day she died.

She and Marge were headed, happily, toward the snacks table. "What's the second job?" said Marge. "Tell me about it."

Without mentioning anything she didn't want to get out to the world, Louise described her work at Whiting Labs. She hoped this would be an entrée into the topic of Polly Whiting, and it was.

"Polly's been through a lot."

"You mean Dr. Whiting's death."

"*And* before . . ."

Would this woman actually stand in the social room of the church and talk about adultery? No, but she might *imply* it, so that her listener could *infer* it.

"Oh," said Louise, "you mean when she got involved—I know she didn't *mean* . . ." There. That could refer to anything.

"No, she didn't," said Marge. "I think she always loved Peter, even when temptation—well, you know about it. Someone saw them at that little out-of-the-way beach resort—they apparently didn't realize there's nothing *that* private left for trysts of that sort . . ."

". . . and the *scientific* community being how it is . . ." said Louise, taking another large leap.

The solemn, predictive eyes gazed at her. "Oh, my dear, I know too well. They *talk*. My husband's in physics at G.W. And when Jefferson brought Conti in, what a splash he made—people watch his every move. He's quite the dashing man. Polly wasn't the only one who would have . . ."

"Yes, I know what you mean; the man has such . . . *vibrancy.*"

"And that job of his, why, he's tops in the country. And then Peter began to lose his spark, as if he had some malady. Polly seemed to get restless—"

"So you knew about the illness." How could this woman keep up with such intimate details of people's lives? Louise was incredulous.

"Oh, I'm just guessing one of those tropical diseases was getting to him. You know how *unsanitary* it is down there, and he was down there every chance he got. Why, Polly even went with him."

"Yes, a number of trips."

"And James Conti accompanied them on one trip . . . in fact, that might have, you know, been the beginning—"

"Yes, it may well have been. It's extremely—sensuous down in Brazil . . ."

"But unsanitary."

"I bet you knew Peter Whiting's first wife. I'm curious. Did *she* ever go on field trips to the Amazon?"

Marge shook her head. "Oh, no. There was a sickly woman, nice, but sickly. Finally she died of complications of a rheumatic fever she suffered from most of her life. Fortunately, he'd found Polly, um, somewhat before the first wife passed away."

"And you must know Matthew, too," said Louise, selecting a long, thin hors d'oeuvre made of salmon, onion, and capers. She took a bite, for she was talking so much she was beginning to feel protein-deficient.

"Oh, *Matthew!*" Louise could not have hoped for more; the woman both knew him and spoke his name in affectionate terms. "Lilly, of course, lives next to the Whitings, and she heard the two of them over the years."

"Fighting, of course."

Marge threw up her hands. "Oh, that's almost not the word for it. Screaming—he was always screaming at him. . . ."

"A son shouldn't scream at his father—"

"A *son?*" Marge looked at Louise for the first time with a trace of suspicion, as if this newcomer to the Women of Northminster had peddled herself as something she wasn't.

"Well, I heard from Polly herself that the two fought."

"But Peter's the one who screamed. That darling *boy* is the one who suffered, not old Peter Whiting. Matthew couldn't do anything right. Why, Lilly watched Peter throw his belongings onto the lawn of that house, and heard him tell him to never come back. Now, is that any way to treat a child?"

"What had Matthew done? Oh, of course, he switched from biology to acting. . . ."

Marge nodded her head. "And Peter was such a diehard: science or nothing. Others of us have had to deal with much more nonconformist children than Matthew—why, the stories I could tell you— and haven't treated them so shabbily. Besides, the dear professor, talented though he was, had the most vicious mouth in the scientific community."

"I can imagine."

"You *knew* him, then, Louise."

"Yes. He could get very cross with me."

Marge Allgren smiled and waved her hand. "Oh, rest assured that was nothing; he rarely turned it on with women, certainly not with his beloved Polly. But men—all men had to measure up to Peter's impossible standards. He had a simplistic attitude toward life. He wanted a beautiful wife, a son who followed in his footsteps, a beautiful home, and repeated successes in his field of ethnobotany. For a while, he was acting biology dean, and he drove everybody crazy, demanding that his colleagues be workaholics just like him. Not content to rest until they had gone after every challenge with the vengeance of a jaguar after a wildebeest. He more or less *devoured* life, refusing to admit to anything less than, as I say, his concept of the well-ordered existence."

"Marge, you know everything."

Marge gave her a tired look. "I'm afraid I do, Louise, and let me tell you, sometimes it's a terrible burden." With that the woman picked a plump, stuffed mushroom from a plate and popped it straightaway into her mouth.

21

The Eldridges' older daughter had stayed on a few extra days in Washington to do research in the Library of Congress for her civics class at Northwestern. Everyone in the house respected Martha's privacy, and let her work in her room in solitude—until she felt like emerging for meals or a little conversation with the family.

Once in a while Louise or Janie came into her room, or "shrine," as Janie dubbed it, with its mauve carpeting and white French cotton floor-length curtains blowing in the November breeze. "I have to have fresh air," Martha explained. They would interrupt her for a moment to bring tea, while she smiled her thanks and continued typing on the computer, surrounded with her opened books and neatly written notes on pads. Occasionally, Janie huddled with her older sister for private talks, and Louise was happy to realize the two were so close.

Tuesday night, Louise had the pleasure of Martha's exclusive company. Instead of letting her study in peace and quiet, Louise exploited her—

learning in the process that her daughter had the instincts of an excellent investigator. It happened because Bill had left town for a brief trip to New York, and Janie was auditioning for a school play. This left Louise and Martha free to do what they pleased for dinner, since turkey leftovers had finally been deep-sixed in the trash.

After Louise told her daughter what she had learned that morning at the Women's Association meeting, Martha suggested going to a coffee pub in the Belleview Shopping Center. "We can get a fast meal, and it's the kind of place where you might pick up more information." She giggled. "I have to warn you, though, that no one over thirty sets foot in the place. But with a little makeup, you'll pass."

Her daughter swiftly drove them the mile and a half to the shopping center, an older, modest-sized business development that would have expanded had it not been hemmed in by houses. She wheeled Louise's Honda station wagon neatly into the center's parking lot, encountering a sudden jam-up of traffic in front of the Seven-Eleven. That was where Louise caught a glimpse of Polly Whiting.

"Oh, look," she said, "there's my boss."

"How chic," commented Martha. Wearing simple black, as befitted a widow, Polly was sitting in the passenger seat of a BMW, staring moodily out at the world without seeing it. Louise was embarrassed to be staring, but she could hardly avoid it, for the other car was stalled right in her line of sight. Polly's eyes gradually focused and she recognized Louise. She raised a hand and gave her a tentative smile. At the wheel sat Dr. James Conti, a proprietary arm draped on Polly's shoulder. He did not see Louise, since he was staring forward.

"So that's Polly Whiting," said Martha, as they finally pulled free of the tie-up. "She's awfully blond, isn't she? Is any of it real—the hair, or those eyes?"

"No."

"And the dude with her, did you know him?"

"Yes. Dr. James Conti, who was her dead husband's boss."

"You have to tell me everything." Probably because Martha had been so engrossed in the visiting Jim Daley, this was the first time she seemed interested in details of Louise's affairs. Louise was anxious to tell her daughter about the little web of people involved in Dr. Peter Whiting's world.

They went into the coffee pub and found a corner table, and Martha pulled a pad and pen out of her purse. By the time their drinks had arrived, she had debriefed her mother, made an organizational chart of the people, and formulated what she called "focus questions."

Louise was beginning to feel guilty. "I thought you were in a hurry to get back to writing your paper—are you sure you want to talk about all this?"

But Martha was now hot on the scent. "As we university students like say, 'Analyze or die.' Let's keep analyzing, shall we?" Sipping her tea with one hand, she took up her pen with the other and poised it at the first question. "You've gone once to the Jefferson University biology labs, and it doesn't sound like it went well. You'd better lay off this Dean Conti, since he's already furious with you. You've passed good information on to Detective Geraghty; let him pursue it. Now, Ramon Jorges: same with him, and do you know why, Ma?"

"No, not exactly."

"Remember that besotted man who used to chase you when we lived in Tel Aviv?"

"You don't have to remind me. . . ."

"He was South American, too," said Martha needlessly. "If I were you, I'd leave him to the cops. . . ."

"Martha, that is so prejudicial. . . ."

"Well, then, leave the South American angle out of it. This Dr. Jorges is a scumbag. I can tell just from what you've told me—trying to seduce someone on her honeymoon. So why get close to him? That's how you've gotten yourself in trouble before. Now, who does that leave? Joe Bateman and Matthew Whiting. Those two seem enough for you to research."

"How about Polly herself?"

"You've done enough on her, Ma—you found that she had an affair with James Conti." She smiled, her big, hazel eyes filled with laughter. "What else can you do, go and break into her house?"

Martha sat there, a beautiful young woman with long brown hair flowing around her shoulders, supremely confident that she knew the right thing for her mother to do. She darted looks around the dim restaurant, then leaned forward and said in a low voice, "You know, this is going to be a great place to find out about Matthew, and I'll tell you why. First of all, you just saw his stepmother out there, right?"

"Right."

"The reason you saw her was be *cause* . . . " It was as if Martha were the wise professor, urging on a slow student.

"Because she lives in the neighborhood."

"Right. This is the closest place to her house to shop. This is where she buys gas from the gas station, groceries from the Giant, and candy bars or whatever from Seven-Eleven. In other words, her *neighborhood* shopping center. And Matthew's, too, when he was growing up."

"So you're saying . . ."

Martha looked around expectantly. "There are probably people in here right now who used to know Matthew, that's what. I'm hampered a bit because I never went to high school here; too bad we don't have Janie with us. But I've met some locals who live in the general neighborhood; I know a lot of them hang here." She reached a slim hand over, put it on top of her mother's, and gave her a brilliant smile. "Now all we have to do is open ourselves to new experiences—"

"In other words . . ."

"*Meet* folks. And the first thing we do," she said, getting up from her dark wood barrel chair and grabbing her coat, "is move ourselves up front where we can see everybody who comes in. C'mon." She scooped up her teacup, and led the way to the table as the waitress looked on in puzzlement.

Martha gave the woman a smile that would have earned her the best table in any restaurant. "We just *have* to sit at this table, d'you mind? We're expecting friends."

They were finished with dinner, and still no one that Martha recognized had appeared in the coffee pub. Louise could see her daughter was growing restless, and possibly regretted plunging herself into her mother's dubious investigations. Then two young women entered the pub, their eyes searching each table of the dim, dark-wooded interior, and recognized Martha. They smiled, rescued from anonymity by a thread.

"Martha, is that *you*?" said a slim blond young woman.

"*Cindy*—and, let's see . . ."

"It's Rebecca," said her heavier companion, who

had carefully permed wavy black hair. "We met, too, last summer at Brian's party."

"Why don't you come and join us? This is my mother, Louise Eldridge."

"Your *famous* mother," Rebecca exclaimed. "*We* know her—the TV gardening lady."

The young women sat down and ordered café au lait. Louise beamed, and decided to let Martha get this conversation rolling. The young women had graduated from college, and now shared a rented condo in the neighborhood. "It's nice," said Cindy, "since it's only a few miles from our parents' homes."

"That is nice," said Louise. She wondered, was it insecurity, or a desire to continue tradition, this returning to the old neighborhood to live? She herself felt little attachment to places, since she and Bill had moved eight times since they were married. From country to country, and back and forth from foreign countries to the States. Furthermore, she knew her children had this same vagabond approach to life—since they'd made the moves with them.

Through tactful questioning, Martha found out that Cindy and Rebecca were twenty-six. Louise felt a letdown. How could they know Matthew Whiting, for he was almost from a different generation. But her daughter focused in further, now pinpointing the two geographically, like one of those computerized location finders in an automobile.

"A*ha*," said Martha, "so when you were growing up, you lived in Northminster Estates, before moving to the Mount Vernon area?" She sent her mother a look that said, *Heads up!*

"Right near your Sylvan Valley neighborhood, Mrs. Eldridge," said Rebecca with a mocking little smile playing around her lips, "which, of course, I always thought was real—interesting. All that kind of *lurid* history, and all those kooky, modern houses . . ."

Louise ignored the not-so-subtle putdown of Sylvan Valley, which had a reputation from the fifties of being a hotbed of liberals and radical newspapermen. "You must have known the Whitings," she said. "I work with Mrs. Whiting now."

"The *Whiting* family!" cried Rebecca, self-consciously shaking her waves of hair. "Living close to them was *too* close."

"Really?" said Louise in her most casual tone.

Rebecca's brown eyes lit up. "Now, I don't like to gossip—and it has nothing to do with Polly Whiting, because it wasn't *her* fault—but that family had its troubles—despite the fact that old Professor Whiting was a very big deal at Jefferson University, y'know. Of course, now he's *dead* and so no one probably wants to know the bad stuff about the family. . . ."

Little did Rebecca know that the Eldridge investigative team longed to know the bad stuff about the family.

"What, in your opinion, was the problem?" asked Martha, leaning forward intently so her brown hair fell around her face.

"Oh, I guess you'd say they were both the problem," said Rebecca, rolling her eyes. She lapsed into silence, playing for complete audience attention before delivering the punch line.

Louise saw a muscle move dangerously in Martha's cheek.

Just as she feared her daughter would reach across the table and strangle the answer out of Rebecca, Cindy decided enough was enough. "Oh, just *tell* them," she said. "Never mind. I'll tell them myself. Keep in mind—we were about ten years younger than Matthew, nosy little brats running around the neighborhood, so of course we knew *everything*. Matthew started out being a little scientific whiz kid, right in Daddy's footsteps. Then, when he was a senior in high school, his mom died. That was the beginning of all the trouble. After that, Matthew changed. He got himself some druggie friends his father hated. . . ."

Rebecca said, "Not the little nerds he used to run with—this was the artistic crowd that liked a snootful of cocaine to go through life."

Cindy continued. "Right around then, Dr. Whiting married this good-looking young woman from the university, who seemed like a pretty good stepmother, even though she was young."

"Did Matthew like her?" asked Louise.

The two young women shrugged their shoulders in puzzlement. "Hard to say," said Cindy, "because he was away at college. Not long after his freshman year, he made the big break and ditched science. He decided to go into the theater instead."

Rebecca leaned forward and said dramatically, "You would have thought that Matthew had committed *murder.* I felt so sorry for Matthew—at first."

Cindy shook her head and said, "The entire neighborhood knew about the final incident. . . ."

"When was that?" asked the ever-analytical Martha.

"About fifteen years ago, I'd say. Professor Whiting became terminally disgusted with Matthew, and *threw* him and his clothing, and his stereo equipment, out of the house."

"What did Matthew do?" asked Louise.

"He'd never fought back before, though his dad was always yelling at him," said Cindy, "but he did that time. We thought he was going to land in jail for attempted murder, or something."

Rebecca interrupted. "What he did was beat up

his father, knock him down, break his arm or his elbow, I forget which. Why, he had to go to the *hospital.* The professor's wife came out with a broom or something and broke things up. Why, I remember they had a new terrier puppy. That dog went berserk and attacked Matthew, so his leg was all bloody."

Dogs have long memories, Louise realized. Herb was still suffering from the trauma of that fight; it was why he couldn't accept Matthew.

"Gosh," said Martha. "And this all happened right there in quiet Northminster Estates," said Martha.

"Well, *sure,* " Rebecca piped up defensively. She shoved her wavy hair dramatically away from her face and gave Martha a superior look, as if Martha didn't know much about life. "And what makes you think there weren't any other big incidents in our neighborhood? Did you ever hear about the time one of our teenagers tied up his parents in the attic and threatened to shoot them and himself?"

"Hey," said Martha. "So what happened *there?"*

"The cops talked him down, so to speak," said Cindy.

Louise decided it was time to wrap this up, lest Martha start bragging about Sylvan Valley's famous forty-five-year-old incident of wife-swapping, or perhaps the more recent murder of her friend, Jay McCormick, in the Mougeys' fish pond. She said, "What a shame for that to have happened—and how hard it must have been on Matthew. Thanks for sharing it with us."

"Actually, Matthew Whiting's doing all right, I guess," Cindy said. "He's with the Rolfe Civic Theater in Washington, and he must be pretty talented—he won that Golden Sphere Award."

Martha smiled. "Apparently, he made the right

career choice, even if his father didn't like it." She looked at her watch. "Speaking of a career choice, I'll have to make a new one myself if I don't go home and finish my term paper." She had told the two young women of the research project that kept her in the Washington, D.C. area.

As Martha said good-bye to her two acquaintances, Louise thoughtfully shrugged into her jacket. The two young women had revealed a new side to Matthew Whiting. He was not only the victim, as Marge Allgren had made him out—but the traumatized victim who'd turned on his father and beat him almost to a pulp.

22

Over the years, Louise had lunched in lots of different venues, at home, in fancy restaurants, in greasy spoons, with her husband on hillsides in Israel, and in tavernas in Greece, but she had never brown-bagged it before she started working at Whiting Labs. No one at Channel Eight would even consider it, the television industry having certain standards to uphold; therefore, most staff branched out to the mediocre restaurants within easy distance of the station.

But Louise found she enjoyed the daily routine of bringing a sandwich and piece of fruit from home and eating with her colleagues. It was a spare and utilitarian way to take lunch, and filled with a special camaraderie, especially since the president of the firm, Polly Whiting, plunked her brown bag down with the rest of them.

Today, however, Louise had retrieved her lunch and gone home to eat it. She decided to phone Jefferson University, and realized she could hardly do it at work under the very eye of the man she was investigating—Joe Bateman.

It was a matter of pride to revisit Jefferson University. She was not about to be hounded away because of one bad experience. Besides, Sarah Shane was the kind of person who would know about Joe. Louise sat at the dining room table, her feet propped up on another chair. The cell phone was cradled in her shoulder, a pad of lined paper and a pen lay before her, and her sandwich and a glass of milk stood handily by her left hand. The house itself was deadly quiet, but with ghostly little echoes of young people's voices. All guests were gone, and Martha had left this morning to go back to Chicago.

Louise should have realized the noon hour was a bad time to catch people. As she munched her sandwich, she kept being transferred within the confines of the Public Relations Department. By the time she reached Sarah, she'd consumed her entire lunch and found a very chilly woman on the other end of the line. Obviously, Dr. James Conti had made Sarah suffer for her sins.

Louise asked if they could meet for coffee and a little chat.

"I don't think so, Mrs. Eldridge."

"Tell me straight, Sarah," persisted Louise, "did I land you in trouble Friday?"

"Oh, it wasn't your fault," she replied stiffly.

"Do call me Louise."

The young woman talked in a quiet, discreet voice. "It's just that Dr. Conti is always difficult, Louise. I should have *done* something about that open office door; that's what he said."

Louise was silent for a moment. "I am so sorry. I didn't think I was going to get you into such trouble. But I still need your help. Could I talk to you if I came to Georgetown?"

"I suppose we could meet somewhere after I get out of work at five."

With an inward groan, Louise pictured the massive traffic jam in Washington at that hour; no one in their right mind entered it without a good reason. But this was a good reason. They arranged to meet in an espresso shop promptly at five.

Louise returned to Whiting Phytoseuticals and put in an afternoon's work, leaving promptly at four. Then she gritted her teeth and set out through the maelstrom of late-afternoon traffic. Parking in Georgetown, she knew, would be a problem. On a whim, she drove up O Street toward the entrance to Jefferson University, where there was unmetered parking. She smiled as if God had intervened. An empty slot opened up on the opposite side of the street. She drove to the university gates, did a quick U-turn, and only then saw a shiny new car hovering beyond the spot, trying to decide whether to take it or not. Without hesitation, she slid nose-first into the space, and with heart thumping in her breast, turned off the motor. Either the driver in the shiny car would come back and shoot her dead, or else she'd just won the prize parking spot in overcrowded Washington. The shiny car slowly drove off, apparently indifferent to the loss.

She hurried down the deep set of concrete stairs that took her to M Street, and immediately saw the sign for the espresso shop. She found Sarah Shane sitting at a back table, her large gray eyes looking worried until she saw Louise; then she smiled. After ordering a large coffee, Louise decided the best thing to do was to level with her companion. She hunched forward in her seat and told Sarah that she was helping the Fairfax police.

"It's not that I'm doing anything really big—I'm just giving them my impressions of the people who were involved with Professor Whiting."

"That's why you came here?" The gray eyes were

skeptical. Wasn't she even going to believe Louise? "But the police already interviewed everyone here— not me, but everyone around Biology. Dr. Conti. Dr. Peter Whiting's teaching colleagues. Even his former secretary. People like that."

"And Joe Bateman, who's running Dr. Whiting's lab now."

"And Joe, I suppose," said Sarah. "I wouldn't know—he left the department about ten months ago."

"I wondered if you knew anything about Joe."

She dropped her gaze and focused on the coffee cup that she cradled in her hands. "What kind of things?"

"I'd like to know what you know, Sarah, without bending any rules or anything—mostly, what kind of a person he is."

"Funny you ask, Louise." Her voice was dreamy. "I dated Joe for a while."

"You must have liked him."

"Oh, I liked him a lot. He's nice-looking and intelligent, maybe not as *colorful* as some of the young scientists, even though he's just as ambitious. But he never seemed to get that interested in me—"

"That's odd right there."

Sarah smiled. "So we just remained friends. He makes a good friend, I guess."

"You sound disappointed."

"I guess I am." She laughed and tossed back her short brown bob. "He was a really good catch: no previous marriages and divorces, or kids. Do you know how few men there are like that? Intelligent, as I said, and not money-mad, like some. And very loyal to Dr. Whiting—he was like a son to him."

Louise liked hearing that.

"He likes sports," Sarah continued, as if reeling off a curriculum vitae that she had memorized, "especially fishing in the Potomac in his little boat, which was great fun a couple of times. He's a member of the Maple Island Boat Club and keeps his boat there. But don't get me wrong. It can't be a very fancy club, because he isn't that sort, you know. He's a real straight arrow, but headed for bigger things, I guess."

"What do you mean by that?"

Sarah looked at the front of the coffee shop with concern, apparently having seen someone she knew. Louise turned around; a middle-aged woman was taking a seat in the front window. "Well, there's someone from our office—I sure hope she didn't see us."

"You were talking about Joe and how he's bound for bigger things—"

"Oh, yes. What I mean is, he could possibly hook up with Polly Whiting someday, couldn't he? Or that job in biotech could play out to an even bigger job with a pharmaceutical company. As far as marrying Polly, I sort of doubt it, as I think about it. He never seemed interested in her that way. Dr. Conti is the one who'll probably catch her first."

Louise could agree, remembering the submissive air Polly had had about her last night as she rode with James Conti in his shiny black foreign car.

"Conti's quite a sportsman, I guess."

"Oh, very big into sailing and polo, when he has time. He likes to take part in yacht races, when he can get up a crew. Poor soul, he apparently spends a great deal of time with his Gene Implantation Team and—well, it's hard right now for those scientists." She met Louise's eyes, then quickly glanced down again.

"Yes, I heard there was trouble with some patients. . . ."

"I don't want to talk about *that*," she said emphatically, giving Louise an anguished look, "even if everyone else at the university *is.*"

Louise got off that track fast. It didn't seem to relate to Dr. Whiting anyway. She was reminded of another troublesome would-be suitor of the young widow. As she sat back, the ice cream-parlor-style chair cut into her back, so she leaned forward again. "Sarah, have you ever met a Dr. Ramon Jorges?"

Sarah's eyes rolled, as if they were now onto a disgusting topic. "How could I forget him?"

"Why do you know him? Why did he come to Jefferson?"

"To visit the biology labs. To meet the famous James Conti. And to renew old times with his old research partner, Professor Whiting. He's quite the lecturer, you know, on phytoseutical plants, but he has a wild reputation. The first time he visited, he even came in the P.R. department and I swear, he picked me right out, I don't know why."

Louise thought she knew why. Those limpid gray eyes, the beautiful young figure, the sculptured face.

Sarah wiggled her hands in front of her, as if each finger were a snake. "He had what you might call 'wandering hands,' which I hated. He'd come in and *touch* me, when he didn't even *know* me. He asked me out, but I told him no. I had the feeling that if I'd said yes, he would have tried to drag me to the Royal Motel down on Pennsylvania Avenue, or something. That's the kind of man *he* is. I don't think Polly Whiting even likes him—though Polly's odd." Sarah's face now wore a wise expression. "She really likes the attention of men—all men."

"You knew Polly pretty well, then?"

"Yes. She was easy to work with—very smart. But she was obsessed with becoming a success. I think that's why she married Peter Whiting, because her success was assured, in a manner of speaking, because of his reputation and what he could accomplish."

"And how about Peter Whiting?"

"Some people joked about the two of them. They said Polly was an angel, and Dr. Whiting was an old devil. Most of the time he acted like a courtly gentleman, but sometimes he was very difficult. He'd *scream* at people." She looked guiltily up at the woman at the front table, as if even across the length of the coffee shop the woman could hear her. "He never screamed at me."

They drank up their coffee, and Louise said, "I'd better let you go home."

Sarah bit her lips and said, "I hope I did the right thing, talking to you. You may be helping the police, Louise, but all the time we've been talking here, I've felt like I was gossiping."

"I don't think this really rates as gossip, Sarah. You weren't unkind. You were just telling the truth. We won't think it's gossip if some of this information helps the police catch a violent criminal."

"You feel strongly about this, don't you?"

"Very strongly. Professor Whiting was a friend. And he was butchered to death one block away from my home."

23

Louise arrived at work Thursday, whistling a quiet little tune, happily anticipating a new day at work with her tiny plantlets.

Polly Whiting intercepted her at the front door of the lab, eyes blazing. "Can I have a moment of your time, Mrs. Eldridge?" she said.

The words were like drops of pure poison. There was no music in the widow's voice this morning. Louise trailed the CEO of Whiting Labs into her plush-carpeted office.

"And close the door, please," she ordered. Louise dutifully obeyed.

Polly's furious expression and harridan-like voice were downright scary, until Louise learned why she was so upset. She had just gotten off the phone with James Conti. "Someone saw you and that P.R. woman in that coffee shop."

"You mean, Sarah was deliberately followed?" Louise was incredulous.

"As a matter of fact, yes," said Polly crossly. "She obviously was gossiping about staff at Jefferson, and about James Conti. Talk about letting the fox in the *henhouse*—I ought to fire your ass right now! But I think I'll talk to Joe first."

Louise, her face red with embarrassment, cringed at the use of "ass." No one had ever threatened to fire it before. Then her thoughts turned to Sarah Shane. It had been rash of her to talk to Sarah in such a public place. Louise getting fired was one thing; she had another job, a very good one, and a husband for support. But what would happen to Sarah—single, and on her own in a city with high rents? For Louise had a feeling that the powerful Jefferson biology dean would see to it that the woman lost her job.

Polly's voice bit into the silence of the office, which was well built but not soundproof. It was impossible for passersby not to hear the import of a loud conversation within.

Matthew Whiting, halfway into his white lab coat, knocked on the door, then opened it and poked his head in. "Everything all right, stepmom of mine?"

Louise noted again how his sharp features resembled his father's, and in his white lab coat, his whole bodily frame must evoke in this grieving widow memories of her deceased husband. Or did the widow think of things like that?

"No, it *isn't* all right," said Polly in a petulant, little-girl voice. "You might as well come in, Matthew." She waved a disgusted hand at Louise. "Louise here is a spy. She's going around asking questions about us—well, about me, and about Joe, and about James. That's why she went over to Jefferson University in the *first* place—the *only* reason, I bet."

Those enhanced blue eyes glared menacingly at Louise, until she backed up a step, lost her balance, and slammed down in Polly's chrome-and-leather visitor's chair.

Now she had two people staring down at her from above. In embarrassment, if not shame, she kept her gaze down. This gave her a good view of Polly's desktop. Absently, she noted the familiar-looking letterheads. Polly had mail from the big pharmaceutical companies, just like the mail in James Conti's office.

"Hey, Louise," said Matthew, "it is *so* uncool to be a fink like that, don't you know that?"

Quietly, she said, "I am not a fink, Matthew. I'd like to explain."

Polly cocked her head, hearing the opening of the front door. She extended the flats of her hands on either side of her, like a director stopping the action of a scene. "Hold on—it's Joe. Let's see what Joe thinks."

Joe Bateman walked by, saw the group in the office, and came in. "Hi. Am I missing a meeting?"

They all stood looking at Louise while the widow reiterated the accusations to the postdoctoral assistant. Louise's stomach clamped with tension. She closed her eyes for a minute and desperately tried to relax, slumping back in the Mies Van Der Rohe chair so it could do its part. She told herself that this was not the end of the world, just the most embarrassing scrape she'd landed in so far.

There was a moment of suspended animation. Then Joe Bateman grinned. "Well, Louise, find out anything interesting?"

She began to feel her tight muscles loosen a little. "I found out very little." That was almost true, she told herself. "Joe, I wish you'd persuade Polly to listen to my explanation."

He turned to the widow and advised her to do just that. "Look, Louise is great in the lab. I'm sure she got into this innocently, and wasn't doing it like a private eye or anything." He asked her, "What happened, did the police ask you to help?"

She nodded. She might as well admit it. She was already caught in the act. Then her stomach pitched, as she woke up to the further consequences of her action. Mike Geraghty was sure to fire her now—unless she could keep the police's role an innocent one.

She would have to fudge this somehow.

They were all looking at her, and she knew that everything depended on how well she did. "Some of you must have realized I knew Detective Geraghty before he came in here the other day. Since he's handling Professor Whiting's murder, he asked me to make some really simple inquiries."

"You mean, that day he dropped in?" asked Polly.

"We didn't talk here," she hastened to add. "He dropped in at my house later and said he was surprised to see me, and then asked me to just keep my eyes open, to pick up, uh, biographical information on people, for instance, that the police might have missed. After all, they are doing everything possible to find out who murdered your husband, Mrs. Whiting."

Polly stood with her hands on her hips. "You make it sound so innocent, Louise."

At least, thought Louise, she was no longer calling her "Mrs. Eldridge," so she guessed she could drop the "Mrs. Whiting."

Resting a hand on her heart, Louise said, "I swear to you that I didn't do any snooping around here"—she wasn't going to enlarge that geographical area, for she certainly *did* snoop in Conti's office—"nor would I ever do so."

Of course, that was not true; when had she become such a smooth liar? If warranted, she'd probably break into this place after hours.

Joe Bateman's response was interesting, the response of a guileless man who believed everyone else to be as innocent as he. "I believe Louise, Polly. I think we ought to let this go. If James Conti wants to prosecute her for wandering into his office and peeking at his grant proposals, or because she asked for a few bits of information from a P.R. flack, well let him go to it. It's ridiculous." He looked down on Louise with an admiring expression. "Louise has made herself invaluable around here, and I, for one, want her to stay."

Matthew chimed in. "She is one of us, Polly, whatever little snooping she's done at police request. I say, we're a good team; let's not blow it."

Louise looked over at Polly. The woman had her hands on her hips, and a distracted look on her face, and she obviously was doing some fast thinking.

After seeing the widow with Conti the other night, and watching her come down on his side on this latest matter, Louise was certain that Polly was beholden to the biology dean. Perhaps she feared she would need James Conti, and maybe even Jefferson University, to bring her ambitious project to success.

Peter Whiting was like a magician; he had discovered, skillfully promoted, and provided the lab resources to make a commercial success out of a jungle plant. But the rest of the work was not going to be easy. His widow, Louise realized, had to hedge her bets with a number of people, certainly both James Conti and the nefarious Ramon Jorges. She didn't want to alienate either man, especially Conti, and the easiest way to make sure she didn't was to fire Louise.

On the other hand, there stood Joe and Matthew, keeping the ax from falling. Polly crossed her arms over her chest. "Okay, I won't fire you. But I *will* if I ever catch you again doing a thing like that."

"Hey, Polly, chill out," said Matthew. "She didn't even *do* any detective work here in the lab; why, I've been with her whenever she's been at work. Louise was like, oh, you know, Watson working for Holmes, or Archie hustling clues for Nero Wolfe—Sergeant Lewis for Inspector Morse—that kind of thing. Don't fixate on it—it isn't worth it. What's she going to find out—that we're all on the level?"

Polly looked hard at her stepson. "She wasn't asking questions about *you*—or was she? How do you know she hasn't been poking into *your* life?"

Matthew laughed. "It'd probably be a heck of a lot more interesting than yours or Joe's, I'll say that—especially some of my earlier years." He beckoned to Louise. "C'mon, Louise, let's get back to work." She got up and looked at Polly, who nodded her head, as if giving absolution after a confession.

The disclosure of Louise's undercover role with the police did a strange thing. It seemed to draw the workers at the lab even closer together. She felt a deepening kinship with Joe, Matthew, and Gina. Joe was a good leader, and a man willing to stand up for what he believed. Matthew could still be difficult in the lab, showing an emerging pattern of wanting to do things his own way, as if he had inherited the tendency from his father. But today he dropped the role of prima donna and acted like a real team player. Gina was a pro lab technician, and just what the place needed. They ate their brown bag lunches together, but Louise wasn't fully recovered from the indignities suffered earlier; her dry cheddar cheese sandwich tasted like a penance devised by an Old Testament God. She discarded it after two bites.

Polly stood on the edges of their amiable lunch group, aloof and bad-tempered; Louise realized the disclosure of her petty spying was not the only cause of this woman's unhappiness.

24

L ouise sprang up the steps at the entrance to the Dixie Pig with an energy fired by her desire for a pork barbecue sandwich. She headed to her favorite booth in the restaurant's back corner, where she could people-watch if she chose.

"Hi, there," said the counterman, as if he knew her. But he didn't, and she was glad for that. She sat down and looked guiltily up at the grease-flecked clock: four-thirty. A little late to eat lunch, but her route home had taken her right by the restaurant and she was starved.

As soon as she sat down, a wave of fatigue hit her, and she yawned deeply. It had been a terrible day, so it was nice to sit in a restaurant where no one else knew her, and probably no one would chew her out or threaten to fire her.

Her eyes glazed over, and she sat and stared contentedly into space.

At first, she hardly noticed the waitress, though she did hear her ask for her order. "What will I have? The pork barbecue sandwich and hot tea with lemon." Then she regained a semblance of decorum and looked up at the woman and smiled.

Her mouth dropped open. The woman's face—never to launch a single ship, never mind a thousand—was a mess. Monstrous shiners around her eyes gave her face a sickly yellow cast, and she had large cuts over her right eye and around her mouth. Her left arm was supported by a light sling. The face wounds—for which her mass of curly black hair made a dramatic frame—were stitched in such a prominent way as to give her a slight resemblance to Frankenstein's monster.

"My *God,*" Louise blurted out before she could stop, "who did that to you?"

The waitress instinctively put a hand to her face. The color of the bruises told Louise they must be a week or two old. "I thought folks wouldn't notice anymore," she said. "But thanks for asking." She leaned over Louise and muttered, "A real first-class S.O.B. did it, and he's gonna get his."

"Well, I hope so," said Louise. She also hoped she could go back to staring into space, but the waitress continued to orbit nearby, and it was impossible to ignore her.

Two bill-capped young men sat down in the adjoining booth, obviously regular customers. Sidling up with hips swinging, the waitress said, "What'll ya have, boys, the usual?"

"Hi, Dorothy," said the stockier one of the two. "How about the São Paolo sandwich," he suggested, and broke out in raucous laughter.

She feinted a move, as if she were going to strike him with her order pad. He obligingly ducked. "How about if you just shut your mouth," warned Dorothy, "or I'll give you a few expressions in Portuguese that will make that wimpy straight hair of yours curl into ringlets."

Louise's internal system had gone into neutral, but hearing "São Paolo" and a threat to spew Portuguese curses around threw her reluctantly back into gear.

She watched Dorothy the waitress saunter down the aisle to deliver her latest order to the kitchen. The woman was not pretty, but she was very sexy; she could swing a hip as well as such legendary hip-swingers of the movies as Marilyn Monroe. An open invitation to men, noted Louise.

It couldn't be possible, could it? No.

Louise's sandwich came, and she set upon it as if she hadn't eaten in a week. In a few minutes, Dorothy wandered back to refill the hot water in her little metal teapot. "Need a new bag?" she inquired.

"Thanks, yes," said Louise, and the woman drew one from her pocket. Before she went off to another table, Louise said, "Could I inquire as to what a São Paolo sandwich tastes like?"

Dorothy laughed, but there was a touch of bitterness to it. "Oh, that's just a bad joke." She brought the two workmen in on it. "This lady thinks there really is a São Paolo sandwich. Wants to know how it tastes." She laughed bitterly.

One of the men cupped his hand and quietly said, "It's not really food—it's a sexual remark." When Dorothy passed him, he grabbed her arm and said, "But we don't really mean it; what we do mean is if we caught this blankety-blank South American, he'd have more than a few cuts on his face."

Louise was pretty sure that Dorothy the waitress had somehow tangled with Ramon Jorges. And the more she thought about it, the less of a stretch it was to think of him picking up a nice warm-blooded woman like Dorothy.

When it came time to pay the bill, Louise realized she either had to put her detective cap on again and face further humiliation, fatigue, and terror, or else decide she didn't care who gave Dorothy all those wounds on her face. But she *did* care. She also realized this could be related, somehow, to Peter Whiting's murder.

The trouble was that Dorothy was getting busier. After Louise brought up the São Paolo sandwich, the waitress had seemed wary; maybe she had made too much of it, and the manager didn't like it.

How would Louise get her to talk? She got a little piece of paper out of her purse and printed, CAN I MEET YOU FOR A MINUTE IN THE LADIES' ROOM? She set it, and a ten-dollar-bill, on top of her check, then busily put on her coat.

Dorothy picked up the check, read the note, and gave Louise a long look.

"Keep the change, won't you," said Louise, and rose and went to the ladies' room.

In a minute, someone knocked, and Louise let Dorothy in. The waitress immediately lit up a Lucky Strike, drew smoke deep into her lungs, and exhaled. She said, "Look, I've got in trouble already with my employers over this beating I took. Too much talking about me, too much jokin' about how it happened—the manager don't like it. What do you want?"

Louise spoke quietly. "I want to know who did it to you. Did you press charges?"

Dorothy sighed deeply, her chest heaving with the effort. "I'm thinkin' about it."

"Did you know his name?"

"Sure—Sanders, Michael Sanders, from"—she said it with a nasty, sarcastic twist—"*São Paolo*, Brazil."

"You're sure that's his name?"

Dorothy took another serious drag on her cigarette and began to talk in a more normal tone. "No, I'm not sure. So just who are you?"

"Louise Eldridge." She stuck out her hand, and Dorothy shook it. "I live about two miles away, on Dogwood Court." The street name didn't register. "In Sylvan Valley."

Dorothy nodded knowingly and poked a thumb out as if hitchhiking. "Oh, yeah—west of here."

"I also help police with a little investigation now and then."

"Oh, *man*—so if I decide to press charges—"

"Let the police know—or call me. I'll be happy to go with you to the station."

Michael Sanders. Could there be two men from the same Brazilian city hanging around this neighborhood? Not likely.

"Dorothy, would you mind describing Michael Sanders?"

"Oh, no. He's a *babe*—nothing wrong with his looks. About six four, quite swarthy, or *bronzed*, you might say. Dark hair and eyes, and he dresses like a million dollars even if he *did* stay in a fleabag."

"A fleabag?"

Dorothy's laugh revealed a lifetime of smoking non-filtered cigarettes. "Is there any fleaier fleabag than Romance Village?"

"So he stayed there. Um, would you mind telling me if you ever went there with him?"

"But definitely—five nights in a row." She smiled. "It was nice—we were in this really pink room that's the honeymoon suite. Bathroom tub leaks a little, but otherwise, it's nice. And Michael was lovey-dovey, at first. Then he disappeared for five days before he showed up *again.*"

"So did you go back with him to Romance Village?"

"Yeah, even though he wasn't staying there any

longer. I think he moved to some fancier place. It was a mistake, I'll tell you that."

"Was that when—"

She nodded her head, and when she spoke her voice trembled. "Things got way out of control. We both drank a lot, and then it got rough." She looked at Louise out of ravaged, dark-circled eyes. Her expression was wary. "Now, I'm not sayin' I didn't give it to him, too. When he roughed me up too hard, I paid him back by scraping the hell out of his pretty little face. *That* made him explode, and he damned near *killed* me. . . ."

Louise was now certain that the bruises and cuts Dorothy received were courtesy of Ramon. She remembered distinctly when the man had come to Whiting Labs with deep scrapes on his face.

The woman was crying, and Louise had an impulse to take her in her arms. She had a feeling that no one had hugged Dorothy tenderly for a long time, so she did the best she could. She put an awkward arm around her shoulder and squeezed on the right side, hoping she didn't hit an injured spot.

"Dorothy, it's terrible what's happened to you, and you can't just make a joke out of it with your customer friends. I think I know who did it—and his name isn't Sanders. When did this happen?"

"Two weeks ago," she said. "And if you need someone else to back that up, just ask that puny little desk clerk at that motel. It's a wonder he didn't call the cops himself, except I think Sanders was paying him off. So—who is this guy, really?"

"His name's Ramon Jorges, Dr. Ramon Jorges. He's a prominent scientist."

Dorothy pulled in her breath in a little gasp, part of the ravages of the cut on her mouth. "He may be a prominent scientist, but he's also a bastard."

* * *

Mike Geraghty peered at her over half glasses as he opened a manila file folder. Sarcastically, he said, "You look awfully happy for someone who has stepped into doo-doo again."

She smiled. "I'm sustained by good food—the Dixie Pig's finest." She had come straight from the restaurant to the station when she picked up her phone messages and found a testy one from the detective. Now she sat in Geraghty's Naugahyde visitor's chair in the Fairfax police substation, her stomach full, her conscience relatively clear.

"Oh, yeah," he said, bobbing his white-haired head, "I like the Pig."

"While I was there, I learned enough to take the heat off me for whatever I've done wrong."

He frowned at her. "I hope so. You're gonna need some leverage. But how come you went back to Jefferson University? I told you not to go back there."

"I didn't go back to the *university.*"

"Dr. Conti's administrative assistant saw you and Sarah Shane in a Georgetown coffeehouse. She reported it right back to him."

"I know—Polly Whiting nearly fired me today over this. They're spying on Sarah. Pretty soon the woman will have a civil rights case against that man—abridgement of the right to free assembly or something."

"Now don't be too clever, Louise. You're in trouble on this. Were you pumping her for information?"

"Yes, but that's my right. This is a free country, and she was off work. But I'm sorry if I caused you trouble, especially since Sarah didn't tell me much that was useful."

"Are you sure?"

Louise pulled a pad from her purse. "I have my

notes right here. Want me to read them?" Before he could answer, she rattled off the information she'd learned. "There, does that tell you anything that helps you at all?"

Geraghty had made a few notes as she talked. "I see what you mean. Nothing much you didn't already know—for instance, about Peter Whiting's bad temper."

"I knew that already—he was a man with terrific mood swings."

"Louise, let's go back to Conti. This is not good when the biology dean at prestigious Jefferson University thinks I sent you out to do these things—even though, in a sense, I did."

"Thanks for adding that."

"I thought you were limiting your research to the Northminster Presbyterian Church."

"I had no idea a little coffee klatch would hurt—and it really rubbed me the wrong way to have them running me off campus."

The big detective leaned forward. "I had to do some real fast talkin' to get us off the hook. And I'm sorry, but I sort of made you out to be a loose cannon. . . ."

She threw her hands up in desperation. "Oh, swell."

"Which you *are*, Louise," said Geraghty, "and we both know it. At any rate, that's the end of your 'research,' as you call it." He put both hands up, with the flat palms facing her. "*No mas,* okay? Anyway, it's too dangerous, and there's nothing left for a civilian like you to inquire into."

"Oh?" she said. "But I bet you want to know what I just learned about Ramon Jorges."

He sighed, giving her a look she preferred not to interpret. "Whaddaya got?"

She related the story of Dorothy the waitress and her misadventures with Ramon.

"*Wait* a minute," said Geraghty. "It sounds as if he was around before Whiting was killed."

"He was. Not only that, he was staying right in the neighborhood, just a couple of miles away from Peter's house. I wouldn't be surprised if he hadn't been hanging around Peter's lab, or his house."

"Or the woods where you and Whiting walked your dogs," he said, sending her a serious look from over his glasses. "Well, he's in big trouble now. We're gonna trace every move he's made since he arrived in the States."

"Where does this leave your theories?"

"I still cling to the idea of the serial killer. We need some way to explain those several different encounters in the woods, that attack on you, even the details of Peter Whiting's death, with the eyes and tongue destroyed, and the body neatly, almost ceremoniously, laid on the path. It sure seems like the work of a sick psychopath—"

"*Ceremoniously laid out on the path?* I didn't know that about the position of the body. Exactly how was he laid out?"

"Like a corpse in a mortuary. Neatly, on his back, with his hands folded on his chest."

She gulped hard. "That's scary," she said softly.

The detective leaned back and folded his hands behind his neck. "This information on Jorges changes things, Louise. Maybe what we got here is this. One person killed Dr. Whiting—maybe somebody you know over at that lab—and maybe a different person altogether staged those other attacks. We'll be workin' on that angle. But right now, we'd better wrap this up; it's gettin' to be dinnertime." He sat forward and grinned. "And your mentioning that pork barbecue sandwich didn't help. So, suppose you tell me anything else you might have found out in the past few days."

She told him what she'd learned about the

Whitings, their family fights, additional confirmation of Polly's affair with the biology dean, and the strained atmosphere at the lab, with Polly angry at Louise, and with Conti and Jorges roaming in and out. She went into the greatest detail about Matthew's attack on his father.

"Five potential suspects, all hangin' around that lab," said Geraghty in disgust.

"Mike," she said tentatively, "I need to tell you something else. What if I told you that I thought the person who went after me in the woods Thanksgiving night knew me. . . ."

"Knew you?"

"Spoke my name."

Geraghty jolted suddenly forward. "What the *hell*," he said. "Why didn't you tell me this Thanksgiving night?" He glared at her from under his thick white eyebrows.

"Because I couldn't be certain. It was just like a voice on the wind, and I thought I might be hearing things. And I didn't want Bill to worry."

"Well, didja hear it, or didn't ya hear it? What did they say exactly?"

"I can't say for certain if I heard it, but maybe I did. The person just said, *'Louise'*—in a kind of murmuring voice."

"Dammit, Louise, that does it," he said, bringing a fist crashing down on the old desk. "I want you to quit investigatin'—and that's an order, not just a suggestion. I also advise you to quit that lab job—*immediately.*"

"Mike—"

"For Pete's sake," he said in exasperation, "can't you see that it's gotten too damned dangerous? I don't want anything to happen to you—Bill would kill me. You gotta go home and get your mind on something else. And I'm sure he'd agree if he knew all this."

She looked over at him. "He's been busy the past couple of nights. I'll tell him everything tonight."

"As for me, I'm getting on this Jorges angle right away." He flipped the manila file on his desk shut and tapped it with his forefinger. "I have a feelin' that this might be the break we need. So, thanks to you, Louise, for that"—and then his face darkened with worry—"but no thanks for holdin' out on that other information."

25

On Saturday morning, Bill went into his tiny workshop off the toolshed for one of his infrequent reunions with his household tools; he was going to erect a shelf in the back hall. Janie went off with friends from school, which left Louise on her own with no place to go and nothing much to do.

She wandered out to the front porch to get the *Washington Post.* Now that they were into December, the cornstalks, gourds, and Indian corn on her front porch looked forlorn; she would have to remove them. But at the moment her body felt heavy and listless, and all she wanted to do was to go back in the living room and curl up on the couch with the paper and a cup of coffee. The only sounds in the quiet house were the comforting muffled thumps of her amateur-carpenter husband in the workshop. Maybe she'd call her daughter Martha in Chicago to get a little sympathy, for a cloud of depression had been growing over her head since last night when she'd realized she had to give up the lab job.

It was silly, really, for it had been only a temporary job, just a fill-in until she went back to WTBA-TV to resume her more dynamic role as a garden show hostess.

Scut work, really, caring for those plants and mice at Whiting Labs. But she had loved it. The very thought of Perky almost brought tears to her eyes.

She set aside the newspaper, and picked up the phone and tapped the speed-dial button for Martha's college apartment. Idly, she realized she should also program in Jim Daley's place on the phone, since Martha seemed to spend quite a bit of time there. The girl had given her Jim's number just in case she wasn't in her Evanston digs. This time, she was.

"Ma, you sound terrible. What's happened?"

Louise liked it that her older daughter was like a friend, and that she could actually listen to her troubles. It was even better than talking to her buddies, Nora, Mary, or Sandy. She filled Martha in on what had happened in the past three days, trying to remember the details of the fiascos at the university and the lab. Louise left out the particulars of the heated discussion that she and Bill had had last night.

This humiliating lecture had occurred after a relaxing and delightful interlude of lovemaking. When Louise revealed to her husband that she had withheld the fact that her attacker in the woods may have known her, he was furious— parading back and forth au naturel, giving her the scolding of her life. "... *lack of confidence in your spouse ... could have been slaughtered in your own backyard ... too damned independent to survive till old age ...*" Since this was her third lecture of the day, she had just sat back in bed, phased out, and admired her spouse's perfect butt.

All she said to her daughter about this was, "Your dad was upset. And now, to his great satisfaction, I'm a stay-at-home mom."

"Well, well," said her older daughter, "I just left town three days ago. You've been busy—no wonder Dad's nervous. I'm beginning to understand what Janie was talking about when she said it was a heavy responsibility just being your daughter. . . ."

"Janie said that?"

"Yes, she did. So—you've been *fired*, fired by everybody, huh? The cops *and* Polly Whiting."

"Polly didn't actually fire me, just disapproved of me in a very public way."

"So you quit because they think someone at the lab may have committed the murder. What do you think?"

"I'm coming around to that opinion."

"Ma, Jim and I think so, too. He thinks you should assume a very low profile."

"A very low profile? Why? Jim hardly knows me."

"I've told him what you've been up to. And he says you're what the police might call a target—like a sparkler on a dark Fourth of July night. You've managed to call attention to yourself—through no fault of your own, more or less—but if it *isn't* a stranger doing these crimes in the woods, then it's someone who sees you out front, snoopin' around and threatening them."

"So that's what Jim says," she repeated in a subdued voice.

"Yeah. And until the police get a handle on this thing, he thinks you ought to be super-careful. Hang with other people at night. I know Dad gets home late sometimes and Janie runs off with her school friends. Go schmooze with your neighbors, then. Maybe you should carry Dad's gun. And never walk in the woods again. And stay out of the way of that Ramon guy—"

Something was wrong here. "Martha, I didn't even mention Ramon Jorges."

"As a matter of fact, Ma, I talked to Dad last night. He shared some of this with me."

"Oh, he did, did he?"

"Ma, it's just that he's worried about you. Now, all we have to do is get you worried about *yourself*." The girl laughed, a lilting sound. "You know, there's a joke being circulated on the Internet that reminds me of you—"

"I hate those jokes. . . ."

"It's about the private eye who didn't know the meaning of the word fear, who could laugh in the face of danger, and spit in the eye of death—in short, a moron with suicidal tendencies." She chortled. "Isn't that *hilarious?*"

"So you don't want me to be a moron with suicidal tendencies, is that what you're saying?"

"Ma, we love you, and we want you to survive." It took a while before Louise got over her irritation with her daughter and her husband for talking about her behind her back, but finally she told Martha she appreciated the advice. What else could she do, for hadn't she initiated the call? She said good-bye, and got down to reading the paper.

After scanning the headlines, she turned to the local news. There was an update on the story of Professor Whiting's death with the headline POLICE PURSUE FOREIGN LEAD IN PROFESSOR'S DEATH. Few details were given; Louise realized the police had dished out this information because of what they'd learned from her about Ramon Jorges. She leaned back in the couch pillows and smiled. It made her feel worthwhile to have had one investigative coup, even though she'd now been laid off.

"Oh, no," she murmured as her eyes went to the byline on the story. It was Charlie Hurd's. He'd succeeded in wresting the story away from the reporter who'd covered it from the outset. She could just see him elbowing his colleague off the assignment with the argument that northern Virginia crime was *his* beat. He'd read the back stories by now and found that the murder took place a block from her house; she was sure she would hear from him soon.

Louise sat there with the newspaper, staring into space. She had completely forgotten Sarah Shane, the innocent victim of her mishandled detecting efforts. She scouted up the young woman's phone number in her notes, settled back on the couch, and dialed the number.

She was not surprised when Sarah disclosed to her that she had been fired. "I was afraid Conti would do this," said Louise. "It seems so unjust."

Then she heard the call-waiting signal. "Hold on, will you, Sarah?" Pressing the "flash" button, she found Charlie Hurd on the line.

In a sarcastic voice he said, "Louise, my little top suspect, how's it goin'?"

"Just give me your number, Charlie, and I'll get back to you." She unloosed the pen attached to the pocket of her denim shirt and jotted the number on the edge of the first page of the sports section.

Then she returned to her conversation with Sarah. The young woman said she wasn't sure she could afford to contest it. "Dr. Conti is totally down on me, and with an enemy like him, how could I win an appeal?"

Louise didn't want to give the discouraged young woman too much hope, but then she thought of the suspicious way that the biology dean was conducting himself. "I would definitely do so, even if you don't decide to return there; you need to clear your name."

She suddenly recalled the flurry at her television station just before she left for her three-month vacation. A veteran employee in the marketing office had announced her retirement at the PBS station.

"Sarah, a marketing manager is leaving the TV station where I work. It's the kind of job that you might like. At least it might be a stepping-stone to something bigger. Why don't I talk to some people there?"

"Public television? Marketing?" The tiniest trace of boredom in her voice. There was a long pause. Was public TV too stodgy for this stylish young woman? Was she thinking she would have to help run WTBA-TV's sometimes interminably long fund drives? Louise's more glamorous job as an on-air personality might appeal, but maybe not this one. Finally, Sarah said, "I *might* like that, Louise—and it's awfully nice of you to mention it, but just remember. You aren't responsible for getting me a new job. I'm the one who talked to you of my own free will—you didn't twist my arm."

She had said good-bye to Sarah and was rummaging for Charlie's number among the newspapers when she heard the front doorbell ring. In the floor-to-ceiling window alongside the door she could see the small, impatient figure of Charlie Hurd, rocking back and forth on his heels. His old-time newspaper fedora was shoved back on his pale blond hair, his hands plunged into the pockets of his roomy trench coat.

Opening the door, she said, "Don't tell me. You called me from your car."

"Doesn't everyone?" he said happily. It was as if Louise were his mother, and he the impertinent, all-powerful child. He swept by her into the living room and then zeroed in on the kitchen. "Ah, yes," he said, sniffing victoriously, "I can smell it. I knew you were the kind who'd have some black poison brewed at ten on a Saturday morning. Can I have some?"

"Sure, Charlie," she said, and she fixed him a cup of coffee and refilled hers.

They settled in the living room. "Now, how about givin' me the skinny on the good professor's murder?" Charlie said. "You swear you didn't do it? I hear you were friends."

"I swear it wasn't I." She carefully told him of her brief friendship with the professor, and of her connection with Whiting Labs. As she talked, she saw Bill walk past the patio windows, hammer in hand, the little white Westie hopping along at his heels, delighted to be outside helping the master of the family. Her husband noted the presence of Charlie Hurd with a mock raising of his eyebrows, and was about to return to his workshop when Charlie turned in his chair and saw him.

Caught, Bill slid open the tall glass door and leaned in. Fella took this opportunity to dodge in the house, tear once around its entire perimeter, then return and leap to Louise's lap. She gently set the trembling little beast on the floor, where he gave one look at Charlie and one protesting bark.

"Hi, folks," said her husband. "I'm a little sawdusty, so I don't think I'll come in—but you get the dog back, I guess."

Charlie got up and hurried to the door, his hand out. "I'm Charles Hurd. Pleased to meet you, Bill."

Bill shook hands and nodded. "Yes, I've heard a lot about you, Charlie. You're quite the reporter."

"And I've heard about *you*," he said. "Well, not a lot. Louise doesn't share as much as I share with her. You and I ought to talk sometime—I bet you have a lot of interesting angles on world affairs and things."

Her husband had an amused expression on his

face. "Well, thanks, Charlie. Maybe we can share some ideas on American foreign policy one of these days—just not today." He slid the door closed and disappeared around the house.

Charlie cocked his head in the direction Bill had departed. "Bet there's a guy with a lot of secrets," he said. "So, tell me what you know, Louise."

While drawing a vivid picture for the reporter of the work done in the biotech lab, Louise left out all the suspicious details she had learned about the various people surrounding the case.

Charlie sat almost somnambulistic, listening, and slumped forward in the antique straight chair opposite the couch, hands cupped around his coffee, sharp eyes taking in every detail of the room. So when the reporter suddenly lurched back and tilted the piece onto its hind legs, Louise wailed. "Oh, *no!*" Fella jumped to his feet and ran over to attack this person who had offended his mistress.

"Hold it there, little dog," commanded Charlie, putting out a hand to ward off the growling puppy. Louise came and picked up the dog.

It took a moment for Charlie to understand why Louise was upset. He chuckled, as he set the legs down again. "Someone would do that chair a *favor* busting it," he said. He got up and started pacing the room. "I've listened, Louise, and I know damn well you're holdin' out on me. And so is Geraghty. *I* think this all-points three-state bulletin is a bunch of crap, frankly." As he made the turn and approached her again as she sat on the couch, he said, "You've got to follow the money!"

"That's partially how they unraveled Watergate," she said dryly.

"That's how they unravel most crimes," said Charlie sarcastically. "There's millions at stake here. So why are police looking for some crazy fool when *I* hear that not-so-crazy people would be set for life if they took over Whiting's plant project? Look at them all: the dishy wife, the disinherited son, the postdoctorate wanna-be—plus, I hear there's some guy at Jefferson University who may be involved, and I'm busy on that angle. In fact, I'm workin' on a gal from the public relations office, but she's pretty close-mouthed. *Plus,* Geraghty talks about a 'South American' connection, but he won't give me any goddamn *details!"*

Louise bit her tongue. She didn't want to get in more trouble with her detective friend by releasing information to a reporter.

Charlie made another circuit of the room. When he returned, he leaned down and tapped her on the shoulder as the Westie, now sitting guard duty on Louise, growled again.

"Look, Louise," he said in a dramatic voice, "there's gotta be secret players—you know who? *Drug* companies, that's who. They'd probably sell their mothers to buy up that little biotech company." In her mind's eye she could picture all those letters from pharmaceutical firms spread on the floor of James Conti's office. How easy it would be for Conti to be in league with one of them.

She sighed. "Not bad reasoning, Charlie. Why don't you pursue all that?"

"I *am,* I am. Now, I bet you know plenty from working in that lab. . . ."

"Very little, in fact. It was just a temporary job. As a matter of fact, I'm quitting. I have too many other irons in the fire. Research for the January *Gardening with Nature* programs. And Bill and I might take off for the islands for a week—"

He looked at her skeptically. "Oh, yeah, sure. Hey, I know there's more here than meets the eye." He wiggled his forefinger at her. "And by God, you know I'm going to sniff it out, whether you cooperate or not."

She grinned. "More coffee, Charlie?"

When he left, she carried Fella and walked with the reporter under the vine-covered pergola, down the flagstone path, and out to the street. She noted that things must be going well for the *Post* reporter, for he had upgraded his high-end Saturn sports car to a low-end Porsche. "What do people think when you arrive at the scene of a story in a car like that?" she asked.

He gave her a self-satisfied smile. "They guess the truth—that my folks have bucks. And actually, I leave it home when I need a low profile."

"Well, good luck, Charlie."

He inspected her from head to toe, and suddenly she could see herself through his eyes. A woman with disheveled brown hair in need of a cut, wearing an old denim shirt, worn sneakers, and Japanese gardening pants, carrying a scruffy little dog.

"And *you* be careful, Louise. Sounds to me, from what you and Geraghty *didn't* say, that you're livin' right in the middle of a den of vipers." He pointed to Fella. "And that little ball of used white yarn isn't going to help you much."

She smiled and scratched Fella's head, for she knew Charlie was wrong about that.

26

Louise sat at the dining room table Monday morning and drank her third cup of coffee while perusing the local-news section of the *Post*. She was delaying going to work, for she knew how traumatic it was going to be. Since she'd failed to reach Polly Whiting over the weekend, she would have the unpleasant task of telling her face-to-face this morning that she was quitting without notice.

It wasn't hard to find a news story to distract her—a story she'd heard about weeks ago. It had a four-column headline: THREE DIE IN JEFFERSON U GENE THERAPY EXPERIMENTS. Two of the three patients had expired more than three weeks ago, on November 8, and the *Post* tsk-tsked in great detail over the fact that the university had kept the lid on the bad news.

Her eyes quickly scanned the story, and there, in the fifth paragraph, were the names of the gene implantation team, or "GIT." Unfortunate acronym, she noted: GIT's got real trouble. Dr. James Conti was one of four prestigious scientists on the team, all of them busily quoted as saying that their protocols did involve substantial risks of which the patients and the families were quite aware, but that these were "terminal" patients in the first place. Unsaid was: *Why not subject the patients to our experimentation? They were going to die anyway, and this just might have saved them.* Someday soon, she wondered, would people begin to picket against human gene replacement experiments, just as they did animal experiments?

How hard this must have been for a proud man like James Conti, thought Louise. How could a man in his position, who occupied the top science chair at Jefferson University, ever retrieve his glossy reputation? She refolded the paper, and realized it was time to go to the lab.

Louise strode into Whiting Labs, and couldn't help feeling the usual excitement, even though this was her last day. The Margaret Mee pictures still vibrated with color. The growing room beckoned her with its enticing brightness. She could almost hear the baby plants growing in their magic gel. And just down the corridor in the mouse room, she knew, Perky and the other experimental mice were frolicking in their cages. She closed her eyes for a moment, as if to blank out the realization of all she was giving up.

First, she went into the CEO's office, hoping to find Polly. The office was empty, except for Herb, the dog, curled in a corner. The ancient terrier wagged his tail a couple of times, and promptly went back to sleep. She went into her normal routine, and donned a lab coat before using her key to gain entry through the double doors to the lab area.

She wandered through the growing room, and still did not find Polly, until she reached the mouse room. Polly and Joe Bateman were hovering over a cage.

"Look," said Polly delightedly, "Perky is showing off on the wheel." The mouse, which was now over a year old, was clambering expertly on the wheel, like a juvenile letting off steam. "It's a real sign that he's maintaining his youth."

Louise's lips trembled and she fought back tears, for she realized she was not destined to see what happened to this winsome animal. Why, he might achieve public stardom if the *Tabebuia* tea proved as magical as it sounded. She could see the headline: RESEARCH MOUSE LIVES TO THE EQUIVALENT OF 120 YEARS OLD. And to think she knew Perky when.

Joe looked at Louise. "Are you all right?"

"Oh, just something in my eye, I guess," she said, rubbing the tears away with her sleeve. "Actually, I need to talk to you both."

"Well?" said Polly archly. Louise knew the woman had forgiven but not forgotten her spying. Polly would never totally trust her again.

She told them that her husband had insisted she resign her job. "It's just not working out at home."

Polly had a strange reaction. Her blue, expressive eyes showed relief. Quite obviously, the woman was thinking, *At last this troublesome woman is getting out of my life.* But she put on quite a show, clutching Louise's arm and saying, "I'm so *sorry* to see you go—and I'm sorry I was rude to you on Friday— you have to believe me when I say I never talk that way. Could that be why—"

Louise shook her head. "No, no, that had nothing to do with my decision. It probably was not a good idea for me to even start this job, because I already have one." The lies just started rolling out of her mouth. "And Marty, my producer, has just come up with a great big three-part show that requires travel, and a lot of research. . . ."

Joe looked at Polly and slowly shook his head, as if to say, *Get a grip—and don't make too much of this.*

"You're right to do this, Louise," he said. "Even the timing is right, since we need to hire several more permanent employees at this point. Don't feel bad. I told you we appreciate your work. You caught on so fast that it hasn't been a loss training you, and it probably did you some good, right?"

"Oh, yes, I love working here. In fact—"

No, she couldn't overrule Bill; she *had* to resign. "Could I just work today, as a kind of a farewell present to myself?"

Polly hugged Louise and said, "Of course you can." It was as if the widow's harsh words of a few days ago were never spoken. The threats to "fire" her ass and the dismay at letting the "fox in the henhouse" were forgotten—just as long as Louise would be safely gone by the end of the day.

But just why did Polly need her gone from this lab?

Today, Louise worked on the removal of contaminated plants. It was the least interesting of the lab jobs, since plants didn't respond, at least as far as the human eye could see. In contrast, those few times she was permitted to clean the mice cages, there was the opportunity to see close-up the effects of the tea that the animals were fed. Obviously, Polly and Joe had been excited this morning to see one of the oldest mice displaying such youthful energy. Within another six months, she'd heard, they would have measurable animal test results. And when that happened, the whole story—the primitive Brazilian tribes, including the one equally dominated by the "Amazon women," the long-lived mice, and the promise for longer-lived humans—would spread across the media of the entire world.

It wasn't until she was well into her work that she remembered to ask Joe where Matthew was.

"He's auditioning for a big part in a play. If he gets the part, I'm sure, he, like you, will leave Whiting Labs." Joe's face was expressionless; apparently the departure of his "temporary" employees was not going to be an emotional jolt for Joe Bateman.

"It's just as well, isn't it?" she said. "As you said, you need permanent help—young scientist types like yourself back when you were starting out."

Joe stood still and looked at her, and she knew she'd hit a nerve. Here was a man with a Ph.D. in science who for almost a decade had patiently worked for another professor without striking out for himself. What had he really gained in those years, and what lay ahead for him here at Whiting Labs?

Red-faced with embarrassment, she turned back to her work, carefully scrutinizing each test tube, and putting the discarded ones into the tub on her rolling cart.

Working by herself, in silence, gave Louise plenty of time to think; it was one of the great attractions of lab work. Burnt out on the topic of Polly and Conti and Jorges, she focused her thoughts instead on Geraghty's more detailed description of Peter Whiting's murder . . . *the eyes and tongue destroyed, and the body neatly, almost ceremoniously, laid on the path* . . .

Without wanting to, she found her thoughts turning to her absent lab partner, Matthew Whiting—Matthew, who had been disinherited both of his father's love, and his father's estate. The actor.

Details of the killing had to have relevance. Who would be so uncivilized as to slash the victim's tongue and gouge out his eyes? It had to be someone who had been personally humiliated by the scientist—someone like Matthew.

And then there was the dog issue. The professor's old dog, Herb, continued to bare his teeth like a young mastiff whenever Matthew approached. Louise was becoming more of an authority on dog behavior since she and Bill had temporarily adopted Fella. She found her little dog had superb judgment about people—ignoring or growling at those whom Louise didn't much like, and making up to those she did. Matt had freaked out that dog years ago when it was a puppy.

Had he done it again recently, as his elderly father and elderly dog walked alone together in Ravine Park?

She left the growing room and took her test tubes to the sink, scooping out the mildewy contents of each receptacle. She felt like crying, for she was almost certain now that the son had killed the father. It was heartbreaking, since she liked him. The wily Matthew had wormed his way into her heart.

Placing the last of the well-washed test tubes into the autoclave and tucking in some tools as well, she turned it on. Glumly, she decided there was no sense sharing her ideas with Detective Geraghty. If there was no evidence to connect anyone with the crime, it probably would go unsolved. What was the good of sitting around discussing more theories? They were as useless as all those gossipy tidbits she had dredged up during the past three weeks.

* * *

Ramon Jorges and Dr. James Conti, who'd apparently entered the lobby together, shoved their way through the conference room doorway, jostling each other like a pair of unruly boys.

"Well, hello!" cried Polly, her face lighting up at the sight of the new arrivals. The widow had gone out for sandwiches earlier, and she, Joe, Polly, and Gina were at the conference table eating them, as Polly told them a story about a dangerous journey up the Negro River during flood season.

By their behavior, Louise knew the two men had arrived separately. They were sartorially splendid, Conti in his Italian suit and tie, and Jorges in more relaxed sports clothes that Louise speculated came from some exclusive shop in Rio.

"Do come and sit with us, you two!" the widow exclaimed. She treated their arrival as if this were just part of the gracious social whirl that surrounded the hardworking lab. Nothing could be further from the truth. Both Joe and Polly discouraged visitors—only wanting them on their own terms when the research mice were ready to do their tricks for the public. They rightly feared that, as the lab's work became known, animal-rights protestors and bioterrorists might picket the place.

In Louise's view, the two scientists were nuisances, rather like the suitors who pursued Penelope while Odysseus was gone on his journeys. Except *this* Penelope seemed very much to enjoy men's attention; it obviously gave her a sense of power.

"O-h-h-h," groaned Ramon, "you've eaten—too bad. . . ."

Conti looked at his watch. "And Polly, *I* thought you knew I was coming by. . . ."

Each man had had Polly in mind as a lunch date; they looked with distaste at the table full of people and lunch detritus.

Conti had lost none of his poise, despite the horrific story in the *Washington Post*; the man must have skin an inch thick, thought Louise. He stared coolly at the assembled staff. As he picked her out of the group, an offended look overcame his handsome face. He said, "Why is *Louise* still here? I thought you said you were going to fire her."

Louise was mortified, but Polly had the good grace to come to her rescue. "James, we questioned Louise, and she wasn't doing anything *hurtful* at Jefferson University—just a little biographical fact-checking, she calls it." She glanced at Louise, who sat there trying to look as innocent as possible. Louise nodded gently, as if Polly had put the thing exactly right. Conti coughed, as if about to choke on the widow's words.

Louise chimed in. "Don't worry about me, Dr. Conti—I'm thinking of quitting the lab anyway. Maybe that would satisfy you." She'd had a sudden whim to make her statement conditional on purpose—*I'm thinking of quitting*, not *I've just quit*—to see what the reaction would be. She was here with most of the players for probably the last time. Polly, Joe, James Conti, and Ramon Jorges, all the people intimately connected with Peter Whiting, and all strangely on edge, with Matthew the only one missing.

"She's conning you, Polly," James Conti burst out. "She's probably spying on everyone here!"

There was silence in the room. Louise's face turned red with embarrassment as she realized not one person here wanted her to continue at the lab. Polly Whiting looked shocked at her statement. The usually impassive Joe Bateman gazed at Louise in disappointed surprise. She'd already *resigned*, hadn't she, this morning? Was she reneging?

James Conti shot her a sullen look and said, "Indeed, I hope you quit. It's time you quit."

Ramon Jorges, leaning against the conference room door as if he owned the place, had observed the exchanges without comment. His frozen-smiled gaze settled on Louise, and she found it frightening as she recalled the sight of Dorothy the waitress's ruined face. It was not a very far reach from knocking women around to killing someone who stood in one's way.

He strolled closer to the table. Leaning down, he shoved aside a container containing residual coleslaw and braced a hand on the table edge. "You have no professional credentials, Mrs. Eldridge," he said, in an ominous, purring voice, "any more than Matthew Whiting does, so the two of you don't really belong in an environment like this one."

The man was deliberately trying to humiliate her, in order to speed her departure. To her mind sprang a defiant little speech. But again, she had no need to defend herself, for someone came to her rescue. Joe Bateman, in his usual dispassionate way, said, "I think you're dead wrong about Louise. Lots of plant handlers have little or no experience. There's nothing in any regulation that says she can't do this work—and she's performed very well. As for her personal background, that checked out just fine. We're grateful to have had her working here."

The Brazilian scientist looked powerless and angry; Louise wondered if Joe Bateman would suffer for this, for Jorges would happily take his place in the lab.

Conti also seemed displeased that Joe was trying to make her look good. After those damning news reports on the gene therapy patients' deaths, he must be desperate to reinvent himself; that apparently meant moving in on Polly Whiting's lab, where he'd prefer not to have impertinent meddlers like herself.

A fact in the *Post* story suddenly took on more significance. Since two of the three patients' deaths had occurred more than three weeks ago, James Conti had known for weeks—even before Peter Whiting's murder—that his whole bright future as a scientist was in a shambles. He must have been hugely resentful of the old professor. Whiting was winning a pot of gold while Conti was losing his shirt.

Slanting a careful look at the biology dean and the Brazilian scientist, Louise realized that either could have murdered Peter Whiting. To put it mildly, Conti's career was in the ash can. But Jorges, whom Geraghty seemed to favor as a suspect, had lied to police about the date of his entry to the U.S. Both men must have figured that with Peter dead, Polly would soon become overwhelmed with the job. Then, she would turn to a man with scientific know-how for support. Both men qualified in this respect.

And Louise was ignoring another possibility: a conspiracy between the beautiful Polly and James Conti to get rid of the ailing old husband. After all, they had been lovers only a short time ago. That would make sex, not money, the motive. . . .

As she mulled over these things, she realized what tricks the mind could play. Until a few minutes ago, she had been convinced that Matthew Whiting had killed his father. Now she realized that everybody present—even Joe—had plenty of reasons to kill. Profit, sex, revenge, she could take her pick. Hovering over them all, like an eight-hundred-pound gorilla, were the nameless pharmaceutical companies.

It was almost as if Whiting Phytoseutical Laboratories, with its "paltry" multi-million-dollar budget, was a little practice game that would soon be interrupted by the professionals announcing that the real game was about to start.

"Oh, do let's break this up," said Polly breathlessly, feeling the strain of dealing with Conti and Jorges at one time. Louise gave a self-conscious start, for her mind had been on her latest dark scenario.

"James and Ramon," she said, "why don't you both come into my office, and we'll have a chat. I'll give you a progress report on how things are going here at Whiting Labs."

Louise gathered up the leftovers of her lunch, and helped Gina clear the conference table. "Wow," said Gina, looking at Louise with new interest, "those guys don't like you very well." She giggled. "What have you done to them?"

"I wish I knew, Gina. I honestly wish I knew. It's as if my very existence bugs them. But it doesn't matter anymore, because I'm leaving."

"I for one will miss you," said the lab technician. Louise thanked her, and didn't express how very anxious she was to get out of this tense environment.

During the ensuing few hours, Louise immersed herself in her work without thinking of anything beyond the individual plant with which she was working. Charlie Hurd had said it, and it was true. She worked in a den of vipers. The place was ruined for her because, as clean and antiseptic as it was, as pure as its air was, its floors and its scrubbed vents, the place dripped with suspicion and distrust. Few if any in the lab trusted her, and she no longer trusted them. She would be most happy to leave—if it weren't for the fact that she loved the work so much.

It was almost four when she gathered her things and said a last good-bye to Perky and the other mice, gave a last long look at the test tube plants and the Margaret Mee paintings, and said her final good-byes to Joe, Gina, and Polly. Tears were close behind her eyes, but she didn't cry.

As if as reluctant to depart as Louise was, the Honda didn't want to start. But with continual tries, it finally coughed into life, and she drove the short distance home.

27

There were silver and mauve layers on the edge of the gray night sky as Louise and Fella left the house to walk around the well-lit perimeter of Dogwood Court. Now that it was December, the quixotic Washington weather had turned mild, and the harsh winds of November were only a chilly memory. Louise wore only a light jacket.

The usual dog rest room in the far reaches of the yard had been declared off-limits by Bill until life returned to normal in Sylvan Valley, so with her plastic sack at the ready, Louise hovered as the tiny pup made his innocent mark on the neighbors' bushes. Then, car lights glared at her.

Mary Mougey was on her way to the grocery store and just pulling out of her driveway. She and Louise stopped and chatted a minute, Louise trying to pull her thoughts away from the people at the lab. She realized that the lab was obsessing her.

Mary sat there in golden-haired, designer-suited glory, but looked tired around her blue eyes. She complained about the arduousness of the daily commute to and from work in DuPont Circle, but

Louise told her she envied her every mile of these hectic journeys. "I'm already dreading being a stay-at-home person," she said. "What will I do here?"

Mary reached a hand out and clutched Louise's. "Yet I'm so glad you're not going to work in that lab anymore. Too dicey now, isn't it, especially after that story I read about 'new evidence,' and 'international ramifications.' "

"It was the job, Mary. I loved the job."

Mary squeezed her hand, and in a typical rush of empathy said, "Dear, I know how to fix things. I'll look at my calendar and call you. We'll do lunch downtown—*that* will surely cheer you up!"

Back in her own house again, Louise knew she should have her mind on dinner. Instead, without even bothering to remove her jacket, she slumped into the overstuffed chair in the living room and re-entered the labyrinth of her own thoughts. With her eyes closed, she could see all the people at the lab again in her mind's eye. Each was an enigma in some way, and there was not a soul there she could trust—except Gina.

Her thoughts began to settle, like sediment in a jar, until she felt the answer close at hand. The cruel desecration of Peter Whiting's face, the orderly placement of his body . . .

The phone rang, and her train of thought disappeared like smoke. She hurried to the kitchen to answer. It was Matthew Whiting, talking in an unnaturally quiet, almost sneaky, voice. "Louise— thank God you're home. I need you to get over here. . . ."

"Get over where, Matthew? You're not at work, are you?"

"Oh, yes, I am. I decided to come back this evening and get in an hour or so of work, and I've overheard a conversation somebody sure didn't want me to hear. Louise, I think I know who killed my *father!*"

Was this the truth, or a trap? If he was sincere, he would tell her whom he suspected.

"Who're you talking about?"

"Can't tell you now," he demurred.

She pulled in a sharp breath. He was lying.

"What do you mean, you can't tell me—" She was giving him every chance. . . .

"Listen to me, Louise," he said in his most cajoling tone, "just get over here. I'll leave the back door open."

How could she say no to him without arousing his suspicions? "Matthew, I don't know. . . ."

"Look," he said harshly, "just come!" There was a click and the line was dead.

The only thing to do was to call Geraghty. She hit the speed-dial button for the Fairfax substation, and found he wasn't in. She told the clerk where she was going and what time she was leaving, and suggested the message go to both Detectives Geraghty and Morton, whichever man showed up first. Then she slammed the phone back on its receiver. Stopping first to tuck her pepper spray in her jeans pocket, she raced to the car.

She had no desire to plunge herself into danger, but it was unthinkable to stay home and do nothing. This might be the only chance to find the person who had maimed and destroyed her elderly friend. Otherwise, he might go free. And then for how long would people in Sylvan Valley continue to be afraid that a killer was hovering about? If she missed this chance, she knew she'd regret it the rest of her life.

She would just have to trust that Mike Geraghty got her plea for help in time.

Sliding into the car seat, she turned the ignition

key and was greeted with a low growl. "Damn," she said, and got out and slammed the door. She was disgusted with herself for neglecting the faithful old vehicle, for she had known it needed a trip to the garage. She ran out to the street and saw that her neighbors' houses were dark, though they would be cruising into the cul de sac any minute. The lab was a scant mile from here. Calling a cab was an option, but she could be there by the time the cab arrived. Hesitating no longer, she began to sprint down the street.

As she settled down into a steady running pace, she felt the terrible disillusionment again of knowing someone who had killed. The fact that it was her lab partner, Matthew, made it somehow more personal, and therefore, worse. He must have sensed Louise was getting too close. And now he thought he could lure her into some trap—he probably had a very careful plan worked out to silence her.

But she didn't intend to face him alone. If Geraghty didn't respond to her call, she wouldn't go in unless Joe Bateman was still at the lab. Joe could help her.

After three blocks, she settled down to a speed walk: no need to expend all her strength. She might need it later.

28

She slowed as she approached the stockade fence that encircled Whiting Phytoseutical Laboratories, and wondered now if she should have come anywhere near this place without the police. If anything looked out of the ordinary, she was going to turn tail and go back home and wait for Geraghty.

Two older vehicles were parked haphazardly a half block from the lab—probably owned by employees of the nearby fast food restaurants. She peered in each one of them. The first had an incredible array of junk including a pile of blankets, as if the person slept there; the second, a stash of empty pop cans, plastic food containers, and bits of paper trash. She moved on, satisfied.

Now she was at the gate. She took a deep breath, and entered. What she saw inside the fence caused a warm wave of relief to flood over her.

In the parking area were Joe Bateman's Chevy Blazer, and two BMWs, Polly Whiting's and James Conti's. Of course, she thought, peering at her watch. It was only five-thirty, still part of the normal workday at Whiting Phytoseutical Labs.

As she made her way carefully around to the back door, she wondered who she'd find inside and where Matthew would be lurking. *His* car was nowhere in sight. Once at the back door, she hesitated. Was she in over her head, suffering again from hubris, that conviction that she could handle things all by herself?

She grabbed the handle of the outer door. It opened noiselessly; she stepped into the back vestibule. Now, she needed to be sure she could make a fast escape. On a utility shelf lay several small boxes; she grabbed one and carefully dumped its contents, some kind of cabinet handles, onto the shelf. She tiptoed to the back entrance to the growing room and quietly inserted the key and opened the door, blinking into the room's bright fluorescent lights. Quickly, she jammed the door open with the box. So far, so good; now she stared into the room, letting her eyes adjust to the light, wondering who and what she might find.

She sighed, releasing the breath she'd been holding, and walked fifteen feet down the aisle before she saw Joe Bateman appear out of nowhere at the other end of the room. He was wearing his usual white lab coat, looking utterly calm and normal.

"Hi, Louise," he called. "What's happening?" Although he should be surprised to see her, he wasn't, and she felt a twinge of uneasiness.

"Hi, Joe. Have you seen Matthew?" She backed up a few steps.

Joe turned and looked down, and it was then that Louise noted a bulge in the back of his lab coat; Joe never shoved things in his pockets like that. "Sure. He's right here."

She moved closer to get a better view. The unconscious body of Matthew Whiting lay at Joe's feet. Blood trickled down Matthew's white face, and he looked quite dead. She put a hand to her mouth and stifled a scream, then pressed a hand against her breast to try and stop the pounding of her heart.

"Oh, my God, what *happened*? Did he try to attack you, or something?"

Then the truth flooded over her as she saw the strange, excited expression on Joe Bateman's face.

"You did this to Matthew."

He chuckled mirthlessly. "Had you for a minute, didn't I, Louise? Yeah, I'm afraid so—I did it."

Her whole body was trembling, and she wondered if her legs would buckle beneath her. She managed one more weak-voiced question. "And what about Polly, and James Conti? They're not here, then, are they?"

"Oh, no," he assured her in a cheery voice. "They left a while ago, with their buddy Ramon. It's just you and me and Matthew, Louise."

It was small comfort to know that she had been right when she suspected the "son" of killing the father, for she'd been focusing on the wrong "son." The vindictive destruction of Peter Whiting's face and eyes pointed to Matthew. But the neat placement of the corpse's body and hands reflected a compulsively organized person—like Joe Bateman.

But it had taken her too long to register that he was the murderer, and it soon would be too late to get out of here. Breathing in little gasps now, she turned and ran for the door, which was jammed open just so she could escape quickly.

Soon she heard a terrible noise behind her.

It was just the noise of rubber-soled feet padding on a floor, but it threw panic into Louise's heart. It was the sound of Joe's feet sprinting down the narrow aisle, covering the twenty feet between them in seconds. But she'd gained distance by running, if only it were enough—

She felt, in fact she knew now, that she'd make it. She took a step through the door, then headed for the back entrance—

The hand gripped her sleeve and he was on her like a large beast.

"Oh, *please!*" she cried, but he grabbed her arms and pinned them back painfully, as he might pin back the wings of a chicken.

"*Ow!*" she screamed. He dragged her back into the growing room, kicking the box aside, so that the back door swung shut with a click.

"Well," he said, gasping for breath himself, "good thing I'm a runner, isn't it? You're quite fleet of foot, Louise." He shoved her in front of him down the aisle of test tube plants. "Careful," he warned, "don't bump the sides. I have some rope—I was going to use it on Matthew, but I'll cut a hunk off for you, too."

They'd reached the other end of the growing room, where the inert body of Matthew Whiting lay. Joe put up a warning finger. "Now, Louise, you just stand there nice for a minute. I won't be so kind to you if you make another break for it." On a workbench just beyond the rows of *Tabebuia* plants lay a coil of rope and a long thin knife. He cut off a section and came over to her.

"Cross your hands in front of you," he ordered.

With sinking heart, she did so, but as he approached with the rope, she suddenly thought of a plan. As Joe entwined the rope around them, she tensed her hands and bent her wrists subtly, as much as possible without him detecting it, in order to leave some slack. Surely, he would notice and be furious—but he didn't. He looked at her when he was done and said, "Now we'll just rope you here to the bench for a minute while I remove some blood spots from the floor." Cutting off another hunk of rope, he tethered her to the leg of the workbench, chuckling. "Not very ennobling, is it, Louise, to be tied up like an animal?"

"What you've done isn't ennobling either, Joe," she retorted. "It's hateful." But trading insults wasn't going to free her from this killer. She was worried, for her body was rebelling from the ten minutes of sheer terror she'd just suffered. She could feel the familiar dull pain of heart palpitations starting in her chest, and knew she had to stop them if she were to have any hope of escape. At this moment, if Joe had chanced to look at her, he would have seen her chest heaving from the impact of her thumping heart.

She propped herself against the workbench and concentrated on her classical remedy for palpitations: *Breathe slowly and regularly, and free your mind from troublesome thoughts.* But her eyes quite naturally strayed down to the motionless body of Matthew at her feet. The rhythm of her heart accelerated.

Joe noticed her staring. "Pretty dire predicament, huh, Louise? There'll be no help from Matthew, that's for sure."

The son, like the father, she realized, was to die in the name of some magic tropical plant. It was surely a deadly harvest.

She looked at the postdoctoral assistant as he busily wiped up stains, and grew angry. "How did you come to this, Joe?" she demanded.

He didn't answer at first, for he was preoccupied with rinsing the stains with alcohol, to assure that there would be not the slightest trace of blood left on the pristine lab floor. As he labored, his light brown hair straggled uncharacteristically over his forehead, and when he finally looked up at her, his pale eyes were weary. He said, "Matthew got into our locked laboratory. He was prying. He must have called you, or I can't imagine why else you'd be here."

"He said he'd learned who killed his father."

"Yes." The handsome face twitched with a smile, but it vanished rapidly. "He's causing me a good deal of work tonight, which I didn't really need at this point."

"Such a burden, having to get rid of people who discover you're a killer."

"Huh, don't tell me *you* understand. At first, I saw you as a threat to me. Then, with your clumsy way of handling things, I realized you weren't a threat at all; you're strictly an amateur, if I ever saw one." He looked over at her with amused disdain, then turned back to make a last check of his work.

"But I was a good lab worker—or was that all lies?"

"Oh, no," Joe conceded good-naturedly, and straightened up and moved his neck in a little circular exercise. "You were damned good, and your working here gave me a chance to keep my eye on you. Of course, I was just as glad when you decided to quit because you wouldn't give up nosing around. I still don't know *why* you quit, though. Why did you?"

"My husband and Detective Geraghty suspected someone connected with the lab killed Professor Whiting."

"Huh," he said. "No more 'random killer' talk— glad to know what the cops are thinking. They have no proof, however."

"Matthew found proof."

The more Louise talked, the stronger she felt,

with the heart palpitations now subsiding so that they only represented a small, steady throb in her chest. She looked down at her tether, and wondered if she could free herself by lifting the leg of the bench.

Joe waved a hand airily. "He just overheard my conversation with Carl. Carl's the mergers and acquisitions specialist who's engineering the takeover of our cozy little lab here by Synthez."

"I've heard of Synthez."

Joe's eyebrows raised. "I guess you're smart enough to know the pharmaceuticals are zeroing in on this place; it's a natural takeover target. Matthew stood right outside my office and eavesdropped. I had no idea that he was able to get in here after hours. And of course I couldn't have him going around accusing me of things even if he couldn't prove them. He would ruin everything."

Her eyes were drawn back to Matthew. Somehow, she had expected him to regain consciousness and talk to her. "What have you done to him? Oh, *God,* you've already killed him, haven't you—" Suddenly everything went out of focus and she felt herself fainting. As she grabbed out for something to hold onto, the flat of her hand struck a tray of test tube plants and sent them flying about the lab and onto the asphalt tile floor.

"Have you taken leave of your *senses,* woman!" Joe yelled, and charged toward her as she stumbled to right herself. But instead of striking her, he turned to the plants and quickly set the remaining ones in neat order in their racks. Then, with his foot he gently shoved the fallen and broken ones out of the aisle under the benches. He glared at her, and his voice was harsh. "You have no idea of how precious each of these plants is, or you would never act like such an imbecile."

"I do know," she said in a low voice. "They're a

gold mine. And I understand why you killed Peter Whiting."

She was feeling faint again. She looked behind her, and realized the workbench would make a good seat. "Please, I have to sit down."

"Go ahead then and sit."

She slid her bottom onto the bench, with so little slack in the rope that she had to hold her hands between her legs.

Finished with his straightening efforts, he turned to her. "So you understand why I killed Peter. Do tell me," he challenged, his pale blue eyes calm again after the emotional experience of sacrificing plants to her clumsiness.

"You worked for him for years and years. . . ."

"Nine years, in and out of the jungle. He taught me what I know, and taught it well."

"And you probably helped him establish that the plant was valuable. Of course, I wonder why you never struck out on your own and became a full-fledged professor."

"You are so naive, Louise, about universities and tenured teaching positions. They're scarce as hen's teeth, and you need connections. And you need a certain kind of *charm* that I don't seem to have— for you see, you don't only teach, you have to go out and kiss ass and raise research funds—that's what it means to be a successful professor in the sciences." He folded up the rags he used to clean the floor and set them aside.

Since there seemed nothing left to lose, she decided to goad him a little. "So, lacking the smarts yourself," she said in a condescending tone, "you hooked your wagon to a star who could do those things."

She was right. Joe didn't like her implication that he was second best to Peter Whiting. "Oh, yeah," he sneered, "Peter could do those things,

that's right. But he was a bloody *ingrate.*" The usually mild eyes flashed with anger. "Whenever anything went wrong, I was no longer the 'son he
never really had,' but the scapegoat."

He pointed his finger at Louise, as if it were a
pistol. "And after I worked like his slave to help
him set up this company, the man would never
agree to give me even the *smallest* share of ownership—even though he was probably going to die of
a disease he wouldn't even acknowledge he *had.*
He couldn't take it *with* him—"

"So when he wouldn't give you part ownership,
you killed him?"

Joe broke into a grotesque laugh. *"No,* not then—
things weren't in place then. I didn't kill him until
I'd made a deal with Carl—which gets us to the
conversation that Matthew heard. Synthez is the
place for this *Tabebuia* research to take place anyway; it has the hundreds of millions needed to get
this certified by the FDA as a *pharmaceutical,* and
not merely as a food supplement."

He turned his attention to Matthew, cutting another length of rope and tying the young man's
hands together. As he did, he went on with his
story. "You probably don't realize the impact of it
all. That means it will not merely be a funky tea like
ginkgo biloba, to be taken by its devotees, but one
of the country's most important medicines—a pill
that will enable people to live healthily up to the
age of one hundred ten or one hundred twenty."
He stared at her, to see if she was impressed, but
she kept all emotion from her face. He continued.
"I told Synthez I could bring Whiting Phytoseutical
Labs into their fold within six months—and they
were goddamned well impressed."

"I'm sure your reward was going to be enormous."

Finished securing Matthew's hands, he rose to

his feet and pointed that gun finger at her again. "*Is* going to be enormous, Louise. And I get a bonus if I meet the six-month deadline."

Louise was getting nervous, for there was no more busywork for her assailant, which meant he soon would be deciding what to do with Matthew and her.

Trying to keep the tension out of her voice, she asked, "How does a big outfit like Synthez justify your killing the principal scientist in this deal?"

Joe waved a casual hand. "Why do you think I have spent so much time slipping on my ski mask and harassing people in your neighborhood?"

"That was *you*? My God."

He smiled, pleased that she finally gave him recognition for something. "That has kept the 'random killer' theory alive and well and everybody off my back. Why should Synthez suspect anything the police don't suspect?"

"And then there's Matthew and me—what if we turn up missing?"

He laughed. "Again, since I am the master of that phantom killer, I'll dream up something. How about a few enticing remnants of your clothes, stashed somewhere, but no bodies? Oh, don't think you've ruined my plans—you've discovered them, but you've not stopped me or even interfered with my schedule."

He came toward her, and her pulse quickened again. Desperate to distract him, she said, "So first you killed the professor, who was like a father to you. But an abusive father—"

Joe stood next to her now, remembering the man who'd called him a son. "You couldn't have withstood it either. One minute he was great. The next minute, the insults could literally pour out of his mouth like poison. I used my fishing knife and shut up that mouth for good . . . cut the tongue literally to ribbons . . ."

"Never *mind,*" she cried, "I don't want to hear it."

But he didn't stop talking. "A fishing knife is very thin and long and sharp, and it did the job just fine. I should have done it years ago."

"That knife—"

"—is the one I came after you with on Thanksgiving, Louise—and the one I used in all my phony attacks."

"What about me—were you serious that time? Were you going to carve me up?"

He slid onto the workbench beside her, as if they were just pals, talking. He was so close to her that she could smell his minty breath. "I even called out your name—didn't you hear me?"

It hadn't been the wind after all. "Yes, I heard you."

"You were watching Polly and me—watching me trying to bend her mind." His voice became a little dreamy. "I'm not sure what I was going to do—just scare you, or maybe slit your pretty throat."

The words were so detached and merciless that they chilled her, and it was all she could do to keep herself from shuddering.

But he was into his story now. "Since Peter's death," he said, "I've constantly worked on Polly. And strangely enough, James Conti and Ramon Jorges are helping, for they both make her feel guilty on different issues. Jorges thinks she and the professor *owe* him for his part in finding those tribes for them. Why, he even told her he thought Peter brought in some of the plant species illegally. That's foolishness. It's just aimed at making her feel beholden to him. As for Conti, you might say the old professor owed him and Jefferson

University something, too, for those years of research grants. The net effect? She's beginning to wear down. One day soon, I'll propose selling out to Synthez, and she'll say yes. It's the best deal for both of us, and there's no need for those other two scavengers to get in on it."

Louise knew she only had moments left to save herself. Maybe she could appeal to some better side of his nature. "Joe," she said, "you sound so cold and heartless. Yet you're working passionately on something that will aid mankind. I don't get it. Don't you have any feeling at all for people?"

He jolted up off the bench, and for the first time his voice was angry. "You should have asked me that before I broke my ass getting my degrees. University of Illinois carries some weight, but not as much as Harvard, or MIT. No one handed anything to me. And then after earning the doctorate, the bitterest pill of all was not landing a teaching job. Why, the privileged Whitings and Contis are *handed* tenured jobs as if it's their *birthright!* Instead, I slaved for Peter Whiting through my best years—I was always the alter ego, never the star. In the end, I was even denied crumbs from his goddamned table. All I *wanted* was a paltry percentage of the company I helped build."

He looked around quickly, then down at Matthew, as if he might be losing control of the situation. He reached for the object in his back pocket that had made his lab coat bulge, and in a second of horror, Louise realized what was coming. She had to get free. She slid off the workbench, straining against her ropes to try and topple it over. In the process, she butted her legs against the precious *Tabebuia* test tube plants, and brought a tray of them crashing to the floor.

Joe was enraged. "You shouldn't have done that," he yelled. "You can't escape—escape is not part of my plan." He raised the long black object in his hands, and that was the last thing she remembered.

29

Louise regained consciousness slowly, trying to sort out what must have been a bad dream from reality. The back of her head felt like molten metal, and hurt so much that her only desire was to lose consciousness again to get away from the pain.

But when her eyes had opened, they'd caught a glimpse of something that forced her back into the conscious world.

A sky full of stars. She was out-of-doors, lying under the open December sky, getting chillier by the moment. Not only that, she felt herself and the whole world under her slowly moving.

Turning her head slightly, she saw a man looming above her, busy with his hands. She was on some kind of raft; she could hear the slap of the water against its side, and her body rolled back and forth a little as the raft responded to the leg movements of the man. Though her muscles screamed in agony with her every move, she turned her head as far as she could to the left and caught a glimpse of trees and water. Finally she understood. She was being ferried by rope pulley across a river, which was probably part of the Potomac.

This was not Charon on the River Styx guiding the dead to Hades, but not too much different. Her boatman, she realized, was Joe Bateman, Ph.D., murderer.

As her sensibilities returned and the little logical connections resumed in her brain, she slowly focused on this man. He was methodically pulling the ferry against the current of the water. But to where—an island? Turning her head to the right, she saw a lump lying beside her that must be Matthew Whiting. *Please*, she thought, *let him still be alive*. Between the two of them, maybe they could save themselves.

There was a jolt as the little raft hit land. It sent a wave of pain through Louise's head that nearly caused her to cry out. Joe tied the little barge to a post on a landing platform, then came and bent over her. She feared the worst, that he would find out she was conscious.

She pulled as far back into herself as she could. *I'm as good as dead*, she told herself—for this was truer than not. She knew Joe's face was directly over hers, for she could smell his minty breath. He held a finger against the side of her throat for a few seconds and learned she had a pulse. But when he slapped her cheek with the broadside of his hand, she didn't respond and let her head roll as if her hold on life was tenuous at best. Apparently satisfied that she was helpless, he heaved her up roughly into his arms and took her up a slight incline. After what she counted as forty steps, he unceremoniously dumped her on the ground. The soft crunch of his footsteps over leaf-covered ground disappeared. Now, she could smell the faint sewer-gas odor of the river, and realized she was lying right at the water's edge.

With a desire for survival so strong that she could almost taste it, she worked with the inch of loose rope she had preserved when Joe had bound her hands. She did not mind the chill of the early December night, nor the raw mess she was making of her hands, but just concentrated on the job. To get loose was their only hope of survival. Using her strong, square-cut fingernails, she tore desperately at the bonds, and could feel them giving way. But there was little time, for her captor soon would be back with his other victim.

Never had she felt so miserable. Searing pain filled her head from the blow that Joe Bateman had administered, and she wondered if she would ever think straight again. With only a light jacket covering her upper body, she was turning colder by the minute; hypothermia soon would set in. And even more grievous, an all-pervasive feeling of nausea had overcome her. Finally, mercifully, she turned her head and was able to vomit into the dirt. A leftover deciduous plant, leaves gone but scraggly stem remaining, tickled her nose and somehow made her feel better.

She lifted her head up so she could get her bearings. The river near where she lay like a piece of washed-up flotsam was probably the Potomac. Turning her head the other way, she could see a skeletal open-air boathouse, with canoes stacked four-high with their bottoms up. On the ground in front of this boat storage she could make out a row of flat-bottomed boats. Louise remembered Sarah Shane's story about Joe berthing his fishing boat on an island in the Potomac. This must be it, Maple Island, with its funky little boat club that Joe had wangled himself into. Dully, she reflected that the club should have screened its members more carefully to separate out the murderers from the rest.

But how smart of Joe: What could make better sense to the man than to rid himself of two bodies in this isolated spot, rather than facing the even more uncomfortable questions that would result if she and Matthew were found dead in a populated area. Maybe he would bury them both on this island, perhaps under the boat racks, where the ground was protected from the recent freezes.

This probably was a beautiful place by day, for even in the light of the moon she could see the tall maples and sycamores rearing into the sky. One of these magnificent dappled sycamores, its branches smooth and beautiful, had been ripped from the ground during one of Washington's fierce storms and toppled into the nearby water. Now, it was left as a pedestal for the birds of the river to use.

Oh, how she would have loved to see this place in the light. Yet she was already thinking of herself as a corpse, for that was where she was headed, and in the company of her colleague, Matthew, whom she had so grievously doubted only today.

She tried to take stock of her physical plight. She couldn't move, with her hands and feet bound. The pounding in her head had to be ignored for the moment. What was more serious was that there was something wrong with her legs; she moved each one of them carefully, gritting her teeth from the pain that resulted. She finally decided nothing was broken; it must be only deep bruises from being heaved in and out of Joe's car. While working on the ropes on her hands, she also worked each leg in turn, trying to bring back the strength and circulation.

As she continued her frantic efforts to get loose, she heard the sound of twigs and leaves breaking under foot. Had Joe spied her wiggling about? He came closer, but seemed not to have noticed. Grunting, he threw down his burden beside her, and immediately walked off again. Soon she heard the rattling of chains, and it was almost too frightening to think about what he was doing.

Then, to her enormous joy, the prostrate form beside her gave out a small moan. "Oh, *Matthew,*" she whispered, "you're alive."

He groaned again, louder this time. "Shhh," she warned. He had rolled over, and his face with its thin features and beaklike nose now pointed toward the December sky. "Can you hear me, Matthew?" she asked. "We're in danger. You have to work on your ropes and see if you can loosen them. Joe could be getting ready to bury us—or maybe he's going to take us out in the river."

"I thought we were his buddies," said Matthew faintly.

"So did I."

In the near distance Louise could hear Joe working somewhere near the boat storage. Soon there were clanging noises. It sounded as if he were dropping heavy objects onto a metal surface. Then she knew: He was stealing anchors from other boats and was putting them into his own. There was only one possible use for them, to weight down bodies. But wouldn't many anchors be needed? How could he carry all that weight in a small fishing boat?

She felt sick again, and closed her eyes and leaned her head back on the hard earth. There was no denying it any longer. They were going to be drowned alive in the Potomac River.

Well, she wouldn't let Joe get away with it. Beside her there was silence. She reached over with her bound hands and pinched Matthew hard in his side. "Wake *up,*" she ordered in a harsh whisper.

"*Stop,* Louise, you're hurting me."

Matthew needed some words that would wake him up, for she realized he was falling in and out of consciousness. "You must wake up, Matthew. This may be a celebrated place to be drowned, just up a ways from the Lincoln and Jefferson Memorials, but I don't want to end up here, and neither do you!"

"End up in the river?" he asked.

"Joe is going to drown us, don't you understand? You have to at least try to get free of those ropes. It's our only chance, so dammit, *do* it. And when he comes over here, you have to act like you've never acted before. Play dead—really dead."

"Okay," he muttered, and at last she could see him trying to move his hands.

In the moment's silence that followed, she became aware of another sound from the river. Not just the peaceful noise of lapping waves, but the ominous sound of rushing water. "Listen," she whispered, "water."

"I can sure smell it—and I can hear it. It's—falling."

"Oh, *God,*" she said, and the horror of it sank in. "He doesn't need lots of anchors. There are falls around here—the Little Falls dam. Have you heard of it?"

"Isn't that where . . ."

"Yes." Everyone had heard of the macabre accident in the Potomac a few years ago when a boating party tried to run the falls and drowned. Rescuers never could recover the bodies despite weeks of trying. The hydraulics of the water kept their bodies churning in perpetuity far beneath the innocent-looking five-foot-high dam.

He turned to her. "Louise, I'm so afraid. We're goners if we're tossed into those falls."

She made her voice as strong as possible. "Stop it, Matthew. Don't think about anything but getting away. How're your hands?"

He moved them experimentally. "I'm making a little progress."

Behind her, she thought she heard a noise, as if someone were calling her. "Did you hear that?"

"Yeah. Is someone else here?"

Joe's voice suddenly came to them from quite another direction, and she decided that acoustics near water were tricky. "All *right*," he muttered, as if proud of a job well done. "I'm ready."

"Careful," she whispered to Matthew, "he's coming. Play dead." She turned her head to the side but kept her eyes open a slit, and could see Joe crouch down over her and grab her up.

"Party time for you plant handlers," said Joe with an unpleasant laugh. He hauled her up like a sack of potatoes, carried her the short distance to the boat, and threw her in. She ducked to try to protect herself, but still her head hit the side of the aluminum craft, and she sank into a semi-conscious state. Dimly, she heard the commotion of Matthew's body falling halfway on top of hers—his pale face only inches away from her face, and cushioned by her body. Good, she thought, through her haze; if she ever had the ability to talk again, he was right there to listen.

Joe went to the front of the craft, which was a modest-sized fishing boat about fifteen feet long, with the motor in front. It didn't start on the first try, and Louise heard him spit out some curse words, something she had never heard him do before. But with a few more turns of the ignition key, it responded. Not a huge motor, it nevertheless broke the silence of the night. Then he turned it on low throttle and slowly moved out into the river.

With his attention focused the other way, Louise might have a slim chance to save them. She began to make out objects around her in the bottom of the boat; the little pile of anvil anchors, all lying close to their heads, and a thick coil of rope. The churning hydraulics of those falls were intended to do most of the work for Joe. But this equipment was further insurance that their bodies would never be found.

Joe was backlit by the lights on his control panel, and his movements seemed fast and jerky. Though he had to run the boat slowly to keep the noise down, she realized he had some time pressures; people would soon realize that she and Matthew were missing. If he'd cleaned up the blood smears in the lab, there would be no trace of what happened to them. They would just appear on the missing persons list in a couple of days. Joe would say he'd left the lab at five-thirty and gone home and had dinner, or come up with some such alibi. And what evidence would there be to tie him to their disappearance, even though she had left that message with Mike Geraghty?

She felt a deep pain in her chest area as she realized that this was all speculation after the fact. They were all things that would happen after she and Matthew were thrown into the tumbling cauldron of water, never to be seen again.

While she was thinking this, she realized her companion was struggling hard with his ropes. "Louise," he whispered, "are *your* ropes loose?"

"They're ready to slip off. I'm just keeping them on in case he comes back here to look. How're you coming?"

"I'm not sure I can do this. And my legs—God, Louise, I think my right leg is broken."

She ignored his complaints. "Look, Matthew, maybe I can shift the anchors, oh, say, a couple of feet back. Then, when he comes to get them, we'll trip him and topple him overboard—"

"All two hundred pounds of him?" said Matthew.

"Louise, c'mon—that's worse than a bad stage direction. It's way too complicated."

Suddenly, Joe looked back, and then shifted the motor into neutral.

"Careful," she warned Matthew.

His large figure clumped back through the boat. He bent down, checked the inert figures on the floor of the craft, and grunted. "Hm, still out—maybe forever." Then he clumped back to the front and proceeded slowly again through the moonlit Potomac.

She expelled a large breath of air. "You're right, Matthew—that plan stinks. Well, there's nothing else to do." And she pulled the ropes off her hands. "I'm *free!*" she exclaimed in an excited whisper. "I'm going to try something. We can't just lie here till he throws us overboard."

She patted her jeans pockets; Joe had divested her of her pepper spray. She needed a better weapon anyway; pepper spray might be enough to stop a bear, but not the obsessed Joe Bateman. With her legs tightly bound, she pulled herself along like the lowly garden creature the worm, and made her way the few feet to the stern. Once she reached it, she could see that the seats on either side were compartments with flip tops.

She opened one and found nothing. "Damn," she said quietly to herself. She dragged her body over to the opposite compartment and flipped up the lid. Lying there was an orange plastic flare gun, with an attached black rubber tube. She knew this was the bandolier, which housed the cartridges. They were going to survive!

Thanks to outings on the Chesapeake Bay in Sandy and Frank Stern's sailboat, Louise knew about flare guns. She opened the bandolier and slid out three red cartridges; just as she suspected,

Joe would have all his equipment in order. But the gun held one flare at a time, and she had need for two cartridges. She was just shoving the first one in when Joe called out, "Hey, what's going on back there?" Something had made him suspicious.

Her heart began racing, and suddenly her fingers seemed to fail her. She fumbled and dropped the other two cartridges, and they clinked softly in the bottom of the metal boat.

"Maybe I'll see if my snoops have regained consciousness," he called. "I'd kinda like them to be conscious and know what's happening to them."

Mean sonofabitch, she thought, and groped determinedly on the bottom of the boat for the shells. Finally, her fingers closed on them, just as Joe put the boat in neutral again and flashed his light back at them. The light hit Matthew first, and of course he was where he was supposed to be, eyes closed, playing dead. Then the flashlight found Louise, where she sat propped up fifteen feet away in the stern.

She pointed the flare gun at the sky and squeezed the trigger, sending a brilliant red meteor to arch high over the Potomac River.

"Damn!" Joe spat out the word, then charged, while with trembling fingers Louise finished shoving in the second red cartridge.

She held the gun high in front of her with both hands. "Stop or I shoot! she yelled.

Already moving, her assailant stumbled and almost fell, then frantically pulled himself to a halt. He righted himself midway in the boat, within easy striking distance, and dangerously close to the helpless Matthew.

"Raise your hands," she ordered, and his big arms stretched upward.

"Now move back where you came from, toward the front of the boat." He didn't immediately move.

"Move *now*, dammit, Joe, or I'm not waiting—I'm just shooting. Take your choice."

He slowly moved toward the bow of the boat.

"Not too far," she said. She didn't want him to try to grab a weapon from up there. "That's right, right *there.*"

"I've stopped," he said nervously. "You can see I've stopped just where you told me to. Please watch your finger on that gun—"

Then she heard a sound across the water, the clank of wood on metal, and her hopes soared. Yet she knew that help could never have arrived this soon, and realized it must be her imagination.

Now it was a standoff, she with her flare gun, and Joe with his overpowering physique. She tried to relax, pulling in a deep breath and then letting it out in a nervous uneven stream that let the whole world know how anxious she was. Her gun hand began to tremble as she watched her adversary standing motionless, the ghostly light from the dashboard illuminating his raised-arm silhouette and making him appear monstrously large.

For a moment, there was only the soft putter of the engine in neutral. No one else could hear the frightened beating of her heart. Would this moment never end?

Then Joe spoke again. "Huh, Louise, do you really think you have this situation under control? And if so, for how long?" It was the old, expert Joe Bateman droning on, trying to psych her out. "After all, you haven't done anything else right yet in the investigation of your old buddy's murder. Why should things change now?"

Louise could feel pain again, and her head was swimming with it. She resisted putting a hand to her skull for fear he would see her weakness. "I've made some mistakes in the past," she admitted, "but I'm wide awake now, no thanks to you. I'd like you to be alert, too, Joe, so you can appreciate just what's happening to you."

"Listen," he said in a wary voice, "I know you enjoyed throwing my words back at me. I won't move. I don't want to make you nervous in any way, Louise. A person could release that trigger by accident. That's why the gun never stays loaded in the boat, did you know that?"

In a minute he would be on his knees, whining. She realized that although she was scared of Joe, he was more scared of the flare gun. At once, she felt more secure. She put both hands on the gun to hold it up, for it grew heavier by the moment. She quickly glanced at Matthew, who was sitting up now but couldn't manage to get the ropes off his wrists. It didn't stop her from making a threat on his behalf.

"Furthermore, Joe, Matthew hates the idea that you killed his father, and he'll grab you and shove you over the side if you should rush me."

Matthew nodded. "Damn right," he said in as tough a tone as he could muster.

She listened for the sound of help coming, and fancied she heard sirens. But nearby was a real sound, the splash of an oar in water.

Like an apparition, a dark mass moved close to the fishing boat—a canoe. What was a canoe doing out at this time on the Potomac on the second day of December?

"Well done, *Louise*," said the canoeist. "I *loved* that red flare." The aluminum craft came alongside and gently bumped the side of the larger boat. She didn't dare turn her head, for she feared what would happen if Joe Bateman decided to charge her.

"It couldn't be. *Charlie*—is that *you*?"

"None other," said Charlie. "And I've got to say you were terrific, Louise. But since I have a pistol here, you can relax just a little; I've got it trained on Joe over there, and like you said, if he moves an inch, he'll get it from both of us." Now she chanced a look at the reporter. He was dressed in dark sweats, sitting in a canoe that he'd obviously snitched from the island. She could see the comforting steel glint of the gun in his hand.

"You mean, you followed us here?" she asked, puzzled.

"He *followed* us here?" echoed Matthew.

"Hey, look, guys," said Charlie, using one hand to pull a small object from his pocket and flipping it open, "don't get in a snit. I'm calling 911 just to be sure the cops make it here soon because, frankly, that big jerk over there makes me real nervous." The murderer's hands were not held so high now, and he loomed like a giant in the modest-sized fishing boat. Louise tightened her grip on her flare gun.

It took a few seconds for Charlie's remark about the cell phone to sink in, probably because Louise and Matthew both had suffered blows on the head.

"Don't tell me he had a cell phone the whole time!" she said.

The canoe was still nudging against the fishing boat, like a baby trying to nurse its mother.

"Yeah," said Matthew, "and he's just now using it."

Charlie was listening to everything they said. "Actually, that's a fact," said Charlie, not quite so cockily as he sometimes talked. Having completed his quick call to 911, he folded his phone and put it in his pocket. "Look, you guys, you gotta understand I am here as a *reporter.* I had to let the thing play out; I didn't exactly know what was going to happen, but I had to let it *happen.* But you should be grateful—why, you two might not be alive if I hadn't come and rescued you."

As if to refute his words, the world began to shake with the vibrations of a helicopter speeding up the river from downtown Washington, D.C. Sending up the flare had produced an almost immediate reaction.

Matthew laughed, a tired, desperate laugh. "Hey, man, listen to that copter. It had nothing to do with you. You're distorting the truth. Louise got the draw on this guy before you ever pulled up. I thought you were a *reporter*, not a liar."

Louise said, "With that caveat, Matthew, meet Charlie Hurd of the *Washington Post*."

30

"I'm Charles Hurd of the *Washington Post*—and this woman is my—Aunt Louise."

She was on a stretcher, being borne to an ambulance, the flashing lights of the police cars and the rescue vehicles almost more than she could bear. She had closed her eyes on the scene, until she heard Charlie's words. Then they popped back open.

"That jerk is *not* a relative," she mumbled to the emergency medical technician, but the man could not understand her.

"I think she needs a shot of painkiller," said the attendant to Charlie. "She seems to be delirious." In a few seconds, someone asked her, "Allergic to anything, Louise?" She shook her head, and a few seconds later she could feel herself twisted about, and a needle going into her hip.

What difference did any of it make, she soon decided, and was drifting off to sleep when she heard his voice. He was holding her hand, and she didn't have the energy to shove it away. The despicable Charlie Hurd, who had let Matthew and her go through the tortures of the damned before he decided to rescue them. But the Demerol was kicking in, and she was beginning to feel euphoric at just being alive. She couldn't discount Charlie's role in this, could she?

"Louise," he said in a stagy little whisper, "did you realize that Joe Bateman was going to throw you over the Little Falls dam?"

"I figured it," she murmured, drifting off.

He squeezed her hand hard to wake her up again. "Know what he told me in the boat after you passed out? There's a little island right out in the middle of the river near the falls. That's where he was taking you. He would have landed there, hauled you two out of his boat, tied a couple of light anchors on you, and then thrown you over the falls. That great hydraulic action would keep you down there *forever.* Good plan, huh?"

She looked up, and saw Charlie's pale eyes sparkling with the excitement of the tale.

"Depends on where you're coming from, Charlie." She wished she had enough strength to swat him one in the face.

"So, before you completely pass out again, tell me what got you over to the lab this afternoon. Did Matthew call you, or something?"

She nodded. "He listened in on a phone call of Joe's—Joe cooking up a deal with a mergers and acquisitions guy."

"To do what—buy up Whiting Labs?"

"Yeah."

"For whom?"

"For Synthez."

"*Bingo!* Synthez!"

"Yeah. Joe'd get, you know . . ."

"A big commission."

She nodded.

"And what did you find when you went inside?

Did you have a fight with Joe? Did Matthew? Set the scene for me."

She cocked her head, as if indicating heads played a part in this story. "He knocked Matthew out; blood was coming out of his head. . . ."

"What'd he *say* to you, Louise?" Charlie's face was so close to her that if he'd had bad breath, she would have suffocated.

"He's a disillusioned postdoc. Nobody'd give him tenure. He doesn't have much personality, you know, and I doubt he's a very good teacher. So he was Whiting's 'slave'—that's what he called it—for nine years." The effort of saying all this wore her out, and she was floating off to sleep, but Charlie shook her firmly on the shoulder.

"*Louise,* dammit, don't forget I helped save your ass. Now, stay awake while I get a few more details. What was he going to do—marry the widow? I gathered there was a line of suitors wanting to marry that widow. . . ."

"Maybe not marry. Just persuade her to sell, and Synthez would presumably keep Joe around to head the research into the *Tabebuia.*"

"*Tabebuia*?" said Charlie. "Oh, so that's the name of the magic plant they're growing in that lab? Nobody ever spilled that information to me."

"Of course not," she said. "It's like the mice that live till a hundred and twenty. . . ."

"Mice?" he asked skeptically.

"In human years, that is. They'll tell people about this when it suits them."

His eyes lit up. "*Methuselah mice!* I can hardly wait to get a chance to see them. What a story! But tell me how a couple of other people figure in this. What about James Conti—I bet you know him."

"Oh, him . . ."

"Is he implicated? I mean, he doesn't have any

connection with Joe, does he? What's his deal with the widow? Is it only because the old professor worked at Jefferson University, and got backed by them for his research for umpteen million years?"

"I guess so. He needs Polly now. . . ."

Charlie looked puzzled. "Whatever that means. Hey, don't fade out on me and get all screwy. Now, there's another character in all this, Ramon Jorges; I heard about him through this chick at Jefferson U—wouldn't be specific, but I take it he's some operator. Do you think he was mixed up with Joe—a conspiracy of some kind?"

She shook her head hopelessly. "I'm so tired— no, I think Ramon hated Joe Bateman, and vice versa. Each of them had their own agenda. . . ."

"I believe you mean to say *his* own agenda, Louise."

"My God," she murmured, "you're correcting my English. And here I am half-dead."

"Look, you're nowhere near dead, Louise, you're just woozy. It's good for you to talk; the medic told me to *keep* you talking, because you might have a bad concussion. I'm doin' my duty. Now, one other thing. What did Joe Bateman do to you?"

"He tied me up. He said he was like a son to Peter Whiting."

Charlie was scribbling furiously with a stylus on his palm-sized computer. "Hold it, hold it, hold it—slow up. Exactly what did he say?"

And so she tried to give him Joe's exact words. ". . . he was like a son, but a mistreated son who gets yelled at a lot and who in the end gets disinherited—just like Matthew . . ."

"Was *Matthew* Whiting disinherited, too?"

"Why don't you ask him, Charlie?"

"So then what happened, after he told you how the old prof treated him like dirt?"

"He knocked me out. I owe that guy a couple of good thumps; he had the nerve to attack me in my own backyard. . . ."

"When'd he do *that?*"

"A couple of weeks ago—back when he thought I was dangerous. My dog scared him away."

Charlie cackled. "Aw, c'mon—that stupid little dog of yours? No way."

"Yessir," she said, trying to rise up on her cot, "Fella scared him right into the water garden."

Charlie raised an impatient hand in a dismissive gesture. "Okay, Louise, have it your way," said the reporter.

She looked at him sourly. "*Aunt* Louise, hadn't you better say?"

"Guess so," he said, scribbling notes. Charlie had no shame. "After that," he persisted, "Joe quit thinking you were a threat to him?"

"Yes."

"What a mistake," said the reporter, smiling broadly. "I would never take you off my enemies' list, Louise." He saw the look on her face and said, "Just kidding, of course. So he conked you over the head, just like he'd done to Matthew."

"Yes. And I'm feeling woozy, in case you hadn't noticed. Can't you let me go to sleep?"

He pulled on her jacket sleeve. "Just a couple more questions . . ."

"*Guard,*" she called in the loudest voice she could muster. Being tied down to a bed in the back of an ambulance seemed like some form of imprisonment, so it only seemed natural to call the attendant a guard. "Charlie's bothering me, and won't let me go to sleep."

"Your nephew was helping us keep you awake, Louise, because we don't like concussion victims to drift off right away. . . ."

"He's not my nephew—oh, never mind.

Charlie, you don't believe the story about my dog. I'm through with you."

"Sir," said the medic, beginning to view the reporter a little less trustfully, "maybe you'd better sit over here while I take over."

Louise watched as Charlie moved to a seat on the side of the ambulance, no longer interested in her at all, just busily scratching away with his stylus.

31

"I can't believe I trusted that man so completely," said Polly, shaking her blond head. She sat gracefully in the apricot-colored chair that was positioned alongside Louise's bed. Louise was propped up with pillows, wearing her pink charmeuse nightie and a fuzzy robe, her white goose-down comforter pulled up cozily around her. A heavy coat of makeup covered the rainbow of bruises and the stitched cut on the side of her swollen face.

The widow was chattering on about how she hadn't a clue that Joe Bateman could be a murderer. Though Louise's head felt like a large ball of fuzz, she tried to follow the words, but most of them were a blur.

"...just didn't realize...trusted him with everything..."

"We all trusted Joe," said Louise, chiming in when she heard something she could relate to. "He always had the right responses to things, so what was there to distrust?"

Polly's gaze slid away from Louise's injured face and dropped demurely to her hands, laced in her lap. "You must have thought me a fool—all those men clustering around, panting after me *and* a part in Peter's business." She laughed. "Their passion seemed equal on that point—for the woman and for the lab . . . though maybe the woman a little more than the lab . . ."

"More passion for the woman?" said Louise, drawing her forehead into a frown.

"Oh, yes," said Polly. She tossed back a long lock of blond hair, and smiled at Louise in a self-knowing way. "Really, it seemed as if I owed each one of them something, on both a personal and a professional level."

Louise sighed and slid down a little in her covers. Polly was trying her patience. Owed James Conti what—another roll in the hay? And Ramon Jorges what—the little fling that he'd been denied years before? She felt like screaming, *Get a grip, woman!* until she recognized that this was the same response that Joe Bateman used to have for Polly. The widow was so caught up in the drama of her own life that sometimes she had room for little else.

For instance, it hardly seemed to matter to Polly that Louise had just arrived home after three days' hospitalization for a serious concussion. The woman had not come here to offer her condolences, but only to talk about herself.

She and Bill had opened the visitors' gates too soon, and after Polly left, they would be clanged shut if Louise had anything to do with it! But as long as the woman was here, maybe Louise could set to rest some questions in her mind. "I've wondered about something, Polly. What exactly did you owe to Ramon Jorges and James Conti?"

"Oh, Ramon helped Peter make contact with the first tribe, Louise." She laughed. "Ramon was a young scientist then; Peter immediately understood the significance of the *vigorous* elders of the tribe and the taking of the *Tabebuia* tea, whereas he told me that Ramon really *didn't* connect the dots."

"But Ramon told you differently?"

"Yes—and for all I know, maybe he was right. What was so perplexing was that my husband never clarified these matters. He tended to let certain things go; he let his *health* go, and it had terrible consequences, believe me." An unhappy look filled her blue eyes. "We had only recently found out he suffered from Mycobacterium avium, a serious type of tuberculosis that would have sent anyone else to the hospital for treatment. Peter, of course, was too busy for that, and insisted pills were enough to cure him. He did the same with people—he'd let his personal relationships sort of—*fester.* Look at the horrible relationship he had with Matthew."

"Poor Matthew," said Louise.

"Yes, I agree: poor Matthew. Then there's James— let's talk about James. You probably guessed that he and I once had an affair. We became involved after Peter's—troubles started. They denied him and me sexual pleasure, and since I am still quite young, it was a blow."

Polly was willing to marry the prestigious ethnobotanist almost twice her age, but not live with the consequences.

"It must have seemed quite a deprivation," said Louise dryly. She could detect her Presbyterian stoicism bubbling to the surface, but she was too tired to fight it. "So with Peter dead, James quite naturally thought you and he could resume, morally, what you once pursued immorally."

Polly lurched unceremoniously back in the apricot chair. "My *God,* you are a judgmental person, Louise. All this 'moral' and 'immoral' stuff. Is adultery really that wrong?"

Louise slumped further down in the bed, so the comforter was now at her chin. It was no time to mince words. She waved a hand out of her goosedown cocoon and declared, "Yes, it's *wrong.* But you don't have to listen to me—the world's full of adulterers. People do what they're going to do."

"I guess you're right about that," Polly said tartly.

Louise painfully pulled herself to a more upright position; she was losing moral authority being slouched down like that. Now that she'd already insulted Polly by practically calling her an immoral slut, she might as well follow up with a blunt question. "Let me ask you something more. Now that you know James Conti had nothing to do with Peter's death, what are you going to do, make him CEO? Marry him?"

Her visitor looked at Louise strangely. "You are so—*detached,* Louise."

She shrugged. "I'm just curious."

"I might marry him. I think I love him." She blushed. "I was sure I loved him when we had our little affair several summers ago."

"A little beach rendezvous, right?"

"How would you know that?" Polly asked suspiciously.

"Oh—just figured it . . ."

"No, you didn't." The blue eyes accused her. "James was right: You snooped into *everything* in his office."

Louise stared beyond the woman, wishing Bill would wander in and save her. "You're right, I covered quite a bit of ground in there. I accidentally came upon some snapshots in his desk. I could tell right away when I saw the picture of you that it was a very—meaningful affair."

"Wouldn't you call that *voyeuristic?*" she primly asked.

Another wave of fatigue swept over Louise, but just because she was running out of strength, she didn't intend to have this woman lay a guilt trip on her. "Darn right, Polly. If I'm detecting, I'm snooping, and I may well be a voyeur in the eyes of others. But that can't be helped. As a matter of fact, I found things that showed that James Conti had more than one reason to kill your husband."

"He'd *never* have done that. . . ."

"Well, *now* we know he didn't. But he had motive. So did Ramon Jorges. So did Matthew. And so did you. That's why I felt perfectly justified in checking everybody out."

Looking uncomfortable, Polly gathered herself to leave. "I didn't mean to confront you, Louise, especially when you're so—wounded. I hope that *face* heals all right. I really came here to apologize. Somehow, I feel it's my fault for getting you into this, and if you ever want to come back to the lab, I would dearly love to have you there. . . ."

Louise laughed and shook her head. "Well, it must be that you respect my work. For after the conversation we've just had, I doubt you like me personally very much."

"Oh, don't say that, Louise—we were just being frank with one another. Now, here's another incentive for coming back. Did you know that Matthew's signing on for more work? With the torn ligaments in his leg, he's no good for the stage right now—he couldn't take that big part he auditioned for."

Polly leaned forward in the chair and fixed her with the blue eyes. "And I think that in all fairness, I'll try to correct Peter's harshness by giving Matthew a part ownership of the company. I know he cares about it, and I find myself caring about him, poor dear. I only regret that he and his father quit being friends."

"Now, that's class, Polly," Louise said. She realized it was the first civil thing she'd said to the woman. "You're remedying the mistakes of the past, and you should be proud of yourself."

"So how about it, Louise, would you come back to work with the plants?"

Louise took a minute to think before she gave her answer. She said, "I love to work in the lab, but Bill wouldn't want me to. Anyway, Christmas is just around the corner; I have to get ready for it. And soon after, I'll be back at my job as TV garden show host. It seems a long time ago now, but I'm anxious to get back to it."

32

Her husband and Mike Geraghty were having a conversation about her. Bill was sitting on the end of the bed, while the Fairfax detective occupied the apricot-colored chair at the side of the bed, not five feet from where she lay with her eyes wide open.

"Don't bother to apologize, Mike. We both know that she would have done it anyway, even if you hadn't asked her to help you."

"Anyway, I'm glad she's okay. *Major* concussion, but she seems better now."

"Can I ask you something?" said Louise.

"Sure, honey," said Bill.

"Why do you talk as if I'm not here? It's as if I'd died and gone to heaven, and all that was left for you to sift out a few details such as what to do with my personal effects."

Bill grinned at the big detective. "She's better."

Geraghty nodded, his blue eyes smiling with pleasure. "That's good—I wondered there for a while."

Her husband patted her feet, which made two small mountains in the bottom of the quilt. "So we see you've come back to the party. You really needed that nap after Polly Whiting's visit."

"Yes. Now I need you two to tell me what's been going on. For instance, there's no question, is there, that Joe will stand trial for Peter's murder?"

"No question. For the murder, and the attempted murder of you and Matthew. We have several strong witnesses—the two of you, who heard him confess to the murder, and the mergers and acquisitions man. The collection of stolen anchors in his fishing boat and the big loop of rope are ample circumstantial evidence that he was going to drown you. And of course there's Charlie Hurd. Since Joe's been caught red-handed, his lawyer is looking for a plea bargain. The prosecutor is not willing to give him one, because of the ruthless way Dr. Whiting was killed—"

"—and the ruthless way my wife and Matthew were treated," added Bill. "Why, if Louise hadn't found that flare gun—I don't even want to think about it." He reached over and squeezed her hand.

Louise said, "Did you know that he set up those other attacks in Sylvan Valley to distract the police?"

"Yeah, he was very clever," said the big detective, "the way he took such great pains to confuse the police, the way he dickered with this guy Carl Rohrig. He's with the mergers and acquisitions firm, and was the point man for trying to take over Whiting Phytoseuticals."

"How'd you find that out?" asked Bill curiously.

"Matthew slipped into the lab Monday evening with his secret master key. He overheard Joe talkin' to this Carl. We started from there, and traced a lot of calls from Rohrig's company. It speaks to Bateman's motive, that's for sure, for he was going to get—"

"—a huge commission," interjected Louise. "Joe told me that. He also explained that Peter never would have been killed if he hadn't wanted to keep the whole pie for himself. Joe thought he deserved a piece, and so did Ramon—"

"And so did James Conti," added Geraghty.

"My God," said Bill, laughing, "I can just see one of those '*After you, dear Gaston*' moments; who gets there first to murder poor Peter Whiting."

Geraghty raised an admonitory hand. "There's more truth there than you know, Bill. Jorges is out on bond for false statements to police, and illegal possession of a gun with a silencer. We have evidence that our Brazilian friend prowled around for almost a week, watching the professor's house and lab. We found some pretty suspicious materials in his hotel room—dark clothing and a ski mask for surveillances, and the gun, of course. Why, he probably followed Louise and Peter Whiting on those walks, just as Joe Bateman did." Geraghty elevated his bushy white eyebrows. "It makes for quite a scenario when you think about it, Louise."

She put a weary hand to her head. "I can't believe we were walking in a woods full of prospective murderers. How will we ever walk in that woods again without thinking of them?"

Geraghty obviously was anxious to go back to his recital. "So Ramon's been charged on two counts, but we're lookin' even deeper, into all this *plant* stuff. . . ."

He waved a big hand in the air, as if "plant stuff" was beyond anyone's comprehension.

She laughed at him. "Mike, this whole case is about plant stuff. What do you mean?"

"Well, Ramon's plant shenanigans have already brought him into the Brazilian courts, as you know. Now we wonder if there was more hanky-panky with this *Tabebuia* plant? For instance, did Whiting get the proper permissions to bring in that plant, or did he sneak it in with the help of Ramon? Was Jorges going to blackmail him? We don't know yet for sure. Obviously, these are big questions, and require the cooperation of the Department of Agriculture."

"Peter Whiting may have been a difficult man," said Louise, "but he was no fool. I can't believe the professor did anything illegal in bringing in those plants. Why would he jeopardize his whole operation? I think it's more likely that Ramon *wanted* the widow to suspect that, just so that she'd feel a moral responsibility to share the project with him."

"We'll see how it turns out," said Geraghty. He raised a hand. "Oh, and I nearly forgot—the waitress at the Dixie Pig will make more charges against Ramon. The woman's daughter took some Polaroids of her injuries the day after they occurred."

"Good," said Louise. She touched her face, yellowing each day as the bruises healed, and remembered what poor Dorothy had suffered at the hands of Ramon Jorges. "Speaking of people who have done wrong, what about Charlie in all this? He could have ended our misery out on that island. After all, he had a gun."

Geraghty tried to put it in perspective. "*He* says he got there just as Joe was shovin' the boat off. Apparently he was hanging around Whiting Labs in his old car, which is how he discovered all this in the first place."

Now Louise realized her inspection of the two cars near Whiting Labs had not been thorough enough; underneath that pile of blankets in the backseat of the first one probably lurked Charlie Hurd.

"He came wearing dark clothes," continued Geraghty, "and armed with a chain cutter, as well as a gun. The chain cutter's how he loosened that canoe so he could follow you."

"And don't forget, he had a cell phone in his pocket—why didn't he phone the police as soon as he arrived at the island?" She was indignant, thinking about it.

Geraghty looked uncomfortable. "Says his phone didn't work until he tried it again out in the river . . ."

She laughed and shook her head. "An answer for everything, that's Charlie. I can't believe it. Granted, he helped cover Joe Bateman until the river patrol came, and who knows, maybe we needed him as much as he says. But he's the kind of person who turns people into cynics."

Bill said, "Let's talk about something more worthwhile than Charlie Hurd."

Louise gave an impatient pat to her white comforter. "Only two of these people are what you'd call worthwhile: Matthew and Gina. The rest of them are out for themselves—Ramon Jorges, James Conti, Polly Whiting. It breaks my heart to admit it, but even Peter Whiting was not the man I thought he was. He was a great scientist, but he was mean and ungenerous. And he planted the seeds for his own destruction."

Bill looked at Louise and nodded. "This is the last time you get into something like this. . . ."

Louise sighed. "I couldn't agree with you more, darling."

Detective Geraghty merely raised his bushy eyebrows and looked at the two of them, as if to say, *Fat chance.*

When the policeman left, Bill returned to the bedroom and sat next to her on the bed. "Suppose you'll be wanting to get up pretty soon. I know there's somebody in his cage in the back hall who's dying to have you take him for a walk in the woods."

"I'm getting up right now," she said, shoving aside the covers and trying to ignore the dizziness she felt. "I've neglected you, you and Janie and Fella—and the fall gardening, as well. There are bulbs that have to go into the ground—if I can find any ground soft enough to dig . . . roses that need mulching. And I need to bring the banana plant in from the storage shed; it doesn't like it out there." She looked at her husband cautiously. "It *is* okay, isn't it, to bring it in the rec room to winter over?" The plant took up at least five square feet of floor space.

Bill shrugged. "That big horse of a plant? Honey, I doubt it'll fit in the house; but I'm not thinking about bananas right now. Did you ever think that after all this excitement, we need a good place to winter over ourselves? There are three weeks until Christmas. How would it be if we sent Janie to stay at Nora and Ron's, and you and I dashed off for a vacation to Brazil? Chris's room is probably available at the Radebaughs, and I already called the travel agent; she has a good package deal on a twelve-day boat trip leaving from Manaus. . . ."

"You're taking me to the Amazon—"

"Honey, you can *revel* in bananas, palms, orchids. . . ."

She put her arms around his neck. "Oh, Bill, you know I've always dreamed of going to the jungle!"

MYSTERY IN THE GARDEN

A GARDEN ESSAY

If you are talented or lucky enough to have mystery in your garden, you'll know it. Passersby will stop and stare, and friends will ask you how you did it.

And you, who either cleverly concocted this garden masterpiece or else stumbled on the good effect, can tell them this: Just as a mystery story keeps us suspensefully turning pages so that we may gradually learn the whole story, a garden becomes exciting when it keeps things hidden and then gradually reveals itself. The suspense lies not only in what can be seen, but in what is still not seen. Conversely, the least interesting garden is the one that is like an open book and can be viewed in a single glance. No matter how many lovely plants, trees, and ornaments it contains, it lacks that key essential, suspense. Here are some of the ways that the experts achieve it:

• **Changing the elevation**. This may sound dull, but it's not—it's the sexiest concept in garden design today. *Nothing creates more dynamic tension than changing the elevation of the land.* In fact, that's the first thing designers do when they look at a yard or acreage, consider how to move dirt. They create hills, swales, berms, pools with waterfalls, bog gardens, and even ha-has. (A ha-ha is a wall that separates a higher piece of land from a lower piece without interrupting the view. It was a popular way to enclose cattle.)

The backyard gardener can get into dirt-moving, too, for bobcat operators are surprisingly versatile and cooperative; in an hour or two, for a couple of hundred dollars, they can fashion a whole new landscape in a small yard. A terrace, hill, bog garden, or pool may make the most sense in a small garden environment. A hill that is engagingly planted with trees and flowers creates an enchanting picture, and leads us to wonder what lies beyond.

• **Paths**. The path is the magic way into the garden. Although it can be narrow, it should never be straight; around each curve should be something new. Think of the path as a work of art—it might be made of large natural rocks surrounded by gravel of the same color; or wood strips interspersed with river rock. Our excited eye will wander down this path seeking further secrets of the garden.

• **Containers**. Pots and urns are part of the Victorian look that has come back into garden fashion. They seem to be made these days in two sizes, big and bigger, and all styles—fluted, ornately carved, plain, rope-bordered, tall, and squat. To avoid the need for fall storage indoors, select containers that are made of new and stronger combinations of materials that withstand winter frosts. They're meant to be filled with flowers, grasses, plants, and even small trees. Some containers lend themselves for use as a small water garden, with the welcoming silhouettes of lotus, arrowhead, and papyrus rising above water lilies and water hyacinths floating on the surface.

Containers are most effective when set in groups. They are like low walls that break the view and create what is called "garden rooms." But in some cases, a single container can transform the garden—for instance, a large urn set on a pedestal at the end of an allée formed from two lines of trees. Many people don't have this kind of space in their yard. For them, even a single planted pot can beget a mood of mystery, if it has texture, color interest, and depth. An example: a large, ornate gray stone urn overflowing with scarlet and gold flowers, variegated-leaved red geraniums, and chartreuse-toned grasses.

Be careful where and how you place pots and urns. The Victorian look can be overdone, as suggested by the very word "Victorian." Mystery is achieved with restraint, not excess.

• **Suddenly changing the subject**. Just as hills, terraces, and swales change the land, the backyard gardener can create excitement by suddenly altering the plants in the garden. For instance, a circuitous garden path might lead us out of a sunny patch around the curve of a large tree or bush, and into a tropical bog garden blazing with bold cannas, gingers, and big-leaved plants like elephant's ears. Still another bend in the path might bring us up a rise to a sunny, high spot swarming with ornamental grasses and dryland plants.

• **Walls, faux walls, and fences**. A half-wall near a house gives the illusion not only of wonder— "What's behind it?"—but also of extended space, rather like a mirror. Yet it takes up little space itself. The wall may be solid, or a lattice-work effect. Trellises can serve this same mysterious purpose. Two partial walls set at right angles to each other can suggest the atmosphere of a Persian garden. Walls can be constructed of many materials. One designer-built wall was constructed of layers of fist-sized gray stone separated by slices of bold brown sandstone.

Garden fences should be artistic, and that means not made of chain link. Yet people often buy houses whose backyards are surrounded with chain-link fences. They find they are difficult to remove and expensive to replace. A solution is to cover them with vines, shrub roses, and espaliered trees. If they are planted in a row more thickly, and with taller trees, we would call this a living wall, perfect for shielding the front of the home from car or foot traffic. These plantings create the height of mystery: a veil of foliage through which the garden is glimpsed, but not fully seen.

• **Trees and evergreens**. These large structures are crucial to making your garden a year-round delight. Two examples: Globular or vertical evergreens, on which snow lies gracefully in winter, are invaluable in designing garden rooms. The incomparable horizontal-lined dogwoods and Japanese maples make ideal "frames" for interior garden pictures. Yet none of these plants should be taken for granted; they must be cared for and pruned. A shaggy Japanese maple tree, for instance, may have no appeal at all, whereas one that is deftly pruned may be a work of art.

• **Gates and arches**. We all know entrances should be dramatic. Gates should have character and drama, for they are the invitation to the garden. Put up a freestanding gate, with shrubs and trees nearby but no attached fence, and you will create an enigma that will attract and delight visitors. Those with a romantic flair might want to construct a homemade arch that stands in the garden like a proud remnant of the classical past. This wonderful entryway should be set in place so that it frames your favorite garden view, then leads you into a new section of the yard.

• **Waterworks**. A waterfall or a fountain pleases the eye and ear and masks traffic and other unwelcome noises. Waterworks can be set in literally the smallest garden, and can transform it magically. One noted designer garden is cheek by jowl with the house, only twelve by fifty feet in size, and features a waterfall made of pieces of narrow sandstone. The homeowners view it through large glass windows, yet cannot see it all at once. An amateur gardener could replicate this garden, which is unified by a winding sandstone walkway to match the waterfall. Three Japanese maples break the long garden view, and tucked in between the stones are low-care shrubs and a few clumps of low grasses.

• **Rocks, shacks, and artifacts**. Big rocks, stone tables and chairs, charming garden benches, gazebos, and sculptures of all kinds—be they junkyard art or something more classical—add depth and interest to the garden, especially when you team them with beautiful plants and set them so they will be discovered by accident. Those lucky enough to have an interesting outbuilding can vault it into center stage in the garden. One homeowner did this with his rustic brown garage. He swathed it with blooming trees and bushes, and then for sheer surprise and drama, hung a curtain on the outside of the garage window. The secret of that curtain intrigues visitors. When it comes to rocks, shacks, and artifacts, the unexpected can work wonders.

Remember, in garden design these days, anything goes. The ideas come from a great many sources—everything from chaos theory to the popular Chinese philosophy, feng shui. Just like the big designers, we, too, can hew the land like sculptors carving marble. We can erect walls, or use a profusion of rocks, stones, gates, fountains, gazebos, stone tables and chairs, and big planted containers—whatever it takes to create *mystery*.